GU00792122

BlacknBlue

MATTIE AND THE HIGHWAYMEN

Get ready for action!

In the 1840s most highwaymen are hanging up their riding boots and putting away their pistols. But there is just time for one last gang of misfit ruffians to attack nervous travellers as they pass through Harewood forest in Hampshire...

And so it is that thirteen year old Matilda Harris is captured and forced to join a stylish, dashing, mysterious highwayman and his band of eccentric bandits. She also finds herself responsible for educating "The Brats" - two young escapees from the notorious Andover Workhouse.

This book combines historical events with a tale of adventure and suspense. Mattie, her pet jackdaw firmly on her shoulder, is determined to survive the dangerous and sometimes crazy happenings, and to unravel the mystery of the highwayman's past.

Ed Wicke has written several books for children, including 'Muselings', 'Screeps', 'Bullies', 'Nicklus' and the tale of magic 'Akayzia Adams and the Masterdragon's Secret', to be published in December 2003.

Front cover illustration by Tom Warne

CONTENTS

Ed Wicke

Mattie
and the
Highwaymen

BlacknBlue Press UK

For my mother and father.

BlacknBlue Press UK
13 Dellands, Overton, Hampshire, England

First published in 2003
Copyright © Ed Wicke 2003
Illustrations copyright © Tom Warne 2003
All rights reserved

Printed in Great Britain by
Lightning Source
6 Precedent Drive, Rooksley, Milton Keynes MK13 8PR, England

Acknowledgements

Amongst the many publications I researched, two were of particular assistance:
  The Scandal of the Andover Workhouse – Ian Anstruther (1973)
  A Glossary of Hampshire Words and Phrases – William Cope (1883)

Chapter 1 The Highwaymen

In the darkest hours before dawn on August the 4th, 1845, a young girl was trotting west on a small grey Arabian mare. Stars in a cloudless night followed her down the chalky Hampshire road, giving just enough light to reveal its many ruts and potholes. She sang occasionally to keep her spirits up and paused once to eat a slice of meat and potato pie, which she shared with the tame jackdaw travelling with her. Then she settled a large black cloak about her thin shoulders, pulled the hood over her short-cropped blond hair, and set off again. The cloak flapped gently against the tops of ankle-high black boots that were several sizes too large for her. After a time the quiet, even pacing of the horse rocked her to sleep.

When she awoke, there was a barely perceptible brightening of the eastern sky behind her. The mare had paused to crop some grass from the verge and moved on reluctantly, only to stop yet again. They were at the edge of Harewood forest now, and darkness breathed from the very trees.

'Come on, girl,' urged Mattie, giving the mare a little squeeze with her legs. 'It's not far to Andover now.' They entered the forest, bearing a little to their right, to the north.

'Why, it's hardly more than a wood!' the girl said reproachfully. 'And the road mostly runs along its edge, in any case!'

5

For the next mile, this was true. But then the road bent due west and the forest spilled across the road from left to right, blocking out the little light that remained. The horse's hoofs echoed and were answered by scuttling sounds from the trees that leaned hard against the margin of the road and met overhead.

Mattie peered forward but could make out only the faint white of the chalky road surface. The mare slowed, then halted abruptly, throwing Mattie forward onto her mane. Ghostly shapes moved in the darkness about them.

'Who's there? Who is it?' Mattie whispered, trembling.

For answer there was a low laugh from the bushes on her left. Then a deep voice cried:

'That's good, then, my fine boys! Let's have a light now and see what's in the net, shall we? Don't sound like much of a catch though, do it? Hey?' The voice was well-spoken, with a rustic edge to it.

A lantern was lighted and held in Mattie's face. Its holder was tall and skinny and wore a black mask covering the top half of his face. Below the mask was a sharp nose, bad teeth, and a filthy, matted beard parted on the left by a wide scar. Behind him, another man held the horse's bridle. There were others waiting in the shadows.

'Just a tiddler, cap'n!' cried the one with the lantern. 'A gel, what's more!'

The leader stepped into the pool of light. He was tall and broad, with dark curly hair and a clean-shaven face. In one hand he held a full-length mask, which he twirled about on a ribbon as he studied Mattie with amusement and disbelief. His other hand rested on a pistol tucked into his wide belt.

'Well, well, what have we here? A minuscule mermaid, is that it, boys? Swimming here amongst the sharks, was she? Well now, young Missy! You must consider yourself becalmed, marooned, boarded, plundered, scuppered and shipwrecked!' He laughed loudly and the noise echoed in the gloom. He made a small, mocking bow and added, 'But you are most welcome, young'un. Dicker am I - keeper, you might say, of the Queen's highway!'

Mattie sat up straight and tried to control her voice. 'I - I would be much obliged -' she said in little more than a whisper, 'if you were to - to move out of my path - and - and -'. The man with the lantern laughed at her. She became angry and her voice rose. 'And I would be obliged also if this - this *creature* here would be so good as to stop poking that light in my face, and if the other creature would release my horse's bridle! I am on my way to Miss Bell's Academy for the Daughters of Gentlefolk, where I intend to continue my studies.'

In the darkness to her left, someone snorted at this speech. Dicker laughed derisively and then copied her refined accent.

'What?' he cried. 'Surely - oh, *shorely*! - you are not going to Miss Bell's Academy? Why did you not say so? We were just going there ourselves, weren't we, boys?' He nodded towards his men and changed his voice again.

'Me and my crew, we was goin' to enrol there and learn how to be wise and good, 'cause our mothers never taught us - did they, lads?'

'That's sure as dammit right, Dicker, me old Mam never taught me nothin' but sinfulness, an' that's a fact!' one of the others exclaimed.

Dicker stroked the horse's mane with a large, hairy hand. 'Aye, Missy, we're poor orphan boys what never had the loving direction we needed, and we reckon your Miss Bell is just the lady to give it us! So I expect you'd be pleased if we was to go with you and protect you from brigands and highwaymen and other outcasts from polite society. Hey? Besides, we knows a shortcut, don't

7

we, shipmates?'

'I don't think -' began Mattie.

'Then you shouldn't be talking! Bring her along, lads! Lump, Stump, Pirate, Scarecrow - on the double now! We don't want her to be late for the wondrous Miss Bell, do we?'

Mattie was hustled off the road to her right and all her protests were answered by bursts of rough laughter. They jogged along a path at considerable speed. Branches slapped her face and strong, rough hands pulled at her until she was lying flat along the horse's back, clinging to its mane. The path dropped suddenly and spiralled to the right, down and down until the trees silhouetted on the skyline were high above her, and she could imagine she was in the dark hold of a steep-sided ship, with rats scuttling about her on every side.

They turned a final bend and stopped. The gang were panting from their exertions and two of them sat on the ground to recover while the growing light restored Mattie's whirling senses. Not counting Dicker, her captors were four. Two of them were bearded; three were scarred about the face; all were filthy. One had large gold earrings, long black hair tied behind his head, and a hook nose set crookedly on a scarred face. A second had an arm that ended above the wrist; apart from a wispy red beard, he had the face of a boy. A third was fat, balding and beardless. He sat wheezing and sweating long after the others had caught their breath. The fourth was the thin, unkempt, scarred man with blackened teeth who had held the lantern. Mattie stared at them: Pirate, Stump, Lump and Scarecrow. Dicker, standing calmly at the horse's head, was biting a fingernail.

'You shouldn't do that, you know,' Mattie told in him in a shaking voice. She hardly knew what she was saying. She was talking just to keep herself from fainting.

'Beg pardon? Shouldn't do what, Missy?'

8

'Bite your nails. Miss - Miss Bell says the pieces get stuck in your - your appendix, which then rots inside you, so that you die an agonising death.'

'Bully for her! I'll wager you a guinea that the lying old bird snuffs it afore I do! Hey?'

The jackdaw, who had dozed fitfully throughout Mattie's adventures, roused himself at this last cry. He crept out from within Mattie's cloak onto her shoulder and fixed the man with a bright eye. 'Heh! Heh!' he mimicked.

'Sblood! It's a devil bird!' exclaimed Dicker. He drew the pistol from his belt. 'Shoo the hell-creature off your shoulder, Missy. I'm good with this pistol, but it does jump a bit when it fires, and sometimes the ball goes astray.'

'It's my bird, and I'll thank you leave it be!' she countered, suddenly fearless.

Dicker stared at her. 'Leave it be? Leave it be?! I'm not having that thing in my camp, my little pretty! But it's up to you, girl. I'll take off his head as he sits there on your shoulder, or else as he flies away. But off it most definitely goes, my lovely! Can't abide witches, ghosts, black cats, haunted houses, the gibbet - or ravens!'

'It's not a raven. It's a jackdaw!'

'Looks plenty like a raven to me in this light, and that's enough!' He cocked the gun and raised it slowly.

'You won't!'

'I sure as hellfire will!'

Mattie snatched Jasper from her shoulder and tucked him inside her cloak again. 'Now try it, you - you great *oaf*!' she raged.

The one called Lump gave a great guffaw. 'Got you there, hain't she, Dicker?' he called out.

'Shut your fat face!' Dicker swung at the man and Lump fell backwards with the weight of the blow. The others laughed. Then Dicker's gun turned back to point at Mattie on her horse, slowly, deliberately, as if it were a live thing moving of its own will.

Dicker looked up at her along the barrel and spoke quietly. 'The only thing that stops me from putting a bullet through the both of you is the thought that you may be worth more to us alive than dead, little Miss Bigboots. Perhaps - so as to save your scrawny little skin - you could tell us who you are, and why you were passing along the public highway in a manner likely to bring danger to yourself at this time of the day's dawning?'

Mattie climbed down from the horse. Once on the ground, her bravery left her as suddenly as it had come. She leaned against the mare and tried to stop her legs from shaking. 'I'm - I'm Matilda Harris,' she said haltingly. 'I am thirteen years old -'

'Now that's bad luck, for a start!' Scarecrow exclaimed, dragging at his beard. 'Havin' a woman on board is bad enough, but one that's thirteen in the bargain is not to my likin'!'

'And - and I was going to Miss Bell's Academy, as I have already told you. And Sir Lucid will be very annoyed when he finds -'. She clapped a hand over her mouth.

'I like that name,' Dicker said. 'Say it again. "Sir" Lucid, I think it was?'

Mattie shrugged her shoulders.

Dicker smiled, pityingly. 'What a poor memory you have, Missy! Can't even recall what you said a moment before, hey? I expect you would be a bit of a trial to Miss Bell, right? So maybe you'd better put off your education a few days, whilst we tries to discover how much Sir Lucid misses you, and how much salvage he's willing to pay.'

'Salvage?'

Dicker was all sea captain now. 'It's what they pays you, my little lubber, when you comes across a ship what's floatin' about lost and helpless on the open seas, and out of the salty kindness of your tender heart you takes it in tow and brings it back to port.'

'I was *not* lost!' Mattie's grey-green eyes glittered a little and her chin came up defiantly.

'You are now, young'un!' said Lump, who had righted himself and was edging cautiously out of Dicker's reach.

Dicker continued, 'But at least you're in royal company, little Clonkaboot: under the protection of Dicker - *Sir* Dicker, I should say! - highwayman by appointment to Her Majesty Queen Victoria!'

'I don't believe *that*!' Mattie exclaimed.

Dicker gave her a warning grimace. 'Seems to me you'd best believe what you're told, my cocky little firebrand! If I say I'm Sir Dicker, it's true enough while I've got a knife in my pocket and a pistol at my belt. That pile of mossy stones over there is my manorial seat, and these here nobly-bred boys with perfect manners and bad teeth are my royal retainers.'

Mattie remembered something. 'Miss Bell says that the age of the highwayman has passed. She says the last real highwaymen were at the beginning of the century. Miss Bell says -'

'I think I'm going to grow powerful tired of hearing of that lady quite soon, Missy. Her name rings no bells with me, you might say!'

Lump, now out of Dicker's reach, turned a worried eye towards Mattie. He wiped his brow and panted, 'Say - Dicker - what'll we do if - if they won't pay ready money?'

'She walks, don't she?' - and Dicker gave his men a broad wink.

Mattie considered this. 'You mean I get to go home, but you keep the horse?'

A chorus of laughs greeted this. 'No, my fine prisoner. You walk the plank! Come this way, sweetheart.' And she was pulled along a muddy path, rough hands pinching her arms and shoulders, until they reached a clearing. On one side of it, a steep chalk wall rose. In the past someone had tried to quarry from it, and made quite a deep cave within - which Mattie could see was now a storage place for the gang. Nearby was a ramshackle timber cottage and in front of one of its two grimy windows was a ring of crumbling stone which rose a couple of feet from the ground. It was to this stone ring that she was led.

'Now, my poppet,' said Dicker in a confiding tone. 'This here's a well. The water's still good for drinking, and I once saw Stump washing with it - only once, mind! Furthermore, it would be a fine place to put things when you no longer need 'em and don't particularly want anyone else to know you've had 'em. Know what I mean?'

Mattie looked at the well and said nothing.

Dicker grinned. 'What d'you say, lads? Reckon she understands?'

Scarecrow answered grimly, 'She needs to be shown, Dicker.'

Dicker grubbed about in the dirt by the well and came up with a fat worm. He placed it on a flat stick, which he laid on the stones. The worm crawled slowly along the stick.

Dicker dropped his voice to a whisper. 'Now you see, Missy. I have no need for this old worm, have I? He's nothing to me. And when he gets to the end of that stick, he's nothing to no one. Right?'

The worm came to the end of its short journey and felt forward uncertainly. Dicker tilted the stick and the worm wriggled clumsily and fell. A few seconds later a tiny splash was heard.

'I understand,' said Mattie quietly. 'You're a bunch of bloodthirsty pirates.'

'Got it in one, little Miss! This here's the finest band of thieves, cutpurses and scoundrels you'll ever meet,'

Dicker confided.

'Led by the last of the highwaymen, aye, Dicker?' cried Pirate.

'And why not? The Dickers have always been pirates, bootleggers, buccaneers, poltroons, highwaymen, throat-slitters and kidnappers. It's what we do best!'

'Except when you're in gaol, Dicker!' Lump said.

'Ah, but I'm out now, see? Out for near on six months and not caught yet! Oh, we've got some merry times ahead of us, lads - merry times! And I've a feeling that our young friend here will give us hours of entertainment, and make us all considerably rich besides! That's right, isn't it, my sweet fireball?'

He leaned towards her until his broad face was close to her own. His breath smelled of raw onions and beer. Mattie tried to pull away, but he grabbed her by the shoulder and repeated his question. She kicked out at him feebly, and he laughed. But his shaking of her had dislodged Jasper from her cloak. The bird panicked and stabbed his beak deep into the man's cheek. Dicker fell back clutching his face while the bird flew into the trees.

'Devil's bird! I swear it's a raven, after all. Where's my pistol, Jack?'

Pirate spoke urgently, grabbing Dicker's arm. 'Don't shoot a jackdaw, Dicker. 'Sbad luck, it is. Like - like killin' an albatross at sea.' Mattie was surprised that his voice trembled a little, as if with fear.

Dicker raised the pistol. He sighted along it carefully, then looked around at his men. He gave a long, exasperated sigh. 'All right, boys. Mustn't tempt fate! The damned bird lives.' He put the pistol away and turned to Mattie. He chucked her under the chin.

'What about your folks, then, littl'un? How rich be they?'

Mattie had recovered her courage once more and regarded him coolly. 'If you think I'm going to tell you anything, you're going to be very, very disappointed,' she said.

Dicker laughed. 'What shall we do with her, lads? D'you reckon she'll talk if we roast her feet on the camp-fire?'

There were laughs of approval at this suggestion but Pirate spoke up again, saying doubtfully, 'She's just a girl, Dicker.'

'Just a girl? She's a clear thousand in gold pieces, you lily-livered babies! But no matter. No matter! We know the name - she gave us that. And I reckon if we look in the pony's saddlebags, we'll discover most everything else we need to know. She wouldn't be travelling to school without taking a few necessaries. Fetch'em, Jack! Stump, tether the pony with our own horses. Scarecrow, you see the girl to the cave. Tie her up, if you've a mind to! I expect she'll stay put until the work'us brats get back with our breakfast.'

Mattie was led away by Scarecrow, wondering what a "work'us brat" was. Pirate ransacked her bags, and Stump - who so far had said nothing to anyone - stroked the mare kindly with his good arm and then whistled gently to her as he led her away.

'Dicker! Come look at this, would ye?'

'What is it, Pirate me old sport? A letter? Who from and who to, me barnacled ship's underbelly?' Dicker turned the envelope over. '*Please send to Sir Lucid*' he read.

'Don't reckon we'll do that, will we, Jack?' He took a thick knife from his belt and slit the envelope deftly, like a man accustomed to much slitting. He extracted the letter and read it, his lips moving silently.

Dear Uncle Lucid

By the time you get this letter, I shall be at Miss Bell's Academy. I know you did not wish me to go back there before term starts, but I would be very unhappy to remain at Druddery Hall alone. I have previously stayed with the caretakers, Mr and Mrs Mills, and they were always very good to me. I am certain that they be willing for me to board with them while you are in Cornwall.

I will write to you again once I have arrived. I remain your dutiful niece

Matilda Harris

'Well, well,' he said, mostly to himself. 'Looks like the young lady ran away, meaning to leave behind a letter telling of her whereabouts - but she put it in her bags instead. So... so he doesn't know where she is. Perhaps he doesn't even know she's gone. Methinks... methinks Sir Dicker could make something of this.'

'What's up, Dicker?'

'What's up, old crewmate, is that we've got some digging to do.'

'Diggin'? What for? Gold? Or maybe you mean diggin' graves? Look, Dicker, I done a lot of wicked things in me time, but -'.

Dicker placed a hand firmly over the other's mouth. 'Put a bung in it, Jack, there's a good tar. No one's to be hurt - at least, not unless it's necessary. I meant digging for *information*. There's for sure a gold mine at the bottom of all this, my friend, but it's maybe a long ways down! But first I need some breakfast - and then I need to don my finest rags and assume a right royal bearing, so as to make a social call on Sir Lucid Somebody. Mayhaps Ay shall be Terence Dicker, Esquire, late of Pall Mall, wishing to make the acquaintance of gentlemen of similar breeding, what?'

Chapter 2 Lord and Lady

It was now five months since the Asian Flu had carried off Mattie's parents and half the village of Old Rookum. Five sad, dull months, in which she had lived with her uncle and aunt - Sir Lucid and Lady Agatha Arbuthnot - and her cousin Hubert. Lucid had come to collect her from her boarding school, the Academy for the Daughters of Gentlefolk, and had broken the sad news to her in his hesitant, stumbling manner before taking her to Druddery Hall.

She would much rather have stayed at school. Apart from her home in Old Rookum, the Academy was the place she was happiest. However, everyone had said it would be best for her to break her studies. So instead she had been bored - and angry, and lonely, and unhappy ever since. She had always been a quiet child; now there was something sombre about her silences. She spoke in whispers to her uncle and aunt, if she spoke at all. She did not know how to speak to the servants, having never had any before now. Only with her cousin was she at ease, and even with him she could not speak of the things she was forever thinking about.

Lucid was her mother's elder brother, but Mattie had rarely met him. He was moderately rich and extremely shy: a shortish, plumpish, kindly gentleman who spoke hesitantly and seemed content to potter about his estates.

His wife however was formidable. Aunt Agatha was

tall and big-boned and somewhat stout, with a great, round, severe, frowning face and plenty of silvery-black hair. This wondrous hair was usually piled high on top of her head, where it swirled around and upwards until coming to a point. It looked rather as if she had mistaken one of the beehives in the cherry orchard for a hat, and was wearing it!

She was not Hubert's mother. The first Lady Arbuthnot had died some years previously, and Sir Lucid Arbuthnot had married Agatha only two years ago. He had taken Hubert on a long cruise to Egypt, hoping it would help them to forget the sadness of losing his wife and Hubert's mother. Agatha was on this same cruise. Somehow - and he was never very certain himself how it had happened - he had ended up proposing marriage to Agatha and they were married on the ship before returning to England. He soon discovered that she was a vain and rather ignorant woman; but he continued to love her nonetheless.

Mattie's cousin, Hubert, was fifteen. He was a gentle boy, sometimes dull, but always kind and (for the most part) terribly refined. In gentleness and dullness, he took after his father. He had no choice in the refinement, for Lady Agatha insisted on it. It was for the sake of this refinement that she tried to keep Hubert from Mattie, for the girl had an "improper effect" on him. Mattie caused him to laugh too much and to talk far too freely – "without decorum, decency and discretion!" Since Mattie's arrival, Hubert had even developed a sense of humour, a property that Agatha regarded as "too, too vulgar".

Hubert had an old tutor who came six days a week to train him in mathematics, writing and French, all of which he hated. For relaxation he was allowed to read books about farming, or to develop his mind by doing jigsaws and other puzzles - which he hated more than mathematics, writing and French put together!

Agatha said that Hubert must learn how act like an important person: a Squire like his father, yes, but better than that – a Squire with *refinement*. He had to learn that it looked quite, quite absurd to stand absent-mindedly on one leg whilst conducting conversations, as his father was inclined to do. Lucid had never quite learned how to behave properly in public - despite being a Knight of the Realm! - and Agatha was going to make very sure that her stepson made a far better job of it!

As for Matilda, Lady Agatha knew the girl would never amount to anything, and told her so. It was true that Mattie's mother had been Lucid's beloved younger sister; but this counted for nothing. Mattie's mother had foolishly and stubbornly married below herself, for love! In shocking (Agatha's word precisely) - *shocking* disobedience to her own parents, she had wed a poor country parson and had given up her many luxuries for a life of simplicity, hard work and horrid, *horrid* ordinariness. The child which had resulted from this poor match clearly belonged to *that* sort of life - *not* to the gentility and order of Druddery Hall.

Furthermore, to Agatha's horror, Mattie was eye-poppingly, expensively clumsy. The girl was good only at breaking things! Teapots, glasses, vases, table lamps, chairs: she had broken them all, with great skill and extravagant noise, and with much puzzlement, for she clearly didn't know how it happened.

'I shouldn't wonder if she does it on purpose, to spite us!' Agatha had told Lucid the evening before, as they sat together in one of the many large rooms of Druddery Hall - rooms crammed with interesting pictures, statuettes, suits of armour, old furniture and everything else to be expected in an ancient manorial hall.

'I'm sure she... um... doesn't *mean* to, my sweet one,' her podgy, balding husband said in a mild tone, looking up from his magazine and meeting her eye apologetically, as was his habit. 'She... ah... always seems so *surprised* when it happens.'

'That's all part of an act,' Lady Agatha said. '*Of course* she isn't going to let on that she means to break things. *Of course* she will pretend it's sentimental!'

'Accidental, you mean,' Hubert murmured from his seat on the other side of the room.

'That is precisely what I said, Hubert!'

'Yes, Mother.'

'Hubert! I have told you *not* to call me that! Call me "Mama", please, with the accent on the second syllable - Ma*ma*, not *Ma*ma. Anything else is too, too common.' She returned to her stitching, making annoyed little tutting sounds all the while.

Hubert sighed and returned to his task. He was sitting at a small table covered with jigsaw pieces. He had sorted them into piles of the same colour, and was now giving them an apprehensive stare as if he feared they might arise and throw themselves upon him.

'But why do it at all?' asked Lucid with a frown, taking off his gold-rimmed spectacles and fiddling with them absently. 'Why break things if, um, if you aren't doing it by accident? Do you think she... she ah... *likes* the sound of breaking glass, or - or the noise of china as it - ah - shatters?'

'Or wood, Papa. Don't forget how she pulverised your umbrella stand!' added Hubert, rolling out the words with great pleasure. 'She crunched that up better than an army of termites!'

'Yes - ah - *wood*. Now, that makes quite a different sound when it breaks. So perhaps it's not the *sound* she likes at all...' Lucid pondered.

Lady Agatha put down her embroidery and sipped her tea slowly, a menacing look growing upon her fat face. 'Sometimes I think you two are the thickest, slowest, dullest woolly-brained peewits I have ever come across!'

she said.

'Surely not!' exclaimed Lucid. 'You must - ah - have come across quite a number of, um - nitwits I think you mean - in your time, dearest. The likelihood that Hubert and myself are the - are the thickest and, ah, slowest of them is small. Very, very small indeed. The law of probabilities, you know.'

'Do you not see?' his wife retorted. 'Do you not see that Matilda breaks things with purposement? The girl does not respect us, Lucid! She thinks *her* family - her lowly, common family - was as good as *mine* - and as good as yours - as *ours*, Lucid. She gives herself airs. She has no platitude -'

'Gratitude!' Hubert corrected.

'- *gratitude* for the care and comfort we have given her since her parents died. We who took her in, fed her, raised her and spent good money on her... *especially* the good money we've spent on breakages!'

'My dearest!' cried Lucid. 'Pray do not upset yourself! I am sure you exaggerate. This child, whom we have cared for, and must teach the difference between right and - ah -'

'Wrong,' supplied Hubert quickly.

'Yes, that's right - wrong. That is, I mean - ah - "wrong" is right.'

'Wrong is right, Father?' asked Hubert as he counted his piles of misshapen wood. 'Surely that's wrong!'

'Is that meant to be a joke, Hubert?' asked his stepmother severely.

'It would be wrong for you to think, so, Mama,' Hubert answered gravely. 'And it would be right for you to think it wrong for me to make a joke about right and wrong.' He looked up and caught his father's eye. Sir Lucid stifled a laugh.

Hubert's stepmother gave him an exasperated look, identical to the look he was giving to his jigsaw pieces.

'You have spent far too many hours with Matilda, Hubert. The girl has been teaching you to say annoying things, careless things! I suppose you think they sound clever and funny. But they are simply *childish*!'

Hubert shrugged his shoulders at this cruel comment and fiddled gloomily with an orange piece, turning it in all directions and studying its back with an air of deep puzzlement.

'What I mean, my dearest,' continued Lucid, 'is that our - our Mattie is a sensible, ah, girl. She will not lightly cast aside our, um, good intentions and - yes, our kindness in ah - adopting her as one of ourselves, only, only not *quite* as one of us yet, I suppose....'

'Of *course* the girl is not one of us! And never will be! You can't make silk pigs from a nurse's cow, can you?' Agatha retorted scornfully. She shifted irritably in her seat with a swish of silk - and wool - and cotton - and a creak of whalebone from her corsets.

There was a pause while Lucid tried to make sense of this. 'Oh - I see,' he murmured after a time. 'Silk purses from sow's ears. But - ah - my dearest, Mattie is a human child, my dear sister's child, not an auditory - er - attachment of a farmyard animal...'

'I like Mattie,' said Hubert, picking up a green piece and trying to fit it into a blue one. It did not work, and he carefully replaced the pieces in their piles with another sigh. 'Mattie's such jolly fun! *And* she's a whiz at jigsaw puzzles!' He made a face at the tidy hillocks of puzzle pieces before turning to raise a cup of tea from a little table beside him.

'But she doesn't *sort* the pieces as well as you do, Hubert,' said his stepmother, wagging her finger at him. '*Nobody* sorts jigsaw pieces like you do, and I'm sure that is a great advancement on your part. Once you have mastered the art of fitting the pieces *together*, you will be a far, far better puzzler that she! Good breeding will

21

always triumph!'

'I *hate* jigsaws!' muttered Hubert fiercely. But he said it into his teacup, so that no one would hear. 'One day I will have a big bonfire in the back garden, and I will throw every jigsaw in the house onto the bonfire, and dance round the flames! Yes, I will dance, dance, dance!'

'What are you saying, Hubert?' his stepmother asked in a cooing voice. 'You know we can't hear you if you mumble!'

'Yes, Mama.' Hubert stealthily took a penknife from his blazer pocket. Turning his chair around so that his stepmother could not see what he was doing, he began trimming the jigsaw shapes so that they fitted one another.

Lady Agatha took up her embroidery again. 'That girl will have to go!' she declared. 'I used to have a stepson who spoke kindly to me, but she has taught him to mumble rudely into his teacup. She breaks all our precious, precious ornaments and can't scrub a floor for toffee!'

'Do we give her toffee for the housework she does, my dear?' asked Lucid absently. 'Surely - ah - surely that is bad for her, um, teeth.'

Hubert paused from his careful alteration of a yellowish piece with green edges. 'Anyway, Father, we shouldn't be making poor Mattie scrub the floors at all. She'll only break the tiles!'

Lucid laughed. 'Say, that's rather funny. Good joke, Hubert, my son! Fine piece of - ah - wit. Funniest thing I've heard all week...'

Lady Agatha stared at her stepson. 'Was that intended to be humorsome, Hubert? Were you making light of a *serious* matter?'

'No, Mama - of course not!' exclaimed Hubert. 'It was an accident, Mama, I assure you.' Two red pieces in his hands suddenly went together with a faint click. He gave a little jump of surprise. 'An accident - just like that...' He laughed loudly, and Agatha glowered at him.

Mattie, who had been listening from outside the sitting room window, decided she had heard enough and tiptoed away. Her great boots met something hard on the dark lawn and knocked it over with a mighty thud. She fled into the stables and from there shot into the kitchen, where she seized a meat and potato pie that Cook had left cooling on the window ledge. As quietly as her huge, clonking boots would allow her, she tiptoed up the back stairs to her attic room.

'What was that noise, my dear?' asked Lucid, looking up from the weekly magazine he was reading, called "Squire". It had interesting pictures of sheep and horses in it, and was his favourite recreation.

'Yes, that was quite a thump. Did you drop a stitch or something, Mama?' asked Hubert. He had fitted together a further two pieces now, and was feeling very pleased with himself.

'Hubert!'

'Sorry, Mama, another accidental witticism. I'm getting as bad as Mattie!'

'Go to bed! And please ring for my lady's maid as you pass the bell-pull.'

'Yes, Mama.' He rose and kissed the hand she offered before sauntering off to his room. He was tall for fifteen and thin, with a narrow, gentle face and a friendly look in his eye.

'He is such a dear child!' said Agatha to Lucid, with a hint of real tenderness in her voice. She added fretfully, 'It is a shame that the other one is such a *caravan*!'

'A - a harridan, you mean, my dear? Or do you mean a polygon - you know, one of those - ah - those many-sided figures that Hubert's tutor makes Hubert draw when he can't think of anything better to teach him...'

Lady Agatha gave him a black look that silenced him

on the instant. 'She is a bad-tempered, undisciplined child, Lucid. *And* she brings disaster to all she touches! I wouldn't be at all surprised to find that she is responsible for the loss of my jewellery. I know I mislay my little treasures from time to time; but my diamond ring really has gone, I'm sure of it!'

'Of course it has, my dear. But we'll have one last search tomorrow, shall we?'

'There you go again, Lucid, trying to talk me down! No one believes me when I tell them how upset I am! But *"fine words butter no parsons"*, as my mother used to say.'

Lucid looked up from his magazine with surprise. 'Did she now? Rather uncomfortable for the - ah - parson, I should say, my dear.'

Lady Agatha picked nervously at her embroidery. 'Lucid,' she began uncertainly. 'Lucid, there's something worrying me.'

Lucid nodded. 'I rather thought so -'.

'We go to visit my father tomorrow, in Cornwall.'

'Are you worried now about leaving Mattie behind? I did propose -'.

'Of course not! My father is ill, Lucid! How can you suggest we have that badly-behaved girl with us, breaking all his china and smashing his omelettes?'

'Ornaments.'

Agatha made an angry little noise, rather like the hissing of a kettle. 'I fear a scene. I - I fear my brother might be there. I don't think I've ever mentioned my brother Robert.'

'Can't say I recall you having done so.'

'Well - he is a *most* unpleasant character. The proverbial back street of the family.'

There was a long pause. Lady Agatha took up her sewing again. She clearly felt she had said enough. 'It's such a relief having told you, Lucid. My mind is quite easy now.'

'It is?' asked Lucid, rather puzzled by all this. 'Oh... jolly good, then.'

He rose from his seat and walked to the window. He waddled a little as he walked, being plump as well as small. With his quiff of remaining light hair sticking up from the back of his head, he looked very like a duck, except when he was standing on one leg, which he did in moments of excitement and was doing now. 'Great shame,' he said. 'Great shame.'

'What is, Lucid dear?'

'Your favourite garden gnome. The green one with a little riding crop and wearing a topper. The wind seems to have blown it over! Broken to smithereens, it is! Great - ah - great pity.'

Chapter 3 Work'us Brats

An hour before Mattie was captured, the Arbuthnots' carriage had sped along the same London to Salisbury Road. It had passed through the edge of Harefield Forest without hindrance, only to suffer a cracked wheel just beyond, still several miles short of Andover.

As the driver was carefully feeling the wheel in the half-darkness and trying to decide whether they could continue on it, Mattie was riding into the Forest and into the waiting arms of her captors, who were cursing one another for having missed the coach shortly before.

'How great is the damage, Jackson?' Sir Lucid asked. He was pacing from one side of the road to the other, peering along its length in hopes of another carriage coming to their aid.

The massive coachman shook his head slowly as he knelt and examined the wheel. 'Pretty fierce, Sir Lucid. Wood's mostly sound, but the iron band has cracked right off. If we drop into too many potholes, she'll smash to pieces. But I reckon we can roll along west'ards - slowly - as far as Andover.'

'And then?'

'Spect we can find a smithy there to repair the wheel. Might even be one this side of the town - I don't know the place that well.'

'Will these two know?' asked Lucid, nodding up the road towards two small figures who had appeared from around a distant bend ahead. They might be two miles

26

away: it was difficult to judge distances by the faint threads of dawn which lit their faces.

'Only one way to find out, sir. If you'd be so good as to take your seat again, sir, we'll set off and meet them halfway.'

Half an hour later, they came up to the walkers - two dirty, ragged children who talked loudly in high-pitched voices as they plodded along the stony, dusty road. Lucid motioned to his driver to stop the carriage and was about to speak to the children when they opened the conversation first.

'Got a penny, mister?' This from the boy, who must have been about ten years old. He was clutching two large loaves of bread under one arm and carried a flask - probably beer - in the other. After a moment's inspection, Lucid decided this was the dirtiest child he had ever seen.

'Or two pennies?' No, he had been wrong there. *This* was the dirtiest child he had ever viewed close up. Her hair was matted and he felt sure it was crawling with lice. At least the girl had made some attempt at washing her face - she had succeeded in smearing the dirt from one side to the other, and had then apparently wiped her hands down the front of her grimy dress. She was around the same age as the boy - no, the exact age: they were certainly twins. She was carrying bread and beer, too.

'I think I could find two pennies,' Sir Lucid promised, feeling in his pockets. 'But you will need to help me first, if you can.'

'Be quick about it, mister. A dang'rous place, this. Crawlin' wi' thieves, it be.' The boy looked about nervously. Lucid found himself staring at the child's hair. Good heavens, what colour was it? Blond, brown, red? It was so dirty that one simply couldn't say.

'Here are your pennies.' Sir Lucid held them up, one in

each hand. 'Now - we are looking for a blacksmith's. Would you know where one is, nearby? If so, I would be grateful to - ah - receive the information.'

'Not on this road, mister,' the girl answered, reaching for her penny. 'But there's one in the middle of Andover, near the Work'us.'

'The Smith's not there, though,' said the boy.

'A'course he is!' his sister turned on him.

'He's not, y' dimwit! Saw him outside the baker's half an hour back, goin' south. You want to try t'other smithy, mister. Go 'long this road 'bout a mile, then ren'ards up the Roman Road.'

'Renwards?' Lucid asked, confused.

The boy looked up at Lucid, puzzled. Didn't the old gent understand him?

His sister spoke up. 'He means you turns to the right, sir.' She nudged the boy and whispered to him. 'The gen'lman may be a bit simple, Tom. Or p'raps he's dunch as a bittle an' has disremembered to bring his ear trumpet! Make it plain, else you'll put him all in a muggle!'

Tom spoke a little more slowly. 'Once you be on the Roman Road, go clever 'long it for a mile or two, an' you'll come to the smithy - just arter the woods ends on your right. I used to run errands for the Smith. But I warn you, he's got a lively temper fust thing in the mornin'. I should know, for he thrashed me reg'lar. Many's the larrupin' I've had from he!' The boy said this with unconcealed pride.

Lady Agatha leaned from the carriage window and fixed the boy with a stern eye. 'Boy!' she commanded, 'Come here, boy! Yes, you! Come along now! Don't be so slow about it!' The child moved a few steps in her direction, reluctantly. She spoke to Lucid over the boy's head.

'I know what common boys are like,' she said, giving the boy a meaningful glance. 'They are not *entirely* truthful! Now – boy! - look me in the eye - are you telling us the truth about this blacksmith's? You're not just making up a story so as to get a penny, are you?'

'Wouldn't lie to a gen'lman,' said the boy in a toneless voice.

'Wouldn't lie to *you*, anyways,' said the girl, talking to Lucid. 'You been polite. Most of 'em ain't.' She had been looking down at her feet; now she glanced up at him shyly.

Lucid cleared his throat. He mustn't start feeling sorry for them, he told himself. But he passed them their pennies anyway. Agatha snorted contemptuously and withdrew into the coach. He spoke to the girl. 'And why are you on the road this time of day?'

'We was up afore dawn, walkin' into town for food,' she answered, tucking her penny into her clothes.

'And where are you going now?' he asked.

'We've a place nearby,' said the boy, nudging his sister into silence and avoiding Lucid's eye.

'Sorry,' said Lucid. 'I wasn't prying. Just - just being neighbourly. That's all.'

There was an embarrassed silence. The boy and girl stood for a moment and then took to their heels at the same moment, plunging into the wood.

'Good gracious!' Lucid said to himself, watching them go. 'I didn't think there were still folk living like that now. I thought the Poor Laws and the Workhouses had solved all that.'

His driver gave an apologetic cough.

'What's that, Jackson?'

'Beggin' your pardon, Sir Lucid. They sent my old Nan into the Workhouse, and it didn't do much for her. She said she would have preferred to live on the streets. Was a blessin' she didn't live long. Consumption carried her off the first winter - it did for a fair few of 'em in the workhouse, that year. They worked 'em hard and scarce gave 'em enough to eat. And they wasn't looked after - no, that they wasn't. 'Twas so cold one day the water froze as they tried to drink it at breakfast, my Nan said.'

'Oh. Sorry to hear that, Jackson.'

'Thank you for saying so, Sir Lucid.'

A few minutes later Lucid asked, 'And - Jackson - what did the child - the - ah - *female* child - mean by "Dunch as a bittle?". I didn't quite follow that.'

Jackson gave another apologetic cough. 'Just a local phrase, Sir Lucid. The girl was wondering if p'raps you was a little hard of hearing - "deaf as a beetle" is what it means. But I don't think she meant any unkindness by it.'

'No - no, of course not. No offence offered, and none taken. The children were - ah - surprisingly thoughtful. Quite - ah - touching, indeed.' And Lucid fell quiet, thinking of the odd little encounter.

And so the Arbuthnots, after a small but important deviation to the blacksmith's, continued on their way to Cornwall. Meanwhile, two ragged children chased each other down The Devil's Eyehole.

'Tom! Tom! Stop a bit!' cried the girl in a breathless whisper. 'You've missed the place!'

'Haven't!' he answered with gruff certainty. But he slowed to a walk anyway.

'It's up ren'ard, I'm sure it is,' she persisted.

'Isn't,' he said, annoyed, but veered to the right anyway.

'There 'tis - see, I was right!'

'So? For the first time ever, you ben't wrong about summat. Don't get in a peel over it, Lizzie!'

They climbed a little until they reached a large, spreading oak. Most of the trees up here were beech, so the oak - once you had spotted it - was a good marker.

Lizzie regarded the moody face of her brother. 'You be

so grumpy, Tom. You got the peezy-weezies today an'
no mistake!'

'Stupid cow!'

'What, me?' Lizzie's eyes filled with tears.

'No - that nasty-faced lady in the carriage! "I knows
what you trash be like," she says. "Kill your own Nans
for the price of a penny loaf, you would!" she says. Stupid cow!'

Lizzie stared at her brother as he stood with his back
against the tree, his head erect, his jaw sticking out defiantly and his eyes sizzling with anger.

'She didn't say none of that, Tom! You mustn't make
things up!'

'That's what she *meant*, the old witch.'

'You shouldn't get so angry, Tom. That's just how
rich folk be! We ben't nothing to them. Besides, you're
not always truthful, are you?'

'Least I ben't a boot-kisser like you.' He mimicked his
sister's voice: '"Oh, good sir, you been so polite and
kind. So gen'rus of you to let me old Mam die of hunger
while you eats roast pork off gold plates!" Why're you so
humble to them, Lizzie?'

'Cos it's right. And - and I'm not talking any more
about it. Except, you shouldn't drag our Mam into it! It
weren't the gen'lman's fault she died. But please, *please*
don't let's argufy, Tom.'

'All right. But you be too soft-hearted, Lizzie.'

'Better than bein' soft-headed, like some I could
name!'

They walked around the tree until they reached a narrow crack in its trunk. They put down their provisions
and she sorted through them, extracting two small
loaves. 'Where's your penny, Tom?'

'Here 'tis.' He handed it over and she wrapped it in a
scrap of cloth. Then he bent down so that she could
climb onto his shoulders. He stood upright and she was

able to reach up to a hollow in the tree, mostly hidden by new growth below it. She pulled out two loaves already wrapped in rags and swapped them for the new loaves, adding the two pennies to some small change already there. She replaced the bundle and stuffed leaves around it until the hollow was filled.

'All done, Tom!' He lowered her to the ground, and they took up the provisions again. The storage place was their insurance. If they had to run off all of a sudden, there was food and money waiting for them. And as long as they renewed the bread every day, the food was fresh enough.

A few minutes later, they entered the camp to see Pirate standing outside the cave. He was busy with a sharp knife and a long wedge of smoked, fatty meat. A wide tin skillet was at his feet and the slices of meat fell softly through the air, each to its appointed place in the pan. Tom's eyes lit up.

'Bacon!' he exclaimed. 'The gaffer's in a good mood, then!'

Dicker himself appeared from within the cave. 'Brats!' he called. 'What's kept you?'

Lizzie was about to speak when Tom trod on her foot and said quickly, 'Saw a carriage on the road, Master.'

'So? So you thought you could take your time, then?'

Tom shrugged his shoulders. 'You told us to keep ourselves hid when we was near the forest, Dicker.'

'I see. So you had to hide till it went past, hey?'

'Stands to reason, Master. Can't keep hid 'thout hidin'!'

Dicker looked at the boy suspiciously. 'Which way was the carriage going, then, Tom my lad?' he asked softly.

'West'ards,' Tom replied, looking innocently into Dicker's face.

'Good lad!' the man said, clipping Tom on the ear. 'There *was* a carriage going west - Ben just missed stopping it. So perhaps the rest of your story is true enough, hey? Did you see what kind of carriage it was, or who was in it, or where it went to?'

'We runned off, Dicker. Besides, where could it go? It's Andover or nowhere, surely!'

'Oh. *Surely*, hey? Or turn off south? Or north, on the Roman Road? Might be worth chasing it a ways then, hey? But it's breakfast soon, and I'll not chase carriages in the growing light just to find they've nothing in 'em but an old biddy and her cat!' He took the bread and beer and waved the twins away.

'And Brats -'

'Yes, Dicker?'

'There's a young lady in the cave. A guest of some honour (for indeed, young'uns, there *is* honour among thieves, hey?). You are to treat her with all gracious propriety and see to her every requirement and desire. Except - except that she's to stay with us for the present. So: you two are her warders, understand? If she lams it, you'll feel the rope on your backs, and worse! You know what I mean by worse, don't you, young Tom?'

'Yes, Dicker.'

'Fair maid Lizzie?'

'Yes, Master.'

'That's my girl! And Dicker always keeps his promises: mind you remember it, hey?'

Chapter 4 Trapped

A fire had been lit in an iron basket that stood in a little recess several paces within the cave, under a natural chimney formed by ancient rock falls: a huge gap in the roof rising in dizzy, twisting stony contortions, twenty, forty, maybe a hundred feet, lost in the steep hillside that the cave burrowed into. The flames from the fire licked the rock, sending iridescent sparks floating high into the air and casting strange shadows upon the faces that surrounded Mattie. The faces seemed unearthly, inhuman, drained of all natural kindliness. The broken, discoloured teeth, the staring eyes, the dirty skin with evil scars, ears misshapen, beards unkempt: they were menacing, disturbing, alien.

Mattie kept telling herself that these dirty, uncouth persons were really quite human - and that if she were to get to know them, they might even prove to be likeable, gentle, reasonable and good. But she could not believe it. She glanced from face to face, seeking some glimmer of human kindness, but quickly dropped her gaze.

She then found herself staring at the smooth pink flesh that formed the end of Stump's deformed arm, telling herself,

'It's not that scary, not really. It's only an arm - part of a human arm. But - but, oh, I shall scream if he touches me with it!'

Fortunately Stump kept well away from her. But Lump

kept following her, moving when she moved, trying to catch her eye.

'Your name Matildy, then?' he asked finally.

'Yes. Matilda.'

'I like that. Nice name, Matildy. You - you're thirteen, right? Nearly a young lady, right?' He looked her over slowly, making her feel uncomfortable. 'Fine young lady already, I'm guessin'. Come sit at the table with me, Matildy.' He tried to take her arm.

'No thank you.' She pulled her arm away. He glowered at her, offended.

The one called Pirate spoke up. 'Leave her be, Lump.'

'Says who?'

'Says my fist! Any messin' with the stowaway has to be agreed with the Cap'n first. And I don't reckon Dicker'll want you pawin' his prize, not till he's finished with her.'

Scarecrow laughed. 'So long as we gets our turn, we don't mind Dicker bein' first!' he cackled. 'But the Ship's Cook's right for once. You best leave off handlin' the cargo, Lump! I 'spect she's the sort what bruises easy. Rich gels has soft flesh. You gotta be careful not to squeez'em too hard!'

Lump pondered this. Finally he shrugged his great shoulders and said moodily, 'I don't see why Dicker should tell us what to do all the time! But I wasn't gonna touch her, not much anyways. Too snobby by half, she is. Thinks herself too good to sit with the likes of me!'

'Thinks herself too good for the lot of us! Up there on the road, she called us "creatures"!' Scarecrow claimed. 'Creatures! That's rich folk for you. To them, we's nothin' but animals!'

Mattie felt she had to put this right. 'Excuse me, but I am *not* rich -' she began. But her announcement was greeted with such an array of hoots and snorts that she fell silent.

Lump copied her. 'Ay ahm nahwt rich. Ay ahm really raahther poor, don't you know?' he chortled.

Just then Tom and Lizzie entered the cave, nearly colliding with Mattie. They stopped and looked at her. Mattie flashed a shaky smile at them, but they returned this with stony stares.

'What's Miss Snobby here for?' Tom asked Pirate. 'Dicker - drot him! - says we has to keep an eye on her.'

'That ain't none of your business,' Scarecrow cut in. 'So keep your nose out of it, Brat! All you needs to know is that you're to make her a place in the cottage for the night, near by you, and to look after her. See to her wants and so on.'

'What?' Tom's face was flaming. 'I ben't a zoo keeper, nor a wet-nurse neither! Don't mind keepin' an eye on the scrimpy so-an-so, but I'll not be her servant!'

Lizzie said nothing, but made a face in Mattie's direction.

Tom pointed at Mattie, but continued talking to the others. 'Met one of her kind this mornin', and that was enow for I. Reckon this one 'ud turn her nose up at us an' all. Fessy rammuck! *She* never had to wear the same clothes twice, I reckon.' He gave Mattie a glance of pure scorn. Jasper, from Mattie's shoulder, gave him an evil glare in return.

'Please,' said Mattie. 'It's not how you think it is. I'm not like that, not at all!'

'An' who ast *her*?' Tom said to Lump. 'Don't she know it's rude to innerupt?'

Lump prodded Mattie in the side with a soft, podgy finger. 'Rich gals is nice to look at, but they've no respect for the likes of us. No respect at all!' he repeated, poking her again, his eyes fixed on her.

Dicker entered and the group fell silent. The men took up seats on rickety stools at the long, rough-hewn table that stood a few steps within the cave entrance. Tom served up the bacon into one wooden bowl while Lizzie sawed at the bread with a long, wickedly sharp knife. The men snatched slices of bread, buttered them from a large crock on the table and - using their dirty fingers, Mattie noted with horror - pulled slices of the sizzling bacon from the bowl and folded them in the bread. Lizzie poured ale for them into an assortment of smeared, grimy mugs made of glass, pewter, wood and tin.

The eating went on for some time. Tom topped up the mugs while Pirate sliced more bacon for Lizzie to fry. Her cooking was not particularly graceful - she burned her fingers several times and swore horribly when she did so - but it was effective. She flicked the bacon over with the point of her knife, then cut some bread into cubes and dropped it into the fat and fried that as well.

The men had seconds of bacon and some fried bread. More bacon went into the pan and this time it was for the children.

'Crimany! Oh, *drot* it!' exclaimed Lizzie. 'Burned meself again!' She took the pan off the fire and danced about the cave, blowing on her fingers.

'Stop puddlin' about, Lizzie!' complained her brother angrily. 'You been right shammocky today!'

'An' *you* been takin' miff all day! What's it for this time?' she snapped back.

'Why - can't you be a tad more perky with that cookin'? Tis eenamost nunch-time and I'm jawled-out from bein' up early. Happen I'd like me bacon and bread, right? 'Spect I could eat a whole dollop on me own, I'm that hungry. Leer as a gallybagger, I be, an' there's you skising about when you ort to be busy.'

She put her hands on her hips and scolded him in return. 'I won't stand no jobation from *you*, Tom Smith!' she cried. 'I been up as early as you has. Happen I walked as far, too. An' I've not seen *you* offerin' to cook, 'ev I? *You've* no call for to be ruffatory! If you be hungry, cut a hunch of bread yourself! And as for bein' busy, *you* best beet up that fire afore it goes out, else you'll have nobbut *raw* bacon to chew!'

Mattie stared at the two children. The words they spoke were clearly English, but some of them made no sense to her at all. She started to ask what the words meant but wisely held back. It would just cause trouble.

The men left the table and Dicker waved Mattie into his place at its head. She bowed her head to say her prayers, which brought snorts of laughter from the departing men. She carefully cut herself some bread and offered to cut some for the Brats. Lizzie did not reply and Tom muttered to himself some insult about 'taffety eaters what's scared to make crumbs!'.

Mattie helped herself to bacon but couldn't stomach the ale, so she asked if there was any water. The Brats ignored her completely, talking to one another as if she was not even in the cave with them. So she ate her bread and bacon without water, and tried the fried bread. It was greasy, but delicious. She tried to tell Lizzie how good it was, but the girl would not listen. Mattie shrugged her shoulders and sat in a miserable, defeated silence. Jasper chirruped to her gently, rubbing his beak against her right ear. She smiled wanly and fed him bacon and bread.

Outside, Dicker was mounting a horse and talking to his men in a low voice. He rode to the cave entrance and bent low out of the saddle to shout to the twins:

'Brats! You're to show our guest the cave, and provide her with sleeping quarters. And they'd better be as good as your own - else you'll find yourselves sleeping in the stream tonight, hear? Show her where to wash and such-like. You know! I'll be back later, and I expect to find her smiling and comfortable. If she's not, I'll make you wish she was! Understand?'

The Brats nodded sullenly.

Once Dicker had gone, they took her to the cottage and then around the camp. Their attempts to make her "smiling and comfortable" amounted to such actions as throwing doors open and remarking lifelessly: 'Your room.' 'Our room.' 'The stream.' 'Where we gets water.' 'We uses this as the privvy.'

'Look,' Mattie tried again. 'I *am* sorry you have to do this.'

'So you should be! This be where the horses is kept. There, you seen it all now.'

'Shall I help you clean the dishes?' Mattie asked.

Tom shrugged. 'Don't bother me what you does,' he said and went off whistling, though with a curious, backward glance at Jasper, who was trying to copy him.

Lizzie stole a quick feel of the sleeve of Mattie's blouse while Mattie was turned away. It felt just as she thought it would - soft and smooth and clean.

'I - I doesn't mind if you helps,' she answered Mattie's previous question. 'I allus does it on me lonesome, 'cept when Pirate starts longin' to be ship's cook agen. Then he chases me out of what he calls the galley and does it all hisself. Make a change if you helps me, like.'

'I'd like to be useful.'

They went back to the cave and collected the breakfast things, which Lizzie put into a sizeable tin bowl. She went with Mattie to the pump at the well and pumped water into a large kettle, which they returned to the cave and placed on the fire. While it was heating Lizzie fetched more cold water.

'God 'a mercy!' she complained. 'Got no cloth! I'll fetch a rag from the cottage. Not that they be at all clean!'

'Is there any soap?' Mattie asked.

'Ain't had soap for weeks now. But we can use soapwort from by the stream. Works near as well.' They went to the stream and Lizzie showed Mattie a patch of soapwort, an erect plant with clusters of scented pink five-petalled flowers. They pulled off some of its broad, oval, fibrous leaves and took them back to the cave. They threw them into the tin bowl and poured hot water from the kettle on them. Lizzie burned her fingers and swore again cheerfully. She dumped the greasy plates into the bowl and stood aside as Mattie washed them carefully, first washing the grimy cloth that Lizzie had provided. The soapwort wasn't anywhere near as good as real soap, but it was better than nothing.

To Mattie's relief, Lizzie chattered willingly about everything and nothing, and though many of her words were incomprehensible or unrepeatable in polite society, they were good-natured and reasonable. Mostly, she wanted to know about Mattie's clothes, and what sort of place she lived in, and - and didn't she have nice, soft skin? And no freckles!

'I'd chop off one of me arms an' be happy to be like Stump if I could be rid of me patchwork,' the girl sighed. 'Is it the bird wot does it?'

'Does what?'

'Gets rid of the freckles. D'you reckon if he sat on me shoulder, me spots would go?'

'I'm sure having a jackdaw on your shoulder would have no effect on freckles,' Mattie advised gravely.

'I tried washin' 'em by moonlight an' saying the rhymes - "Out damned spot" and such-like. But it never made no difference, nohow!' Lizzie exclaimed. She looked over her shoulder at Tom, who was peering into the cave.

'You comin' with me?' he asked Lizzie. 'She can finish the washin' while we has a game in the woods.'

'But we's supposed to watch her!' Lizzie objected.

Tom glared at Mattie. 'She's nowhere to go!' he said sullenly. 'You come with me, Lizzie.' His sister shrugged her shoulders and followed her brother, giving Mattie half a smile as she left.

It was a thoughtful Dicker who returned to the camp at around noon. He dismounted from his large black horse and passed the reins to Stump without a word. He pointed across the clearing to where Mattie was sitting alone, gesturing for her to come to him. As she rose he turned his back and retreated up the path a little. She followed dutifully.

'It's not polite to point,' she remarked when she stood before him. It surprised her that she could speak so boldly to a highwayman, when she could hardly whisper to her aunt.

A flicker of a smile crossed his face. Mattie thought that he looked almost pleasant when he smiled. Certainly, he looked much more presentable now - he had changed his rougher clothes for a green velvet jacket, dark leggings and a spotless white shirt with frills at the cuffs. She wondered where he kept his fine clothes.

'I'll try and remember that, Fireball!' he promised. 'Not that old Dicker is unaware of social conventions - he just picks and chooses, hey? Now, I've been putting on the style at your home, Druddery Hall - though the word "home" may be a misdescription where you're concerned, might it not? Why run away otherwise?'

'I - I was going back to school.'

He laughed unkindly. 'I have too much experience telling lies myself to believe *that* one! You're unhappy at Druddery. Your aunt is a bully but you don't stand up to her, and you take it out on the china instead. Then at the first chance you get, you turn tail and run like a little girl!'

Mattie felt herself growing pink. 'That is quite unfair!' she cried.

'But it's what the servants tell me! Oh, the housekeeper was voluble. And voluminous. And volatile. And Irish.' He put on a gentle Irish accent the very double of the portly housekeeper's. 'Ah, for sure, once she knew I was a relation of your dear father's (God rest his soul!), and had come over from Dublin for the particular pleasure of seeing how my cousin's daughter was faring, she couldn't have been more helpful, especially seeing as she was an Irish lass herself (some twenty years ago, mind you - and a good three stone lighter then, I'll warrant!).'

'Really, Mister Dicker -'

'*Sir* Dicker.'

'*Sir* Dicker, then, if you insist -'

'I do, child. Stand and deliver, there's a good obedient relation!'

'Really, *Sir* Dicker. I must object to your pretending to be a relation.'

'*Must* you? To which part do you object, Fireball? To the pretence itself, or to the stomach-churning idea of filthy old Sir Dicker being kin to yourself? For indeed, all men are related through Adam and Eve, are they not? And so, why not yourself and I?' That smile which might be frank amusement flashed across his face again.

'But to the facts, little one! Your uncle and other relations have withdrawn to Cornwall. The servants of the house think you went with them. It seems that your aunt was adamant that you should stay behind, whereas your uncle wanted you to go, and there was a glorious fight 'twixt the two, which the whole house knows of. They reckon the redoubtable Lady Agatha relented at the last moment and agreed you could go; else why is your bed made and some of your clothes gone? The stable boy - who by his account was just waking then - says he saw you going into the stable at about the time your people were leaving.'

Mattie's face clouded. 'And I didn't leave the letter as I'd planned,' she reflected. 'So - so no one knows I'm missing.'

'No one! And I ask myself, do I want them to know? And I answer in the negative, right? For we don't want a search just now, do we? And you don't want your uncle and dear old auntie to be pacing the floors, in agonies of distress for you, wondering what kind of villains might be holding you, and what they might be *doing* to you, hey?' His smile was not so pleasant now, and the stubby fore-finger he poked into her shoulder was hard and insistent.

Mattie refused to back away. 'What are you going to do, then?' she asked.

'I've done it, lassie! I've sent your letter to your uncle, at the address the housekeeper gave me, with a post-script added by Miss Bell herself, welcoming your early return to your studies. And I've sent a second message from Miss Bell to the full-figured housekeeper, reporting that you were delivered there by your uncle as they passed on their way to Cornwall. When next I visit Drud-dery, Mrs Murphy will no doubt pass on to me the sur-prising news that you are happily in residence with the most glorious Miss Bell! So - everyone is happy, Fireball. Everyone is happy! Even Dicker!' He gave a grim smile.

'Everyone except myself.'

Dicker was all surprise and hurt. 'What?' he cried. 'Don't like the company? Don't appreciate the homely comforts? The good outdoor air? The communing with the natural world? The plenitude of ants and lack of aunts? Well... there's a cure for that, stripling, there's a cure!'

'You have no right -'

'I care little for that!'

Mattie crossed her arms and gave him a hard stare, trying to appear calm and strong. Jasper spoilt the mo-ment somewhat by arriving suddenly and trying to land on her shoulder. He missed his footing and nearly tum-bled to the ground. Mattie's small, nervous hands flew to his aid, settling him gently on his perch. The genuine smile reappeared on Dicker's face for a moment, and he murmured:

'But the Raven still beguiling all my sad soul into smiling,
Straight I wheeled a cushioned seat in front of bird
    and bust and door;
Then, upon the velvet sinking, I betook myself to linking
Fancy unto fancy, thinking what this ominous
    bird of yore -
What this grim, ungainly, ghastly, gaunt and ominous
    bird of yore
Meant in croaking "Nevermore".'

Mattie stared at him. He was evidently as cracked as the china teapot she had dropped last week. She said feebly, 'But - but Jasper is not a raven.'

'Lord save us!' he cried. 'You are treated to a private recitation of a verse from an extraordinary modern poem (printed scarcely a few months back) and all you can do is gape at me like a fish in a bowl! Do they teach you nothing at the fearful academy you attend?'

Mattie said nervously, 'Not - not that poem. We do study modern poetry there. We are even allowed to read Mr Browning's poems. And - and Mrs Browning's poems, too.' She blushed a little.

'Romance and moonlight? Soft voices and gentle eyes? But no grim, ungainly, gaunt and ominous ravens? The Academy is not quite modern enough to allow Edgar Allen Poe's poetry?'

'I had to leave school before the end of last term. My parents - they - they -' Mattie left the sentence unfinished.

'The vociferous Irish housekeeper told me about that, too' Dicker said. He paused as though uncertain what to say, and then changed the subject. 'But we were speaking of your raven.'

'He is *not* a raven!'

'You forget, young'un, that if I say he's a raven, he *is* one, until I allow otherwise!'

Mattie could not decide whether the highwayman was serious about this. 'I do wish, Mister Dicker - *Sir* Dicker, I mean - I wish that you would explain what it is you have in mind for me and my - my *raven.*'

Dicker gave a little laugh. 'Now, now, Missy. Old Dicker hasn't anything particular in mind. Just - just that you *co-operate*, you know, hey? Perhaps we'll go for a ride together, in a carriage, say - and you'll pretend to be my niece? Or maybe you'll write a letter to your uncle, easing his mind, telling him how happy you are at Miss Bell's? Or maybe you'll take the Brats under your wing and teach'em to be young Gentlefolk and to wash the bits that show?'

Mattie stroked Jasper and pondered. There was something more to all this, but she couldn't yet see what it was. 'I thought I was a thousand gold pieces to you,' she said.

Dicker kissed his fingers and waved the money away. 'Kissed it good-bye, Fireball. Maybe - maybe your uncle will give us the price of your food and lodging once he knows how well we've looked after you. Maybe Miss Bell will do the same. Maybe your housekeeper will tell us where the family treasure's hidden! But as for yourself, Missy, have no palpitations of the heart. Dicker has no plans for you but what are congruent with your position as his adoptive distant relation.'

'And -,' his face became cunning, 'and think of the consequences if you can't bring yourself to help old Dicker. I'll have to send the Brats back to the Workhouse - ask 'em about that, young Fireball. Perhaps I'll have to send you with them! Would they believe you were a proper young lady, I wonder? Or would they stick a uniform on you and have you pounding bones with the others? And I'd have to take to violence to support myself, murdering and maiming poor innocent travellers. I might even have to make use of that deep, deep well - and a terrible waste of good water *that* would be, hey?'

He gripped Mattie by the shoulders, dislodging the unfortunate Jasper, and forced her to look at him. Her heart pounded. She was sure he meant his threat of that long, final drop down the well. She forced herself to speak calmly.

'But - but I can't look after the - the Brats. I can't!'

'Why not? Too proud? Too ignorant? Or just too *scared*? You can't run away from everything you don't like, girl!'

She flamed up at this. 'It's nothing of the sort! I'd - I'd love to help them. But they don't like me!'

'And why should they? Why should you expect it? Surely a man - or woman - should do his best, whether he's liked for it or not! Even a highwayman knows *that*! A shame it is that a well brought up rich girl doesn't.'

Mattie nodded numbly. What Dicker said was unjust, but there was a strange, twisted truth to his words. She said, biting her lip, 'Until my aunt and uncle return, I will - I will co-operate. But -'

'No "buts", Missy. That's one word I never allow. Never!'

Chapter 5 No Mitchin'

They walked back to the broken-down hovel. A rotting door hung unevenly in its frame, between two grimy windows. Dicker pushed the door open and Mattie passed before him into a dark, damp hallway. At the end of this, she knew already, was a kitchen with a coal stove. The stove still worked but since the chimney was blocked, it filled the house with smoke if you tried to use it. To the left and right were rooms that were bare save for piles of rags and scattered trash. At night the rag pile in the left hand room was the bed of Tom and Lizzie; in the daytime it was their sofa.

It was this grimy, cluttered room they now entered. Dicker waved the Brats to their feet. 'Don't you know to stand for a lady?' he asked gruffly.

Tom shrugged his shoulders. 'She ben't much of a lady,' he said sullenly.

Dicker turned to Mattie. 'See there, Miss Matilda!' he exclaimed softly. 'You've a fair task before you, civilising that one, hey? But you'll manage it, I don't doubt!' He took a long step and grasped Tom by the shirtfront, lifting him from the ground and shaking him hard.

Dicker shouted in Tom's face. 'This here's your new governess. Don't know what one of them is, Tom lad? It's what the rich hire to teach their blasted snivelling children how to grow up with enough manners and learning to keep them out of gaol! Now, you're going to be *polite* to this girl - whom I have engaged at great personal expense - if it kills you! Because, by God, if you *don't* behave, I'll kill you myself!'

He dropped the boy, who tumbled to the floor and stayed there, scowling up at Dicker. Dicker looked back over his shoulder to Mattie. 'They're all yours, Fireball. If *he* -' (here Dicker gave Tom a firm kick) 'is any trouble to you, just let me know. I can promise he won't be troublesome twice!' The highwayman pushed his hat to a jaunty angle and left the room.

Mattie looked at the two children worriedly. She had never been responsible for anyone before. Up to now, people had been responsible for *her*. And she would not have chosen these two waifs as her first experiment in child-raising.

Two dirty, cunning faces met her gaze. Lizzie was biting her lip and screwing up her eyes a little, as if trying to calculate the cost to them of their enforced education. Tom was glaring at Mattie with pure hatred.

'Won't do a thing you ask, so you may as well tell Dicker to come baste me now!' he announced from his awkward position on the floor.

'If Tom won't, I can't neither!' added Lizzie quickly.

Mattie gave a sigh and sat down on the dirty floorboards. 'This is all very difficult,' she said. 'I didn't ask to be put in charge of you. And I don't want to be your governess -'

'That's good,' observed Tom. 'Dicker's like to bannick *you* instead, then. Serve you right, that will!'

'I beg your pardon?' Mattie asked. 'What do you mean, it will serve me right?'

Tom mimicked her voice. '*Ay beg yore pardon?* It's us as begs, snobby Miss! And if you feels the rough of it for once in your time, it's not too soon!'

Lizzie turned troubled eyes upon her brother. 'Oh, Tom! Don't be so hard on the girl! She's only a child like we!'

'Bloomin' large child. Bloomin' stuck-up one, too!' Tom sneered. But his eyes softened a little when Jasper suddenly fluttered into the room and settled onto Mattie's knee, cawing to himself in a grumbling sort of way.

Mattie stroked the bird thoughtfully. 'I understand how you feel -' she began.

'I doesn't think you do unnerstand,' said Lizzie suddenly. 'Really I doesn't!'

Mattie looked into the other girl's eyes. Lizzie was chewing her lip again and trying to find the right words: 'It's just that, Miss, your sort can't. You *thinks* you can, but it's all cobwebs an' moonshine. It's like lookin' in a wormhole an' thinkin' that 'cos you can see his nose down there that you unnerstands how he feels an' how he lives. We's worms to your sort, Miss, an' - beggin' your pardon - your sort is birds.' Lizzie finished her sentence at high speed and stood before Mattie with her thin, dirty fingers twisted together. She was gasping a little, as though exhausted by the effort, or perhaps frightened by what she was saying.

Mattie reddened. 'I'm as human as you are -' she began.

Tom snorted loudly at this and then wiped his nose on his sleeve. But his eyes remained on the bird and Mattie changed her approach.

'Would you like him to come to you?' she asked.

Tom shrugged his shoulders as if he could hardly care less, but he sat up and held out his hand.

'You'll need to turn your hand over. He won't sit in your palm, and he doesn't like to be held onto. He likes to hop about freely.'

Tom turned his hand over, holding out the back of a dirty forefinger to Jasper. The bird peered at suspiciously, muttered something like 'Tch, tch, tch!' to itself in a disapproving, schoolmasterly tone, and then stepped gingerly onto the boy's finger. Tom gently brought his arm into his chest and looked down at Jasper, who stared up at him in reply, his dark eyes glossy, curious, bold.

'He ben't frowted at all,' Lizzie observed, sitting down beside her brother.

Mattie was puzzled. 'Please, what's "frowted"?'

'Scared. Frighted.' supplied Tom.

Mattie nodded. It was a good word. 'And when we were sitting down to eat a little earlier, you said something about being... *leer as a gallybagger*? What on earth does *that* mean?'

'Empty as a scarecrow, a'course!' said Tom, his eyes never leaving the bird. He was examining the creature from every angle, turning his arm round slowly to see each side, raising it above his head to study it from beneath, staring into the glossy black eyes and touching with gentle fingers the sturdy beak. 'This jack, he's just about beautiful, y'know?'

'Yes, I do know,' Mattie said softly, wondering why Tom with a bird on his hand was suddenly a far nicer person.

'All God's creatures is beautiful,' stated Lizzie, but she added quickly, ' - all 'cepting slugs! They makes I all gaggly to look at 'em!' She shivered at the thought. 'An' big spiders wiv goggly eyes, an' spit-bugs an' most of all earwigs. Can't 'bide earwigs!'

'I likes all of 'em,' Tom said steadily. 'Could watch spiders for hours. Y'seen how the littluns makes their webs all dewy in the grass like diamanty in the autumn?'

'My cousin's like you, Tom,' Mattie observed. 'He goes crazy over moths and beetles.'

Tom considered this. 'No, he ben't like I. I spect he's in a big house wiv a bed of his own. Spect he's more'n one set of clothes, too! An' he eats meat more'n once a week, I 'low.' He handed the bird back to Mattie.

Mattie did not reply, but passed Jasper to Lizzie, who trembled as the jackdaw perched self-consciously on her arm. He was staring into the middle distance, looking for all the world like a movie star pretending he didn't know his adoring public were all watching him. Lizzie smoothed his neck feathers with a tiny finger and Jasper was suddenly not a star at all, but an affectionate little creature with a tiny itch on its back which it desperately wanted someone to scratch. He began chirruping to himself as Lizzie riffled his feathers.

'I can see why you be so took wiv him, Miss. He be so main janty! All neat an' nifty an' perky - an' proud, like he thinks hisself a prince, y'know?'

Mattie smiled. 'I don't know what I would do without Jasper,' she confided. 'He's been such a good friend. My father gave him to me a only a few months before he – before, that is -'.

Mattie could not say it. She took a deep breath and continued. 'Jasper had a broken wing and my father found him and put a splint on it, and Jasper decided he was one of the family. And now he's all the family I -'. She stopped again. 'I'll have him back now, if that's all right, Lizzie.'

'So what ort we to be doin', Miss?' Lizzie asked, passing the bird to Mattie.

Mattie shook her head hopelessly. 'I don't know. I've never been a teacher or - or a mother, either. Or a governess!'

Tom said gloomily, 'We'll be in trouble wiv Dicker if you don't do summat. He'll be right huffled!'

'*I'll* be in trouble, too!'

'If Dicker ast you to governess us, you better do it proper-like, else we'll all cotch it, I s'pose,' Tom concluded philosophically. He put his hands into the pockets of his ragged trousers and began to whistle.

'No mitchin' then, Tom!' his sister warned.

'Depends how good the schoolin' is! Us'll not listen to rafty lessons, or stand bein' treated like dummles!'

Mattie held up her hand, like a child at school. 'Please, sir!'

Tom allowed himself the ghost of a smile. 'What does you want?'

'I don't understand some of those words!'

Lizzie giggled. 'Us'll have to learn *you*, Miss! But you'll have to promise not to mitch neither.' She paused as Mattie continued to stare at her in confusion. 'Are you still caddled? Mitchin' is truantin': missin' lessons you know.'

'Oh.' Mattie looked her charges over. She felt a flutter of anxiety. They didn't even speak the same language! But at least Lizzie was smiling now, though Tom's face was still a picture of gloom.

'Tom - Lizzie - do you think you could help me make a bed for myself in the other room?' she asked. It might help if they could do something together, she was thinking. And if her hands had something to do, they wouldn't keep shaking as they were just now.

Lizzie leapt up immediately. But Tom stayed where he was.

'I can help you, Miss,' Lizzie said. 'But Tom's not much of a hand at woman's work, an' that's a fact! Thinks it below him, I dare say. He gets the ragin' peezy-weezies if Dicker makes him do any tidyin' or cleanin', that he does!'

'Peezy-weezies?'

'I mean he sulks like a pig what's had its trough taken away!'

'I does not!' cried Tom. 'But woman's work is for wo-men!'

'An' what be man's work, Tom Smith?' demanded his sister. 'Sittin' on your backside?' She turned to Mattie,

'Leave him be, Miss, you won't get no help from he!'

Mattie tried to be conciliatory. 'I wasn't really expecting either of you to help,' she said. 'I was only asking in case you wanted to give me a hand.'

Tom said gruffly. 'And I doesn't!'

'But I does,' said Lizzie. 'I ben't a lazy toad, see? Unlike some! So – what'll we be doin' then, Miss?'

Mattie looked at Tom again: he was scowling once more. 'Well - for a start, you can both please call me "Mattie". I don't want to be "Miss" to you.'

'Wasn't going to call you that anyhow,' commented Tom.

Mattie continued. 'And next, I'd like Tom to come give his opinion about what we should do to make the other room liveable. He might have some ideas.'

Tom rose. 'Don't mind givin' folk my mind on things,' he said. '*That* be man's work!'

Lizzie caught Mattie's eye and a smile passed between them.

They spent some time putting the room to rights. Well, not quite "to rights": that would have needed a week with a sledgehammer. At least the larger insects had been sent scurrying away down cracks, and the nastier rags were thrown on the fire, the pile of rotting grass from one corner following it. If the floor was not what most people would describe as clean, it had at least lost most of the patches of dried mud. If the window was not quite transparent in places, enough of the smears had been rubbed away for Mattie to look out onto a little clearing surrounded by oak, hawthorn, beech and hazel; bramble and nettle; wild thyme, wood violets, honeysuckle, and the delicate purple heads of ragged robin. For a moment she forgot her predicament and felt only that it was beautiful.

'Here, Miss Mattie!' cried Lizzie, breaking into her

thoughts. 'What'll we do wiv *he*?'

She was pointing to an uncommonly large spider hanging from the ceiling above Mattie's head.

Mattie pondered. 'Is this man's work, do you think, Lizzie?' she asked.

'Reckon so, Miss! Tom - come earn your supper!'

Tom removed the spider with a manly grumble.

'See, Miss, he's gettin' the peezy-weezies already! He can't even move a spider 'thout querkin' about it!'

'Stop calling me "Miss"!' Mattie cried.

'Sorry, Miss!'

That night Mattie lay on lumpy rags beside a sleepy Jackdaw, whispering her prayers and gazing out the curtainless window into a sky spangled with stars. The cottage faced south and she could just see - around to the left a little - Orion the Hunter striding across the heavens, his sword at his belt, stalking Taurus the Bull. And there was the Little Dog, trotting along at the hunter's heels. Mattie's mother had made her learn the easier constellations when she was quite small - and how she had resented it then! Now, it was a comfort to look into the sky and see familiar, distant friends: and to wonder whether somewhere, somehow, her mother was up there, too.

Chapter 6 Some Argufyin'

Days passed. Mattie dedicated herself to teaching and gentrifying the "Brats", without a great deal of success but at least without too much hostility on their part. In the mornings - once Tom and Lizzie had returned with the bread and beer - she would give them two short lessons on mathematics, which a grumpy Tom absorbed with ease. Lizzie however often burst into tears, exclaiming that she was "All in a tizzy-woz!" and that the numbers simply would not stay in her head. Then they would have one rather longer lesson on writing and drawing, for which Dicker had reluctantly provided slates and chalk. The early afternoons were for reading, which Lizzie excitedly found she was better at than her brother.

The reading primers had arrived the day after Mattie's kidnapping, but only because Mattie had insisted that she have some "proper" books to use - and some soap! The next morning Dicker had ridden into camp, removed three books and several bars of soap from his saddlebag, and dropped them at Mattie's feet with a muttered oath.

'And don't ask me for more!' Then he took out a fourth book wrapped in brown paper and handed it to Mattie. She removed the paper carefully. The book was "The Christmas Carol", by a Mr Charles Dickens.

'Published less than a year ago,' Dicker said. 'But an expensively cultured young woman such as yourself has no doubt read it already at Miss Bell's Female Factory!' And, giving her no chance to thank him, he turned on his heel and led his great black stallion towards the make-shift paddock by the little river.

The Brats' books were babyish and dog-eared, and on their covers was plainly stated the fact that they were the property of a well-to-do private school in Andover. Nevertheless, Mattie snatched them up with a squeal of delight and spent hours that evening planning how to explain the mysteries of reading to the ignorant Brats, who up until then had not more than a few months of learning between them.

Lastly, there would be a language lesson for Mattie. She rarely enjoyed this as much as she had expected. Lizzie and Tom would try to teach her "proper 'Amp-shire" by means of shouting a stream of words that she had to try and identify. Before she had time to learn one word they would rush on to another - and then one child would argue heatedly with the other about what a particular word meant, and there would be blows, or tears, or both, with plenty of new swear words that they seemed to think Mattie should learn as well!

'I can't say that!' she exclaimed once when Tom was trying to teach her some extravagant, eye-popping oath he had known all his life.

'Why not?' he asked, puzzled. 'Me Mam used it every day!'

As for learning to act like well-bred children, Lizzie was eager to please but couldn't see what all the fuss was all about. Tom was sulky, or downright rude. They soon reached a compromise: if Mattie and Lizzie would leave him pretty much alone, he would wash briefly once a day, change his clothes when he felt they really needed it, and speak politely when absolutely necessary. He might even consider wiping his nose somewhere other than on his sleeve.

The first time she suggested that they wash themselves all over - perhaps in the stream? - she was greeted with disbelief.

'What for?' Tom wanted to know.

'Because being clean makes people more pleasant to know.'

'You means we ben't pleasant *now*?' asked Lizzie suspiciously.

'I mean you will be *even more pleasant* if you are clean. And you'll be more comfortable, too.'

'Couldn't be more comfly than what we be just now,' Tom judged. 'We be fair burstin' wiv comfort! Can't take in no more wivout explodin' like puffballs!'

'You *does* mean we ben't pleasant to know!' Lizzie insisted stubbornly.

'Well, you *could* smell a little more spring-like, I suppose. And your hair must itch famously, matted and dirty as it is.'

'I likes it this way!'

'So does I!'

Mattie gave it up.

On Saturday morning, Dicker rode down the Devil's Eyeball, whistling merrily. He waved the men to him and they held a long meeting in the cave, accompanied by the sound of corks being pulled from bottles - or, when the corks proved troublesome, the sound of bottle necks being broken off. Mattie and the Brats took themselves and their dirtiest clothes down to the little stream. Mattie distributed soap and they rubbed, squeezed and pounded with more or less good humour. Jasper sat at some distance, regarding the procedure with dismal interest. The day before, he had tried eating the soap and it had not agreed with him.

'So what do you think Dicker is up to, Tom?' Mattie asked. She knew Tom liked to be treated as a source of special knowledge of the gang's activities.

'Well - you seen all them barrels in the back of the cave?'

Mattie nodded.

'They's full of smuggled brandy and such-like. Dicker and the gang, they picked it up from Portsmouth a month back, an' I know for a fact it cost 'em a fair sum. Ever since, they's been argufyin' about how best to sell it on. Well now: the gaffer's got a plan figured, that's what it is,' Tom pronounced. 'He's like that - he's one for goin' out and lookin' things over and doin' a spell of ponderin' afore he decides what to do. Then he spends a mornin' in camp goin' over it again and again till the others un-nerstand it proper-like.'

'Specially Lump!' said Lizzie.

'As for Lump,' Tom expanded, 'well - his head's empty like a cobnut what's had a mouse to it. He's that stupid! He's what they call a right gaby. A hudgy, hulkish sort is Lump. I 'spect he was dropped wrong way up when he was a nipper.'

'You don't know that, Tom!' put in his sister.

'Oh, don't I, Lizzie?'

'No, you -' but Lizzie broke off and place a finger to her lips. Stump was approaching. They turned to face him.

Stump's walk was usually shambling, his manner shy and apologetic. Mattie had not yet heard him speak a full sentence. Two bottles of sherry had changed all that. He grinned and nodded vigorously to the three of them, go-ing so far as to tug at his forelock of wispy reddish brown hair as a token of respect for Mattie. He mumbled something, giggled, turned, clasped wildly at a branch and fell over. He crawled to his knees and tried to rise in a dignified manner. Jasper fluttered down for a closer look.

'Shoo - shoo, bird. Ju-just you shoo off, y'hear?' he gurgled, trying to wave the bird way. Jasper scolded him, just out of reach. The Brats roared with glee.

'Lizzie! Tom! Have some respect!' Mattie scolded them. But they were not to be controlled. Stump crawled after the bird, trying to catch it with his one hand and falling over in the process. At each attempt by Stump, Jasper would hop nimbly just out of his grasp.

'It's as good as a circus, ain't it, Tom?' gasped Lizzie. 'I swear I shall wet meself in a moment!' And she collapsed into a small, giggly pile. Next to her, Tom was whooping and trying to splash the drunken Stump with water from the stream.

Mattie was distressed. 'Do stop that, Tom!' she cried. 'This is *not* funny! It's - it's quite sad, really. Do you hear me, Lizzie? It's a sad matter, this drunkenness. The poor man!'

Lizzie looked up at her, tears of mirth standing in her eyes. 'For sure it's sad, Miss, if you say so. But it's rampagious funny, too! Look at him! The old sot! He's all bosky and bibble-eyed!'

Mattie went over to the groggy, bemused man. She gave his shoulder a gentle shake. 'Stump! Stump!' she remonstrated gently.

'Y'wha?'

'Let me help you up. Leave that bird alone now. He's mine anyway, so don't you lay a hand on him, do you hear?'

'Not lay a han'on'em!' Stump nodded gravely

'And you'll let me take you back to the cave, won't you?'

'Back to cave. Right. Oh -' He screwed up his eyes at her. 'Came - came to tell you - Dicker says, he says you can come do some inner-innertainin'. Sing songs, like, an' do some dancin'. Says to come now.'

Mattie's heart fell. She had been fearing this. She took a deep breath and drew herself erect. 'Oh, he says that, does he? Well, we shall see about *that*, shan't we? Lizzie

- Tom - you stay here and finish those clothes. I'll see to Dicker.' With that she pulled Stump into an upright position. 'Forward, Stump!' she commanded.

He swayed a little, hiccupping. A sorrowful look came to his eyes. 'Jeremiah,' he whispered.

Mattie propelled him forward slowly, the drunken man lurching from side to side. 'What about Jeremiah?' she asked sternly.

'M'name. Used to be. Called me Jeremiah. Me Mam did. W-when I had both - when I w-was -'

'Oh.' Her voice was softer. 'Shall I call you that?'

Yes, please, Missy... God, I'm drunk.'

'So you are, Jeremiah. I expect you all are. It's a silly way to behave, especially with children about.'

Stump shook his head, but whether in disagreement or to clear away the cobwebs, Mattie couldn't tell. 'Me old Dad used to get drunk a lot. Used to w-wallop me Mam, then. Used to w-wallop the lot of us, even me little sister.'

'So you see how stupid it is, getting drunk!'

Stump shook his head again. 'It's - it's just - the w-way things be,' he muttered.

'Nonsense!' Mattie replied coolly. She pulled him to the entrance of the cave. 'Now you sit here - on this log - while I see what's up.' And she left him perched there, swaying gently from side to side and singing softly to himself.

Inside the cave, Pirate was arm-wrestling Lump while Dicker and Scarecrow urged them on with oaths. They fell silent as Mattie entered.

'I understand you wish to see me,' she said in her primmest, most grown up manner. She was pretending to herself that she was not thirteen, but thirty.

They looked at her and then at one another hesitantly, much in the manner of a group of cattle confronted with an unexpected sheet of coloured paper fluttering in the grass.

Lump broke the silence with a knowing laugh. 'You was goin' to do us a show,' he said in a thick, slurred voice. 'Pretty girl like y'self - oughta give us a dance now an' then!'

'I don't do dances.'

Dicker fixed her with a level stare. Mattie could see that he was less drunk than the rest - perhaps not drunk at all. Pirate looked down at the table, as if he had suddenly found an interesting scratch on it. Ben the Scarecrow cackled and gave Lump a poke. 'She don't like you, Lump! You ain't handsome enough for her!'

'Or else -' Dicker said provocatively, 'or else she reckons she's too *good* for you, Lump! She may be keeping her maiden favours for a better class of men than we: men of good breeding, good manners, good teeth - and owning good fortunes. Hey?'

Lump spoke ponderously. 'I'm - I'm good enough for any woman. I worked all me life. I'm good as any man!'

'But ugly enough for two!' Scarecrow exclaimed. They all crowed with laughter and looked at Mattie, expecting her to say something.

Mattie was dumb for a few moments. She had found Dicker's words strangely hurtful. As before, he had managed to put her in the wrong, and yet she had done nothing to deserve his cruel analysis. She felt the colour rising to her face and was suddenly very angry. She squeezed one trembling hand inside another, straightened her back and glared at the lot of them.

'It's hardly a matter of being handsome enough, or well-bred,' she began in a severe tone. She was surprised to hear herself speak so confidently: she had hardly spoken to adults at all since her parents had died. Now, the words were coming out like bullets from an automatic rifle. 'It is more a matter of being *drunk,* or not. And of being *respectful*, or not. You wish to be entertained? I am sure that I can manage that, but *not* in the way that Lum- - that this gentleman - suggests. One evening, when you are all cold sober, if Ben can provide his fiddle, I can sing for you. But I am *not* going to dance, flirt, flounce, flap, canoodle or floozy for you! Is that understood?'

They stared at her. Ben's scarecrow jaw had dropped. Pirate looked abashed; Lump angry. Dicker bit off a fingernail and - mockingly, she thought - applauded her. His handclaps jarred and echoed in the high hollowness of the cave.

'Well said, my little spitfire,' he drawled. 'Well said! You have put us in our lowly places and no mistake! Gentlemen, the morning's show is ended. We've much to do this afternoon and more tomorrow. I suggest a few hours' sleep. Lump, give the horses some water. Jack my friend, the fire needs to be covered. Ben, put the food away - and what remains of the drink! Fireball, I'll see you later. I've a favour to ask.'

With that, Dicker took up his large, black three-cornered hat, placed it over his face, and lay back along the bench by the cave wall. The others went to fulfil their orders. Only Jack the Pirate gave Mattie a glance - a sheepish, almost boyish look.

She turned and walked back to the stream, her legs trembling. She rejoined Tom and Lizzie, hoping to teach them some manners before lunchtime.

Late that afternoon, a bleary-eyed Stump hitched Dicker's horse to a carriage. He waved away Tom's offer of assistance and turned his back on Mattie's enquiry as to whether his head hurt.

'Course it hurts!' cried Lizzie. 'Pounds like a hammer on an anvil, don't it, Stump? Me dad used to bang his head 'gainst the wall after he'd woke from a drunk, he would. Go stick it in the stream, you old sissy!' And she ran off before he could turn on unsteady legs and berate her.

Dicker emerged from the cave, his head dripping from a quick dip in the water butt. He smiled wickedly at Mattie.

'Throw on your pretty things, young Queen Victoria, there! We're off to Andover town for a spell of shopping.'

'Shopping?' Mattie was astounded.

'After a visit to Druddery Hall.'

'Druddery?'

'And you must show me where the estimable Miss Bell resides.'

'Miss Bell?'

He eyed her coldly. 'What are you? A girl, or a parrot? A gentleman offers to take you on a tour of the local sites - at some danger to himself, I must tell you! - and the best you can do is to repeat what he says, like a pea-brained macaw.'

She flushed. 'I am sorry, Mr - Sir - Dicker. It's just that I was surprised. I promise I shall be as - as *loquacious* during this tour as you could hope.'

He flashed a smile. 'Then I am honoured. Loquation is always a pleasure.'

He drove the carriage with hardly a touch of the reins. The remarkable horse responded to soft whistles, the snapping of his fingers and the occasional muttered oath. Mattie was entranced.

'Why, Mr Dicker, you'd almost think the animal understood you - that it respected your every wish!'

'And what's wrong with that, young pretty? Cannot a highwayman have pets? Must he be bereft of friendship? Must he know nothing of companionship, or love? Is he to have no culture? No learning? Is he to be less of a man just because he lives by relieving his fellows of their surplus riches? Is he to be *totally* despised?'

'Really, now!' Mattie exclaimed. 'I didn't say you were despised. But you *are* living outside the country's laws - and God's laws, too.'

Dicker laughed. 'Her Majesty's government takes money from the rich. As does the Church, my little friend! Dicker only copies what he sees his betters doing!'

'That's not the same thing at all! They use money for others. For good things. And people are happy - well, not happy exactly, but *willing* - to give money in taxes and tithes. *You* take money by force!'

Dicker clucked once to the horse, which responded by breaking into a gentle trot. On the highwayman's face a curious smile appeared. 'So you think the Church uses the money it collects only for the good of others, rather than to satisfy the greed of its leaders? And you think the government does the same? Why not old Dicker? Why can't it be that he also uses his gains for good?'

'You were using it this morning to get drunk.'

Dicker shrugged, unconcerned. 'I've known more drunken vicars than drunken highwaymen!' he claimed.

'My father was a clergyman,' Mattie replied coldly.

This seemed to have some effect. Dicker gazed off into the distance for several minutes, muttering to himself. Then, turning to Mattie, he removed his hat respectfully and waved it, bowing from the waist, in a token of penance.

'Apology accepted,' she said.

'Thank you,' he murmured, replacing his hat.

She suddenly burst out, 'My father was a good man. The people loved him. The poor people especially. He gave away almost all his income from the Church. He - my mother, too - they wouldn't buy new if old would do. Perhaps we *were* rich, compared with others. But we never put on airs. We were always visiting the poor. My mother went into their homes. She helped them when they were sick. Whatever Aunt Agatha thinks about her, my mother was a good woman. She... I don't know why I'm telling you this, it means nothing to you.'

Dicker gave her a grave, almost gentle look. 'Don't hold back for that, fireball. Even ruffians have hearts! It's just that they have to be kept a mite deeper than those of other men, for safety's sake - deeper even than the hearts of the gentry, though not as far down as the heart of a hanging judge.'

Mattie drew a deep breath. She had never talked like this. 'They used to take me with them, when they went visiting. Do you know, sometimes the new-born babies had nothing to wear? And there were homes where the husband had no work, and they lived on handouts, and they hated it. I used to see the hurt and anger in their eyes, even when they were taking a loaf of bread from my very hands. And sometimes they made it worse for themselves by drinking away what little they had - women as well as men - and the children hungry, fighting for scraps, while the parents stared drunkenly into the fire.'

She paused, then continued in a small voice. 'But the worst thing was that even after we had visited for years, not one of them came to visit when my parents were - were ill. Does that mean no one really cared for us?'

'No, lassie. It only means that no one likes to scrape and beg and bow.'

'But we didn't make them do that! When we gave them what we had, more than the parish was supposed to give them, we gave it willingly!'

'I believe you. But it wouldn't have seemed that way to the poor: they would have felt you were simply being condescending. And yet - perhaps I'm wrong. Perhaps your parents *were* beloved. It wouldn't be the first time a vicar was truly loved, though it's most uncommon in my experience. But see how unreasonable you are! You expect the poor to show their love for your parents by calling on them. Don't you see that they could not dare to assume the social equality which is implied by that action? Heavens, child! If the Queen was ill, would *you* presume to visit her with a bowl of soup? Beloved amongst the poor you may have been, but you were also the Holy Church to them and the Rich to them and the Educated, Stuck-up Noses in the Air to them - and Lord knows what else.'

'But that's unjust!' Mattie was indignant. 'We weren't like that at all!'

Dicker snapped irritably, 'I never said you were! But how many people - rich or poor - can see further than their own noses and their own tiny, shrivelled, bigoted imaginations? In this very hour, I will provide an example of the blindness we've just been talking about. I can prove to you that it doesn't matter who you are: what people see is what they make themselves see!'

Mattie wiped her eyes. 'I try to see things as they are,' she complained.

'Ah, but then you're still young, my friend. Growing up makes people hard and blind inside, till they can't see what's really there - am I right? You'll see in a minute!'

They turned into the drive of Druddery Hall. Dicker brought the great horse to a stop with a gentle pressure on the reins and a few soft words. The black stallion tossed his head and then leaned over to snatch at the grass growing beside the drive. Dicker leapt to the gravel and handed Mattie down. As they passed the horse, he paused to stroke its mane thoughtfully and whistle to it.

At the great oaken front doors he pulled the bell and then stood to one side, leaning on his cane. Mrs Murphy opened to them, and her face lit up. He snatched his hat from his head and gave her a fine bow.

'If it's not you again, my dear!' the woman exclaimed.

'And I was just wondering this morning if you'd be calling on us!' She caught sight of Mattie. 'And with the young lady, too! How are you, my pet?'

Mattie gave a little nod. Mrs Murphy had never called her a "pet" before now.

'Oh the child is fine, fine,' exclaimed Dicker, in a passable copy of Mrs Murphy's own Irish accent. 'Would you be having a cup of tea for us both, Mrs Murphy? For it's sure I am that we've a considerable thirst on us!'

She laughed merrily at this. 'Come in, dears!' she invited. 'I expect I can find tea for you - or better than tea, if you're wanting it, Sir Dicker?'

'Madam,' he said with just the right mixture of regret and resolution, 'I never touch liquor before sundown. A vow to my sainted mother, you know.'

Mattie stared at him. He gave her a warm smile and ushered her into the huge front hallway as if he owned it.

Chapter 7 Plots and Proverbs

It had been a most unusual visit, Mattie reflected afterwards. Nothing had been what it seemed. She had acted
the part of a visiting young lady of good family, and had
been treated as such: with much bustling about by the
servants, the subdued clatter of tea things, and respectful bows with many a "Miss Matilda, would you like -"
and "Sir Dicker, have another slice of plum cake, do
please."

To be treated as something approaching royalty here
was excessively odd, and she could only assume that
Dicker's apparent gentility and excellent manners had
brought it about. From the moment that they stood at
the door of Druddery Hall to the moment they drove out
the gates, he had assumed a regal bearing that Queen
Victoria herself would have found difficult to better.

Dicker had been shown all over the house and outbuildings, and had praised much of what he saw. In particular, Mattie noticed he was impressed by the size of
the main barn and the extent of the house's cellars. He
had surmised the existence of an underground passage
that led from one to the other, and the head gardener
had been only too pleased to show it to him. The two
had talked at length.

'What was it you were discussing with the head gardener?' Mattie asked Dicker as they turned out the gate
onto the Salisbury Road.

'Mr Mason?' Dicker asked. 'He's rather more than a

gardener. He's your uncle's property manager - in charge of the farming, upkeep of buildings and so on. In fact, he runs pretty much everything. He's your uncle's *bailiff*, to give him his proper title.'

Mattie noticed that Dicker had not answered her question, so she asked again, 'And what were you discussing with him?'

'Oh, a private matter.' Dicker gave Mattie a cautioning look. 'Nothing for you to concern yourself with.'

'Should I not be concerned?' she persisted. 'Should I not be trying to look behind the things that - that *seem* to be - and seeing things as they really are? Is that not what you were telling me as we drove here?'

He laughed. 'And was I right, my noble companion? Did you discover that folk see only what they expect to see? Then perhaps *you* are seeing only what *you* expect! You see a broken-down highwayman, bursting at the seams (as you believe) with evil intent, and you therefore suspect all innocent conversations with gardeners to be groaning with the heavy fruit of iniquity - double-dug with violent schemings - overgrown with the rank weeds of treason, butchery and debauchery - a harvest of malefaction and mayhem!'

It was Mattie's turn to smile. 'I do think, Mr Dicker, that you believe you can make wrong things right just by dressing them up in fine-sounding phrases!'

'Dressing up? Why, I had nearly forgot! It's into Andover we go next, young'un - for frocks and fiddle-faddle fashion! But we must pause briefly at Miss Bell's factory for fine frisky females. 'Tis on this road, is it not?' He set his horse to trotting and made no reply to Mattie's further comments. He settled back into his seat and concentrated on the road - though from time to time his face would break into a smile and he would chuckle to himself or whistle gaily an Irish-sounding tune.

At Miss Bell's they paused for only a minute - long

enough for Dicker to introduce himself charmingly to the caretaker as one of Mattie's relations and to beg leave for Mattie to receive letters there. Then on they went to the centre of Andover.

It was a hot afternoon and the Andover streets were dry and dusty. Mattie's great boots kicked up clouds of dust, which hung lazily in the still air outside the shops she visited - as if they were shadowy dust-dogs tied by wispy streamers to the railings, awaiting their lady's return.

Dicker's way in the shops was quick and direct. He would ask Mattie whether she could see anything needed by herself or the twins. He would then point to the article in question and demand of the shop assistant how much it cost. If dissatisfied with the price, he was likely to walk out on the instant. If the price was reasonable, he withdrew a few paces while Mattie assessed the sizes and quantity required. He then paid the bill with no further comment. They rushed through a dozen shops in this fashion and acquired undergarments, shirts, skirts, shoes and even a few requisites for washing.

'And you'll need to replace those clonking old boots,' he observed.

Mattie looked down at her dusty boots. 'They were my mother's,' she said quietly. 'I don't wear anything else.'

Dicker growled at this but let her have her way.

She looked over their large pile of purchases. 'These will become soiled and ragged very soon, living as we do,' she commented.

'They can be washed,' Dicker grunted. 'There are enough washerwomen in Andover to go around, and to spare!'

'But what is the point of putting on new clothing, when the twins are so grubby themselves?'

Dicker dismissed her concerns with a wave of the

hand and a sarcastic grumble. 'If dirt bothers you that much - for it doesn't bother me! - take them to a wash-house. Take a scrubbing brush with you, too: the dirt will no doubt be difficult to dislodge, being engrained in their skins by now rather than merely clinging to the surface like rich persons' dirt. Hell's birdbath, child! Surely you must have some idea as to how the poor manage to keep themselves reasonably respectable?'

Troubled, Mattie shook her head. 'No, I *don't* know!' she complained. 'How *do* the poor keep clean?'

'The very poorest don't, as a generality. Washing day is but once a week and if you've only one serviceable set of clothes, you wear that all week and have a wash yourself while your clothes are drying. You can tell what day of the week it is by the smell of a poor man!'

'But if as people say, cleanliness is next to godliness -'

'Then only the rich get into heaven - if you believe all that nonsense!'

Mattie stopped dead. Her face flushed red-hot with anger. She turned on Dicker, stamping her foot in the middle of the street, sending a plume of dust into the hot, sticky air.

'You - you - you *stupid* man!' she cried. 'Oh, if only my father were here! He'd soon make you take that back. Nonsense? *Nonsense?* Well, maybe heaven *is* non-sense to people who have never bothered to look in its direction. But it's not nonsense to me, and I'll thank you to - to -'.

She paused, aware that a number of passers-by had halted and were listening to her outburst with uncon-cealed curiosity. She drew herself upright and took a deep breath.

'I'll thank you to keep a civil tongue in your head and to treat serious matters with sincerity and courtesy!' she concluded. She swept past him and began to load her armful of purchases onto the carriage, her back to him.

71

He was standing with his mouth open, dazed and furious. Then he recovered himself, bowed to the various gaping onlookers, and meekly followed Mattie to the carriage. They took their seats and Dicker gathered the reins. In response to a whispered command, the horse backed the carriage into the street and pulled away smartly. Dicker said not a word to Mattie and stared straight before him; but his eyes were alight.

Once they were off the main street, he turned to speak. But catching sight of the fire that still blazed in Mattie's own eyes, he thought better of it and let the horse walk on to the edge of town. Then he brought the carriage to a halt.

'Let's put one matter straight, my little bolt of lightning,' he said - and by his voice she judged that he was very angry. 'Persons who have any respect for one another do not brawl in the middle of the marketplace. In particular, they do not wrangle about politics and religion. In further particular, the young do not berate their elders. And let me list one more specific (here he pointed a finger at her face): no one attacks me as you have just done. I have as much right to my opinion as does the Queen herself and woe betide the man, woman or child who thinks to shout me down! Is that understood?'

'Yes.' Mattie let out the breath she had been holding. She had expected much worse. She had expected to be slapped across the face. She wondered why he had not done so. 'I - I *am* sorry. I didn't know what I was saying.'

Dicker smiled wryly. 'Ah, but you did, child. And, what's more, I was coming off worst! That's what I most disliked! Did you not know?' He gave a great laugh. 'A snip of a girl standing up to a man like myself - browbeating me in public! - and me stock-still like a tailor's dummy, lost for a reply! Why, it beats all!' He laughed again, wiped his eyes, and chivvied the horse to a trot.

'Besides,' he continued, 'I owe you an apology. For I did not mean what I said - at least, not the way it came out. Is the idea of heaven a nonsense? I decline to say so. When a man has seen hell as I have, he's more likely than ever to believe in a heaven, though he may conclude he has no chance of arriving there. My comment about "nonsense" was directed at the common proverb you were quoting - about cleanliness being next to godliness.'

'I wasn't saying I agreed with it!' she put in quickly.

'I am pleased to hear it. I expect my adoptive relations to reject all heresy!'

She stared at him. 'Heresy? Why do you call it that, Mr - Sir - Dicker?'

He thought for a moment, while the horse trotted on steadily. 'Does it never strike you, Miss Matilda, that the churchmen - *some* churchmen, I mean - have got it all backwards? They treat the rich and clean of this world with great respect. But as for the poor man, living in the unavoidable dirt of poverty, they treat him as being of no importance. Yet I do not find that in their Bible! Does it not bear consideration, that Jesus and his disciples must have been a ragged, dusty band of men of little distinction? Only two of the twelve disciples were likely to have had any education; the others were simple peasants. And did not Jesus say, "Blessed are the Poor" and "Woe to ye Rich"? And was not Jesus himself of a poor family, and born to a despised and oppressed people? And was he not famous in his time for going about with just the sort of low, common persons as the Brats are?'

Mattie nodded.

'You do not disagree?' Dicker seemed surprised.

'Father often said things very like that,' Mattie replied gravely. 'Some people were angry to hear what he said.'

Dicker looked hard at her. 'No doubt they hated him for it! And - judging the father by what I know of the daughter - I expect he paid them no heed.'

Mattie nodded again, looking down at her hands clasped in her lap. 'Please, Mr Dicker, we have spoken enough of my parents for this day. As Miss Bell would say, one can have too much of a subject. Please may we talk of something else? Or of nothing?'

He grunted and turned back to the road. They exchanged not a word for the remainder of the journey.

Chapter 8 Rafty Lessons

When they arrived back at the camp, Mattie persuaded the Brats to wash themselves well enough to try on their new clothes. Once dressed they paraded before Dicker's gang - Lizzie hardly able to stand still for pleasure, Tom gloomily resigned to wearing something clean and fine.

But Lump complained. 'Why'd you do it for, Dicker? Why spend our hard-fought earnings on a couple of vagabonds? It's like puttin' a pig on the wall for to see the band go past!'

Dicker gave him a cold glare that silenced him. 'Our earnings? *Our* earnings? While I'm leader here, *I* divvy up the spoils. As on a pirate ship, it's even shares: but only because *I* say so! Tell me, you lumpish brute and brutish Lump, who was it that saved your half-washed neck in the first place? Who sees to your continuing safety? Who organises the little expeditions that bring us money? Me, or you?'

The others looked uneasily one to the other. Stump, usually so silent, supported Dicker at once. ''Tis true you allus shared everything with us, Dicker. Treated us like equals. You allus did us fair. I ain't complainin'. Not I!'

'Nor I!' Pirate said. 'Nothin' more democratic than pirates on board ship - nor down the Devil's Eyeball, neither!'

'But Lump do have a point, master,' Scarecrow added cautiously. ''Tis *our* booty you're spendin' on the Brats as well as yourn. Tain't much you're wastin' for maybe. But what it is, comes for certain sure from our pockets, too!'

Dicker exploded with rage. 'You stingy, black-hearted, mean-spirited snakes!' he shouted. 'You greedy, ungrateful, trough-swilling, mud-brained swine! No - why am I comparing you to innocent animals? Even the nastiest, yellow-toothed plague-infested mob of rats is like a band of angels compared with you two! You blind, witless, whining pair of overfed maggots! Do you not understand? The Brats have *earned* their keep. Who goes for bread, beer and cheese each morning? They do! Who keeps lookout when we're dead tired or dead drunk? They do! They've earned their wages and by God, not only shall they have new clothes, from now on they shall each of them have half-shares in our ill-gathered gains. And so shall little Miss Clonkaboot here! Does anyone disagree?' He rested his hand on his pistol.

One by one they shook their heads. Dicker continued to rail at them, calling them every hurtful and fantastic name he could think of and adding a number of memorable swear words for effect.

'You want your share?' Dicker cried. 'By what right do you ask it? By what law? *Whose* law? Like Cutpurse Moll herself, I know more laws of cheaters, lifters, nips, foists, puggards and curbers, with all the devil's blackguard than it's fit a man should even guess at. I know more orders, offices, circuits and circles, into which a man is bound, in which his own damnation grows and festers like a cankerous wound. And yet I have treated you honourably! Damn and blast you!'

Dicker's voice rose yet higher. 'I am leader here - *leader*, do you hear? I'm not your snivelling slave, your obsequious servant, your cringing, fawning patsy, your stooge, footstool, errand boy, grandma, governess or gimcrack godparent! I am your LEADER! And if I say we buy ballgowns, top hats and a set of china teacups for the camp, we buy them and you thank me kindly for them, or else you clear out! Do you understand?'

'Yes, boss,' said Stump quietly.

'Aye, aye, Cap'n Dicker, sir.'

'Yes.'

Lump just nodded and walked away, his face pink with what might have been either shame or fury.

'Come on, Lizzie, let's go across to the cottage,' Mattie said in a subdued voice. For her, the argument had taken some of the pleasure out of the new clothes. Lizzie however had not been in the least upset and had watched the stormy scene with great excitement.

'What for, Miss Mattie?'

'I think we ought to tidy up the cottage a bit. You know, get rid of some of the - the things lying about.'

'You mean all me rattle-traps? Me jags and tags?'

'If that's what you call the clutter of old rags, bits of metal, glass jars and rotting wood, yes.'

'Oh but Mattie! I collects 'em!'

'They've been growing in dark corners and spawning deviant offspring.'

'What?'

'Your bits of wood are all over slugs. The glass, when it doesn't cut you, hides the most amazingly bloodthirsty spiders and those flea-blown rags are cold and clammy, like they've just come off a freshly-dug mummy!'

'Ugh! Oh, don't say such things! I'll not be able to sleep in the same room as they, now!'

'Good! Come on, let's get tidying. You too, Tom.'

Tom joined them amiably, though this was clearly "woman's work". Grinning all over, he called to his sister, 'Did you hear what the gaffer said? We be highwaymen now, Lizzie! We gets a share of the loot - Mattie too!'

'You can have mine,' Mattie said. 'I won't take money got by evil means.'

Tom and Lizzie stared at her open-mouthed, disbelieving. 'Why on earth not?' they cried.

Mattie furrowed her brow. How could she possibly explain? She shook her head at them. 'It's just wrong!' she cried.

Tom gave her a hard look. 'If this has summat to do with what you calls bein' civilised,' he said, 'I don't reckon much to civilisin'. It seems to mean stayin' poor!'

Mattie gave him a hard look in return and thumbed her nose at him, for good measure.

They spent hours shifting rubbish from the rooms. Mattie's bed, which up till then had been a lumpy mess of rags, was remade using reeds from by the stream, armfuls of fragrant watermint and springy ferns - all of which she first minutely examined to remove unwanted wildlife. She would have to put the bedding out in the sun each day to finish drying it out; but it would do for now.

'And we ought to do something about that anthill by the front door,' she said.

Tom made a face at this. 'Never move an emmet-hump,' he warned. 'They be your guard. They be like them soldiers at the Tower, wearin' big hats.'

'Don't talk rubbage, Tom! Emmets don't wear hats!' cried Lizzie.

'He means that the Beefeaters wear hats – big, round black hats. They guard the Tower of London,' Mattie explained. 'But I don't see what that has to do with the ants. If they start coming into the house -'

'The Beefeaters?' asked a shocked Lizzie.

'No, the ants. The emmets, I mean. If they come into the house we'll have to remove the anthill - sorry, the emmet-hump.'

Tom still disagreed. 'Don't you mess with they, Mattie!' he advised. 'If you don't be riled with *they*,

they'll not be riled with *you*! Besides, emmets be wise creatures. If they's there, 'tis for a reason!'

Mattie yielded on this point. But she ruled that some of the rags used for covering the new bedding needed washing, so they spent some time at the stream doing this. Then the Brats decided they wanted 'proper' beds too, and the whole process had to be gone through yet again. They slaved until night fell and then climbed into their new, soft beds with many a tired sigh.

Mattie tucked Lizzie into her bed. 'Shall I tell you a story?' she asked.

'What for?' Lizzie replied.

'Didn't your mother tell you bedtime stories?'

'When we was little, p'raps. You mind that, Tom?'

'No. If ever she did, I disremembers now.''

'You tell us one anyhow, Mattie.'

'Don't be so soft!' Tom muttered. But he added, 'Go on then, Mattie! What's stoppin' you? Flittermouse swooped down and took your tongue?'

She told them the tale of Hansel and Gretel. When it was done, Lizzie gave a shuddering sigh.

'They was even worse off than we! At least we hadn't been cotched by a witch and fattened for roastin'! But I liked most the part where they gets home an' finds their real mother wasn't dead after all!'

Mattie smiled to herself. She had changed the ending just a little, to the one she would have wanted. 'Did you enjoy it, Tom?' she asked.

'Tis better even than the colt-pixey,' he said dreamily. 'That's t'other story I remembers. Our granddad told it us afore he died, years agone.'

'We knows two stories now!' Lizzie said proudly. 'Tom can tell you 'bout the colt-pixey another night, an' if you knows a second story, you can tell it us back. Then maybe Dicker and the gang can tell a story each. That'll make -' she counted carefully on her fingers '-

eight stories. Be that right, Mattie?'

'That's right, Lizzie. And now it's time to do your prayers.'

'Our what?'

'You mean you don't -? Oh dear.' Mattie sat a while in silence. It had never occurred to her that there were people in England who didn't say their prayers at night.

Tom was dismissive. 'Prayin's for vicars and rich people with full bellies sittin' in church hearin' that God likes 'em.'

'Oh, Tom!' Lizzie cried. 'Don't be so ornery! Let her tell us how to do it. Then mayhaps we'll have full bellies too, an' a carriage to ride in!'

Mattie laughed. 'You don't get things like that by praying!'

'Then why bother?' asked Tom, yawning.

Mattie paused again. She didn't want to talk about this. It reminded her, painfully, of that one prayer that had not been answered, her prayer for her parents' lives. But she had to say something.

'I mean you don't pray to God because you want frills and fancies. But you do ask him for your daily food. You ask him to make you good. And you say you're sorry for anything you've done wrong.'

'Ain't never done nothing wrong!' Tom exclaimed.

Lizzie reached out and thumped him. 'Tom, be serious! Go to, Mattie. Tell us how you do it! Which way d'you hold your hands?'

Mattie groaned at this. 'It doesn't matter about the hands!'

'An' if you says it wrong, does you get the oppysit of what you asked for?'

'Of course you don't!'

'If you says it wrong,' Tom said to Lizzie with a wicked glint in his eye, 'the devil comes up from outa the ground and sticks his big pitchfork through you and drags you back down to hell with him!'

Lizzie shrieked. 'That ben't true, be it Mattie?'

'Of course it isn't. And you just behave yourself, Tom Smith! This isn't something to make jokes about. Now, settle down, both of you. If you don't know how to pray, at least let me do it for you this time. You close your eyes. You put your hands together -'.

'I knew there was summat about the hands,' whispered Lizzie to herself.

'Next you tell God about all that happened today and thank him for everything good in it. Then you ask him for what you need.' Mattie paused. It was hard to put the prayers she had been taught into ordinary words the twins would understand. She took a deep breath and tried. 'Like - like this: "Dear heavenly father, we thank you for loving us this day and caring for us. We trust you for our daily bread and ask for - for your forbearance for our sins. Amen."'

'Amen!' said Lizzie. She settled into her bed. 'G'night, Miss!'

'Goodnight, vicar!' said Tom.

'Goodnight.'

Mattie crossed the corridor to her room. She paused at the doorway when she heard Tom's voice.

'Lizzie!' he whispered.

'Yes, Tom?'

'Why'd we ask for 'em? We ain't got none, I know, but why'd we need 'em?'

'Need what, Tom?'

'What she asked God to give us for our sins - you know, the four bare aunts.'

'I doesn't know, Tom. Reckon there must be a reason, though!'

Mattie gave a great sigh and went through to her room.

Then she giggled. Four bare aunts, indeed! She climbed between the covers and curled up happily on her springy mattress of ferns and reed and watermint. She felt one or two spiky branches that needed to be removed: and while thinking of this, she fell asleep.

Chapter 9 The Danger of a Little Gold

A week after Mattie's capture, Dicker took her again to Miss Bell's Academy to check for letters. This time there were two, sharing the same envelope. The first was from Uncle Lucid and read:

My dear Matilda

I was pleased to hear that you are at Miss Bell's. I have written separately to the good lady to express my gratitude and to confirm that I will of course pay the requisite fees. On reflection I feel certain that the steps you have taken would be congruent with the wishes of your parents, who always spoke highly of Miss Bell and her excellent establishment.

I have not mentioned to Agatha that your plans have changed, believing that in this difficult period it is best for her to be spared the various domestic concerns that appertain to your new position. Perhaps it would be wise for you not to broach the subject with her either. I leave that to your own judgement, of course.

I expect we shall be here another week, at least. Do please pray for us, and particularly for your aunt.

I am, as ever, your affectionate uncle

Sir Lucid Arbuthnot

The second letter, set out most untidily, was this:

Dear Cousin

Did you know, there are Puffins here? I've spent absolute hours spying on them - no, better than that, I've positively infiltrated their ranks! It took me several days of crawling about on my stomach like an obese fledgling, proffering bits of stinking fish I'd obtained from a fishmongers in the town, but they now accept me as one of their own. I'm sure if I opened my mouth wide and flapped my arms and made those awful baby puffin noises, the older birds would feed me! It is, quite without doubt, absolutely wondrously gorgeous to be here.

On a more dismal note, Mama's father continues not to recover (does that sentence make sense?). He seems to be a queer old bird - very old, in fact, around ninety I think. House full of naval curios, loops of tarred ropes, ship's compasses, odd stones, a wonderful collection of shells and a mess of items best described as piratical: cutlasses, earrings, even a hook-hand and a parrot's perch (no parrot to go with it, unfortunately!). One of his prized possessions is a great conch shell, which he keeps at his bedside. Books about the sea abound, and I must admit I've spent absolute ages devouring them.

Mama is unusually quiet and unobtrusive. Seems really to care about the old chap. Has stopped bossing us about, spends a lot of time reading to her pa or sitting in his study. Touching really.

I haven't done a stroke of homework. And (ha ha!) I haven't touched a jigsaw piece since coming here. Hooray!

Wish you were with us. Expect you're having adventures enough of your own, though.

Your cousin

Hubert   PS There are cormorants, too!

Dicker held out his hand for the letters once Mattie had read them. She passed them over reluctantly. He glanced through her uncle's letter first.

'Another week! Well, well, Mattie, we must make good use of this unexpected extension! The Brats will be pleased: another week of your civilising presence will raise them - let's see - to something approaching that of the African savage, I expect! Your uncle writes a good letter. Learned, yet sensible and humane. Is that what he's like? He is? Good! It is a pleasure to be able to approve of one's adoptive relations. Now to your cousin's missive....'

Dicker read Hubert's letter through carefully, then again.

'Is something wrong?' Mattie asked.

Dicker gave her a fierce look and handed back the letters. 'Wrong? What could be wrong? An eccentric old man dying in what appears to be a naval museum, in the bosom - the capacious bosom, indeed - of his nearest family: what could be more fitting? Why do you ask? Now we must be off! I have business to conduct, and you have a troupe of performing midgets to train. I will drop you at the camp.' He set the carriage in motion.

Mattie suddenly exclaimed, 'You've a house somewhere, haven't you? You go there to change clothes and sometimes to sleep. You - you "conduct business" there. Where is it?'

Dicker was annoyed. He growled at her fiercely, so fiercely that she actually jumped in her seat. 'Poking a nose into *my* business is neither ladylike nor safe, and I'll thank you to keep your curiosity within limits! You are in danger of forgetting that I'm not a pleasant person to know. I am one of those who thieve, lie, batter and murder to get what I want! I do not sit by the beds of failing relations, reading them verses from scripture and waiting for their fortunes to fall into my lap! I have to strip *my* fortunes from the living, and a dirty, bloody business it is, too! And the less you know about it, the better for you!'

'I only asked,' Mattie replied meekly.

Dicker snarled at this. 'People are always "only" doing things. Sometimes they "only" die as a result. Remember that!'

Yet that afternoon he was all kindness. He rode down into camp a couple of hours before sunset, bearing new boots for Pirate, clothing for Stump and Lump, and food for them all. He praised the clean clothes of the Brats and listened with evident satisfaction to a song that Lizzie had been learning. When the late afternoon shadows deepened and cooled, he called Mattie to him.

'Well then, girl, want to see a little of the smuggler's craft?'

Mattie shook her head, not trusting his apparent friendliness.

'Be ye frowted then?' he mocked in a passable imitation of Tom's Hampshire accent.

'I am *not*!' she flamed.

'Don't be huffled 'bout it, gal. Why not prove it, just? Oh, come along, ye fessy gammock - leave the bird to Tom there and make ready the carriage!'

'Oh - all right. But I'll not do anything wrong!'

Dicker opened his eyes wide. 'As if I would dare to ask you!' he exclaimed.

As they travelled along the main road towards Basingstoke, Mattie ventured to ask about his gang of men.

'What will happen to Stump and the others? I mean, eventually?'

Dicker scratched his head. 'You see, Mattie, they're all outlaws one way or t'other. Pirate and Stump, I crewed with for a time. We made our fortunes - and lost 'em again - somewhere down around the Canaries and further south still. Then a spot of smuggling went wrong near Southampton and they made scarce while I made for Winchester Gaol. The other two - they were gaol mates and when I was sprung they joined me. I expect one will drift away, one will be caught and maybe one will catch a bullet and turn up his toes - as is the way of things in our trade.'

He looked about at the trees, whose glossy leaves reflected the late summer sunshine. 'Winter's a hard time for men like us. The Devil's Eyeball is a pleasant enough place while the sun shines, but just you imagine it with an icy wind slicing off your fingers and the stream frozen over, and no food, and no entertainment save for picking the ticks out of your matted hair!'

'What will happen then?'

'Maybe I'll find them a place in town. But folk are downright nosy these days, and if your landlord doesn't turn you in, your neighbours might. And in town there's Public Houses a'plenty - and a sore temptation they are for men of the sea and for men brought up to drink hard and long. A few drinks, some boasting, some brawling, and so back into prison, or worse. Perhaps a rope about the neck. You can be hanged for trivial things in England!'

Mattie looked at him severely. 'Now, *that* is clearly nonsense!' she exclaimed.

Dicker thumbed his nose at her. 'A man like myself never exaggerates to a lady, save about one thing - and we won't discuss *that*, young'un! As for hanging and imprisoning, you'll know that scarcely ten years ago, they sentenced ninety-nine poor, half-starved local labourers to death for having the impudence to riot for higher wages. You may have heard of the Tolpuddle Martyrs, which happened a few years earlier: well, this was the same situation, but in Andover. I expect the Andover magistrates were especially angered because it happened during the annual fair and took a bite out of their profits!'

'*Were* ninety-nine hanged?' she asked suspiciously.

'No, it was only about ten in the end. The others were transported across the world to penal colonies, where they would slave and sicken and die somewhere out of sight of the sensitive English public!'

He continued. 'You may also have heard what happened to a boy from this area not long ago. About your age, he was. He got himself sent to a reformatory for five years for taking turnip tops from off a field so as to feed his starving family. It had to be an especially long sentence because he'd been caught stealing eggs before, and for the same reason. When a small child is so depraved as to steal twice in order to keep his mother and little sisters alive, there's nothing for it but to put him in prison for a long stretch, right? That'll teach him, won't it? I expect he'll come back a reformed character, don't you agree? He'll be mayor of the town all of a sudden, and hold down a respectable job - as a solicitor's clerk maybe? He won't be at all hindered by not having had any education, will he? Only half the children in Andover go to school at all, you know, and he's in the other half, the poorer half. No wonder the poor bug- - the poor boy - couldn't do anything but steal! No jobs available, only a pittance paid to paupers, and winter coming on!'

'The poor child!'

'And now they have the Workhouses! Do you know the foundation of the modern Workhouse system? It's to save money for the parish! Let's say you're destitute. There's no food in the house, not a bean. You go to the Relieving Officer (who lives four miles out of Andover, by the way - a long walk on an empty stomach, probably through the snow and without shoes!). Before the Workhouse came to Andover, he would give you food. Now, he offers you the Workhouse, or nothing. If you enter the

Workhouse, you must say good-bye to your home, your clothes, your pitiful clutch of possessions: so you make sure you don't go there until you've sold everything you've got! And when you do get to the Workhouse, there's hard work, and little food, and no gentleness. By law, the Guardians have to make sure that the Workhouse poor are fed no better than the most impoverished of the poor outside the Workhouse. And in any case, the Board of Guardians in Andover are mean, cruel sons of bit- - sons of their mothers, I mean. They'd see their own grandparents starve before they'd raise a finger to help the poor! No, I tell a lie. There's one good man among them - named Munday. But only one, out of about fifty.'

'You are very hard upon others!'

He snarled at this. 'Am I unfair? This is a nation that *hates* its children! By the new Cotton Mills Act, children can legally work as many as seventy-two hours a week. Seventy-two: think of it! That is twelve hours a day, with Sundays off only because the Church would object! What a tender-hearted Church, to insist on one day for God but to leave six days to the devil: seventy-two hours of hell! And until three years ago, children as young as five were working the mines. Did you know that they - and gangs of young girls - were chained, belted and harnessed like dogs to pull the trucks of coal?'

'You said that was three years ago. So it is better now? Have people realised it was cruel, and changed their ways?'

Dicker looked at her with a cold fire in his eyes. 'So the world has turned Christian, has it, now that nine year old children cannot work the mines? Is England a good, compassionate, generous place of joy now that it is only at the age of ten that a child can be made to live underground during every hour of day, returning to the surface to sleep only at night, seeing the sun but once a week? And working each day in cold, narrow, dangerous caves until his young bones bend and his joints swell and his lungs fill with dust?'

'It is very wrong.'

'Wrong? Is that all? It is not wrong, but evil! And equally evil is the fact that nothing is done about it! You have read your Dickens: you must have read his *Oliver Twist*, written not many years ago. A popular book! But did it change those who read it? It did not! They praised it to the skies, but ignored what it taught them: the cruelty of the workhouse system, the evil of poverty, the degradation of child slavery - in the mills, in the factories, down the mines, and up chimneys! Politicians, who know more about it than most, do nothing; churchmen, who should know - or at least, *care* - best of all, do nothing. They are all deceived by the greed of the factory system - a system that demands workers who will labour for next to nothing and die in their labour. Only by creating a nation of slaves can some men become grotesquely, filthily rich.'

Mattie could think of no reply to this. But the lines of a poem came to mind.

> *"For all day long we drag our burden, tiring,*
> *through the coal-dark underground*
> *Or all the day we drive the wheels of iron*
> *in the factories, round and round."*

'Mrs Browning wrote that,' she said. 'We read it at Miss Bell's: it was only published last year. I - I didn't know what it meant when I read it, though.' She sat in silence for a while, suddenly missing her mother very much.

They had turned off and were heading north. Half an hour more brought them to a hill overlooking Overton.

'They hold a fine sheep fair here, in the autumn I believe,' Dicker said. 'See how broad this street is? It curves down to those thatched cottages, and there's a great medieval square where they can pen thousands of the creatures. And just beyond is the White Hart, where the coaches scurrying between Exeter and London are like to stop. It's a turnpike road of course - has been for near on ninety years now, and carriages pay a fee to pass through here. But there's a railway passing through Micheldever now, a few miles to the south: that will put an end to turnpikes, they say. And to highwaymen, too!'

'Why are we here?'

Dicker laughed. 'There's a wealthy man who travels on the London coach this day or the next, and I'm anxious to meet him.'

'You're not going to hold up the coach?! You promised –'

Dicker shushed her angrily. 'Hold your tongue, girl! No wrangling in the streets this time! If I said there's no danger, that is what I meant! The gentleman wishes to purchase a little gold. He's never met me before, nor I him. If he's on the level, there's a deal to be struck. If not, you and I are on a pleasant excursion through the local scrolls of history.'

They swept down Winchester Street and came to the White Hart, standing at the crossroads. To the right, some fifty miles hence, was London; to the left and far, far off, Exeter. Straight over, the road led downhill for perhaps fifty paces and passed over the River Test. Then it swung uphill and to the right a little, passed a large grey flint church and continued rising and falling gracefully on its way to Watership Down, a few miles north.

The White Hart Inn was not a particularly beautiful building, though Mattie thought its sign wonderful: a glorious white stag leaping a broad ditch, leaving in its wake a bedraggled train of panting dogs and dispirited hunters. Dicker caught her gaze and glanced up at it.

'Now then, lass, that's how *I'd* want it to be, always!'

They passed into the coach yard. Dicker went inside and brought out ale for himself and water for Mattie. They sat in the carriage until the light faded and a servant came out to light the lamps. Then they took the carriage out again, this time continuing past the inn and up to the churchyard. The sun was falling fast now; in a few minutes time it would ease itself below the horizon and sink into its groggy summer slumber. The moon would give little light, for it was waning and presented the thinnest of crescents to view. The church clock was chiming nine o'clock - or was it ten? Mattie lost count and could not make out its hands in the dark.

They crossed the road to the right of the church and found a place to tie up the horse. Dicker lifted his saddlebags from the carriage floor. Feeling inside one, he removed some carrots and fed them to his black stallion. Then he and Mattie crossed the road and walked about twenty paces to the gate. Passing in, they followed the path around the church to the left. Dicker was still holding the second saddlebag.

'Fairly old church. The nave - you know, the main body - is reckoned to be Norman, and the chancel part is lovely; but they spoiled it all a few hundred years afterwards by building a bell tower at this end! An ugly big lump constructed for the sole purpose of making dreadful noises at regular intervals, stopping the living and the dead from enjoying the music of the earth - birdsong and wind through tall trees, the splash and murmur of the River Test. Did you know there are kingfishers along the river here?'

They walked once around the building, and then Dicker stood quietly at the large, bolted church door, listening.

'You pass around clockwise again, girl; I'll go the other way about, and you wait for me around the back.'

Mattie set off slowly. Even so, she had a minute's long wait before Dicker joined her.

'Now, my little firefly, there's two things you should know about Overton churchyard. First, there's a hidden tombstone to an Overton boy named William Franklyn. Heard of him?'

'No.'

'He was claimed to be the Messiah, back in 1650. He wasn't though, and plenty of people were annoyed when he turned out to be an ordinary mortal like the rest of us! Are you not interested in latter-day Messiahs? The second fact will interest you a little more, perhaps. Come to the rear of the churchyard and keep your eyes on the ground as you walk.'

They passed along grassy paths and wound in and out of gravestones set on humped graves. There had been a few raised tombs around the front and side of the church, but only a few of them stood here.

The sun's last feeble rays were fast fading. Mattie peered through the gathering darkness at the short, thick grass. Suddenly she saw a small light at her feet, and stopped.

'What is it?' Her heart beat a little faster. 'It's so ghostly!'

Dicker knelt and parted the grass. He raised cupped hands to Mattie, hands from which an dim, ethereal glow was escaping.

'Hold out your hands then,' he whispered.

'No!' she whispered back. But he placed his hands upon her own anyway and let roll into her palm something small, cool and dry, something shaped like a short, fat wingless moth, but glowing with a cold, greenish-gold light.

'Tis a glow-worm. It's all right, it can't hurt you. It's the larva of a little beetle. The female larvae make the light so that the males, who can fly, can find them in the grass. The poor females don't move very fast!'

The glow-worm lay quite still in Mattie's palm: at this speed, it would never find a friend. She put it down gently. Then she saw another - and another. And as her eyes grew attuned to the night, there were hundreds of tiny lights within view, glowing with an eerie coldness that made her think of light rising through seas of ice to gleam unwinking at dazzled travellers.

'Why, they're beautiful!' she exclaimed.

'True enough,' murmured Dicker. 'But there's another light on the way now. Be scarce for a moment, my little glow-worm. Try the other side of that high double tombstone.'

Mattie looked up and saw a covered lantern approaching from the dark end of the churchyard wall. She turned and scuttled a few steps away and seated herself behind the tombstone. A minute later, a voice came out of the gloom.

'Are you the gentleman I was to meet?' asked the new voice. The accent was well-bred, but perhaps too well-bred: as if someone were putting it on.

'That rather depends on what you've come to find!' replied Dicker pleasantly.

'Come now! No need for that sort of talk. What are *you* here for, if it comes to that?'

Dicker laughed. 'For something that glitters and glows, and which brings a wealth of pleasure to them that hold it in their hands. I've some in *my* hand now, in my pocket. You want to see it? For a price, I'll show you!'

For reply, Mattie saw the other man put his hand to his lips and blow a whistle. Immediately, half a dozen other forms rose like the dead from their stations about the distant graveyard wall. The man at Dicker's side removed the cover from his lamp and let its light blaze in Dicker's face. The shadowy forms drew near and became men.

'Don't I know you?' the lantern holder asked.

Dicker studied him. 'I should hope not,' he answered haughtily. 'I rather expect that those in my position do not mix with those in your own. Unless by some chance you happen to have a house in Pall Mall!' He felt with his right hand in the small outside breast pocket of his coat. Mattie noticed that he kept his left hand deep in his coat pocket. He produced a card, which he gave to the man.

The man held the card to the lantern. 'Terence Dicker, Esquire. 78 Pall Mall, London,' he read. 'And what brings you to Overton churchyard, Mr Dicker? Gold, perhaps? Something that "glitters and glows"? We were informed by another gentleman that he was offered gold in - shall we say - suspicious circumstances. What are you holding in your pocket, Mr Dicker?'

Dicker laughed. 'Why, young man, for a local man - I assume you *are* local from the dreadful accent you have - you are particularly ignorant. My niece and I were viewing one of the glorious phenomena of this churchyard. Mattie, stand up and let the gentlemen see you!'

Mattie rose sharply from behind the tombstone. One of the constable's assistants actually gave a sharp groan of terror as she suddenly appeared as if out of the ground itself.

'Yes, Uncle?' she asked.

'Explain, if you would be so good, what we were doing.'

Mattie turned to survey the small group of men who gawped at her. 'Good evening, gentlemen,' she began in her primmest voice. They wished her a good evening in return, some of them knuckling their foreheads respectfully. 'I am enrolled at Miss Bell's Academy on the Andover Road and live nearby at Druddery Hall with another of my relations, Sir Lucid Arbuthnot.' She paused to allow this to sink in and was gratified to see the young constable with the lantern bite his lip in consternation.

'Mr Dicker kindly offered to show me some of the interesting sights in your village, and we came here to view the glow-worms. You do know about glow-worms, do you not? They are beetle larvae which, in the summer months, give off a wonderful icy green-gold light. They do this, by the way, so as to -'

'That's quite enough of that!' the constable interrupted. 'A fine story. But what have you got in your pocket, Mr Dicker? Something that glitters and glows and brings a wealth of pleasure, I think you said!'

Dicker slowly removed his hand and opened it. In his palm were what looked like two ordinary-looking dull grey woodlice.

'If you were not holding the lanterns, gentlemen, you would see them glowing. As it is, they'll have switched off their little lights. But look across the graveyard, out of the ring of lantern light, to the graves of your forebears. There is upon them the sparkle of living gold and the fine jewels of nature, the only wealth the dead may enjoy. I suggest we leave them to it, gentlemen!'

'Not until you have emptied all your pockets!'

Dicker turned out every pocket and shook out his cuffs. There was nothing remarkable in any of them. The constable chewed his lip and swore profusely (which impressed Mattie no end, for it must have been remarkably difficult to do both actions at once).

'There is a lady present!' Dicker reminded him, retrieving his card.

'Sorry, sir.' The constable looked miserably to his men and said to them, 'You'd best go off duty, now. And Mr Dicker, sir, I hope you won't take this unkindly.'

'Of course not, constable. You were only doing your duty!'

'And I am sorry, sir, that I - I caused you any distress. You see, these were unusual circumstances and - well -

not having been in this post for long, it seemed the chance to make my mark, if you understand my meaning, sir.'

'How did it happen, constable? You said you were "informed". What does that mean?'

The constable seemed grateful for Dicker's interest. 'I heard a man talking in the White Hart yestereve - he was two sheets to the wind and I was near enough to overhear what he was whispering - rather loudly - to his girl. I expect I heard the day wrong; or maybe he meant another part of the village altogether. He was proper drunk, he was. The lads had him watched but he gave them the slip early this evening, so I expect he guessed we were on to him.'

'I am sorry to hear that. Did you get the man's name?'

The constable ground his teeth. 'Got a name and address in Southampton, but it was false. But someone must know him. He had plenty of money, too. Reckon he's on his way across the channel, out of harm's way.'

Dicker stood a while in silence. Then he said, 'I won't be keeping you, constable. Keep up the good work! And do not bother yourself about this incident. A man in your position must take some risks. Granted, you would look very foolish if any of this were to be repeated in some quarters; but I haven't a vindictive nature, and can be quiet about it if you can. Besides, this evening has been most diverting. Has it not, Mattie?'

'Undoubtedly, Sir - Mr - Dicker.' She nodded to the constable and he began to move off. He stopped however before he had gone several steps.

He exclaimed, 'Dicker! Now I recall! Did you know, sir, that there's a couple of gravestones with the name Dicker on them? I've seen them myself. One of them, a big raised family tomb, they say the old man rises up from, and he snatches anyone crazy enough to be in the churchyard after dark. He drags 'em down into the grave and then -' The constable halted. 'Oh, pardon, Miss! It's just a story.'

'How interesting,' said Dicker. I must have a look at them some time. But not just now. Good night, constable!'

'Good night, Sir. Good night, Miss. But mind how you travel. This is a small village, a few hundred souls all told, but there's five public houses and it's been a long, hot day. Half the local men will have drunk long tonight, and with them a fair number of gypsies and visiting drovers. You'd best be wary.'

'Thank you, constable.' And this time the man did go.

Dicker and Mattie sat on for a while, until the clock struck eleven o'clock. Then Dicker signalled to Mattie to follow him around to the front of the church. There they crept up to a raised tomb standing in a dark corner. Dicker motioned to Mattie to be quiet. Then, shockingly, grotesquely, he raised the lid of the tomb and eased his arm inside.

Mattie held her breath to stop herself from screaming as his hand brushed around in the tomb, dislodging something that rattled dryly and scraped along the bottom of the raised grave. At last he found what he was feeling for and pulled his arm back, clutching his saddle-bag. They crept back to the far end of the churchyard.

Mattie sat beside him as her heartbeat slowly returned to normal. He smiled at her, his white teeth glinting in the light of the slender moon.

'Now, isn't the Dicker tomb just the best hiding-place ever made?' he asked.

But all she could say in reply was, 'Horrible! Horrible!'

'Not that he's any relation of mine. My family comes from a good ways west of Hampshire - Cornwall, as it happens. But it's a pleasing coincidence, do you not agree, a Dicker casket being available just where it's most useful?'

'Horrible!'

'Shh! I think our man is coming. The real one this time.'

'Surely he'll not turn up!'

'Oh, he'll come all right. He needs gold badly. The constable is right for once. Travelling under an assumed name, fearing for his life: I expect he'll be across the channel to France snappish-like, and gold will be far more use to him there than English paper money. I'd go so far as to say the man is desperate for gold. He'll pay twice what I was expecting. Now off you go again. This time, sit beneath that small fir tree. There's no need for you to rise from the grave again!' He gave a ghostly cackle.

Mattie hid beneath the low boughs of the tree and counted glow-worms. A man - a small fat man this time - climbed cautiously over the churchyard wall and stood in the shadows there. Dicker moved across to him and they engaged in a long, urgent conversation. The fat man made as if to go several times; Dicker did not hinder him. Finally, the contents of the saddlebag were exchanged for several papery bundles. The man left as he had come and Dicker crept back to Mattie.

'Well, then, fireball. Had enough of nature for one night? Or what do you say to a little moonlighting?'

'Moonlighting? What is that?'

'I'll show you another time, when the darks are over. Let's find the carriage and be off.'

As they drove back the way they came Mattie asked, 'What do you mean by the darks?'

'Moonless nights - an old smuggler's term.'

'But "Sir Terence Dicker of 78 Pall Mall, London" is not an old smuggler's name, is it?'

'No, my little detective. But then, my name is not Terence, but Robert. And I've no house in Pall Mall - though I wish I had, young'un! One needs these little disguises in my trade. In other circumstances I might have been -' (he put on a refined, melodic, hesitant voice) 'the Reverend - ah - the *Right* Reverend I should say - Jeremias Green of Aldwich. Do - yes, *do* come in for a glass of sherry some teatime if you are passing the vicarage, officer...'

'Oh, Dicker! You sound quite like one of those queer old churchmen who used to invite us to high tea!'

'I thank you! Did you know there was a Hampshire clergyman who was also a highwayman, and not so many years ago, either? A Reverend Derby, in Yateley - some forty miles from here. Now, for a vicar to pretend to be a greedy, self-serving son-of-a-bishop is arguably not so difficult for some of them (I exclude your own father from that judgement, of course!). But for a highwayman to play at being an elderly bachelor cleric is harder than one might imagine. One has to be eccentric, inoffensive and ineffective all at the same time!' He held an imaginary teacup before him and changed his voice again.

'Oh, dear, dear me. I - I *do* hope you are not disappointed to have to drink out of an ordinary china cup, Lady Carthorse, but I seem to have misplaced the Spode teaset. So - so *forgetful* of me.'

Mattie laughed. And because Dicker seemed to be in a genuinely mellow mood, she ventured a question.

'Were you - please do not be offended, I do not know how to ask this - were you ever married?'

Dicker's face became expressionless. 'And if I was?' he asked in a cold voice.

'I'm sorry,' said Mattie miserably. 'I wasn't prying. Please forget I asked.'

Dicker said nothing for some minutes and the look on his face did not change. Then he looked at Mattie, sitting unhappily with her hands clasped together, and half-smiled at her.

'No need for apologies,' he said. He smiled again, ruefully. 'I should be accustomed by now to squirming on the inquisitioner's rack of your curiosity! Accustomed to your dictatorial, pedagogic intrusion into all my private thoughts, your weighing of my every motive, your dissection of my mode of life!'

'Really, Mister Dicker, I think that is most unfair -'

'It is not in the least unfair! But have no regrets, my little conscience-creature; as my only honorary relation, you have every right so to intrude!'

'I wasn't -'

'You were, and I am not offended. Now stop disagreeing with me, and I will answer your question.'

Mattie nodded and closed her protesting lips.

'I *was* married. It was the most happy time of my life. And for that reason, it is no pleasure to discuss it.'

'What happened?'

'She died. And many fair things died with her. All that was bright became darkened. All that was already dark dropped away into a black, bottomless pit. All things - but you would not -' He stopped himself.

'Not understand? But I do, Dicker. I know about the pit. And - and all the rest of it, too.'

He did not speak for a long time, and then he said in a quiet voice, 'Yes. You do understand. And I thank you for that. But, as you once said to me, one can have too much of a subject.'

She nodded at this, and they fell silent.

It was a long, dreamy, uneventful drive back to the camp. Mattie dozed for most of it, but at one point she woke to the sound of a gentle voice reciting softly one of Lord Byron's verses:

'She walks in beauty, like the night
Of cloudless climes and starry skies;
And all that's best of dark and bright

Meet in the aspect of her eyes:
Thus mellow'd to that tender light
Which heaven to gaudy day denies...'

She stirred and opened her eyes. Dicker was driving the carriage silently, his eyes upon the road, and if it had been him speaking, he gave no sign of it.

She settled again to doze and soon they were at the camp, where he handed her down from the carriage and busied himself with unharnessing the horse. Mattie crept into the tumble-down cottage and found her pile of rags and sweet river rushes. She fell immediately into a deep sleep.

Chapter 10 The Lives of the Poor

Two mornings later - a Friday - Mattie awoke to gentle but unrelenting rain. She struggled out of her lumpy bed and pushed it back into shape. The rags and their stuffing always started off in their proper places - ferns and reeds underneath all bunched together nicely, held in springy bundles by strips and sheets of cloth. But as she slept everything would collapse and spread out, as if the vegetation was trying to creep back to its native habitat.

'Would you like some breakfast, Jasper?' she asked while dressing. He pretended not to hear her and continued with his investigation of the disused fireplace. He was fascinated by the inch-thick grimy soot, which he would peck at hopefully until it made him sneeze. Then he would give a dismal croak and parade back and forth on the hearth, slowly shaking his head as if he felt himself to have been gravely offended by what had just occurred.

Mattie threw on an extra smock, shoved her stockingless feet into her boots and ran for it. She managed to avoid stepping on the anthill to the left of the cottage doorway but caught her ankle on the dripping nettles to her right instead. She gave a little cry of annoyance and slapped at her ankle as she ran, but neither action made any difference to the stinging.

Tom and Lizzie were alone in the cave, sitting at the rough wooden table near the entrance. Mattie settled herself beside Lizzie with a yawn and looked about.

There was only bread to eat and nothing to drink but at least the fire was crackling cheerily, sending sparks and smoke wandering up into the cave's roof, to disappear in the many cracks - which must lead out into the open air somehow, though no one knew where.

'Flisky rain,' Tom announced with dismal satisfaction. 'Be like this all day, I reckons. Drops so tiny you'd think they'd not do more'n wet your hair. But it'll drench you top to end, y'know?'

'There's butter in the crock to go on the bread,' Lizzie said. 'And ale to drink, if you can 'bide it. Nasty stuff, I thinks!'

'Can we make something hot to drink?'

'Hot ale!' Tom suggested.

Mattie made a face. What she really wanted was tea, and there was none of that. Oh, for a cup of real tea in a proper teacup! She sat at the table and tore a chunk from the bread. Lizzie passed her a knife that was three parts clean and Mattie spread butter with it. The butter was almost clean, too. She rescued from the crock a tiny gnat that had wandered there by mistake.

'Where are they today?' she asked.

Tom yawned - nearly swallowing the hapless gnat as it resumed its tiny airborne journey across the cave. 'Dicker's off west, lookin' for deep-dug treasure,' he said. He left on horseback last night and we can 'spect him back Sunday, afore the sun's up. The others has took advantage and gone to town! Reckon they'll be drunk by now, though it be hardly mornin'. We won't see 'em again till midnight, if then!'

Mattie rubbed her ankle again and Lizzie peered under the table. 'You been and hurt your leg?' she asked.

'Nettle sting.'

'I'll get a dock leaf!' Lizzie bounced up and bounded out into the drizzle, leaving the poor gnat spinning giddily in her wake. She scrabbled about in the bushes and returned with a dripping leaf. 'Hold out your leg, then!'

Mattie obeyed, pointing to the rash on her ankle. Lizzie applied the leaf, firmly rubbing it all around the stung area and repeating:

'Out Nettle, in Dock.
Dock shall have a new frock,
Nettle shall have never a one!'

'It's working!' Mattie reported, surprised.

'It allus works when you says the rhyme!' claimed Lizzie. Tom sneered at this a little and grumbled about 'superstittytus little girls'.

'You ben't no better, Tom Smith! You be silly as a toad in Spring when it comes to rhymes! You've done "High buck, Low buck" - I heard you! And that one 'bout Ladybirds, too!'

'That's where you be wrong, Lizzie! My rhymes ben't superstittytus. They just be the proper way of addressin' a creature!'

Mattie laughed. 'Tell me the one about the ladybird!' she begged.

Tom held his open palm before him and addressed an imaginary bug:

'God a'mighty's colly-cow flyin' up to heaven:
Take up six pound and bring down eleven!'

'That's what you must say to a ladybird. An' when you wants to cotch a stag beetle, you must bow to him and say, "High buck, low buck, buck come down", else he'll 'spise you and not come to your hand.'

'Does it work?'

'Course it does, else I'd not do it, right?' Tom asked, and Mattie judged it best not to "argufy" the point.

After breakfast she cajoled them into their daily lessons. Although they claimed to hate learning, she thought she could detect sparks of interest from time to time. Yesterday Tom had been fascinated by the life cycle of the ant; today Lizzie was enchanted with Blake's

105

poem about the Tyger.

Mattie was suddenly envious of the poor girl. Mattie had written essays about the poem at school, but had never been moved by it. Yet Lizzie - silly, uneducated Lizzie, who hardly knew what a tiger looked like - Lizzie was enraptured.

'Oh, Miss! You can jus' see the Tyger, Miss - I mean, Mattie - he's standin' there full of pride an' power, an' there's so much to 'im, like he's a great factory or one of them steam engines made all minnyature, he be so perfect and complicated an' all. An' yet he's so much more, the Tyger's what they calls a Mystery! All creatures be great mysteries, don't you think so, Miss, an' when you watches 'em they makes you feel full of - of awe, and scared even, an' like the whole universe is inside 'em, like as if you can see God's fingermarks where He squeezed 'em out of clay, an' that scares you even more:

> '*When the stars threw down their spears,*
> *And water'd heaven with their tears,*
> *Did He smile His work to see?*
> *Did He who made the Lamb make thee?*'

And so Mattie had to dredge up the whole poem from memory and repeat it often enough for Lizzie to learn by heart, while Tom amused himself at whittling a bit of wood into the shape of what might, in a good light, be considered to resemble a rather scrawny tiger with three legs.

'If only I was back at Miss Bell's!' Mattie exclaimed. 'She has a whole book of his poetry - with his own drawings in it.'

'He did drawins?' cried Lizzie. 'The man what wrote the poem? Oh, Mattie, I'd just *die* for a sight of it! You must be so happy when you be there, allus bein' able to pick up a book like that. I'd want for nothin', I know I would, if I could be you!'

Mattie hugged her gently and said nothing, wondering indeed whether Lizzie might be right: maybe people like her *should* always be happy.

Tom interrupted her thoughts. 'What we doin' now?' he asked.

Mattie took a risk. 'I thought we might all go to Andover and find a place that provides hot baths!'

'What for?' Tom asked incredulously.

'To - well, to get clean! Hot baths are very pleasant, you know. And if you go to a good establishment, they are clean and quite private, I understand. And I would pay, of course.'

'Has you been and had one of them baths?' asked Lizzie.

'No. But I'm ready to try! We don't really have the chance to wash properly here, do we? And I *hate* being all grubby. I feel uncomfortable when I'm dirty; I itch; and I don't suppose I smell very nice! Besides, it would be good to be clean when wearing our new clothes, wouldn't it?'

Tom considered all this and suggested a compromise. 'We ben't proper dirty, not yet by a long chalk! Let's say we goes to the baths. But not till we be dirty all over!'

Mattie gave an exasperated howl. 'Tom Smith! Look at our hands and faces! How dirty do we have to *be*?'

Tom grinned. 'As dirty as ever we can get, I reckons! I says we takes the rest of the mornin' gettin' fair plastered wi' dirt, for to make the baths worthwhile!'

Lizzie squealed with delight. 'We can make mud pies! An' have a mud fight! An' rub soot on our faces and play Indians in the Wild West of Amerricer! We can dig fer gold and have chasin' games in the woods! We can climb trees!'

Mattie felt suddenly shy. It had been a long time since she had done any rough playing. Being an only child, and a quiet, studious one at that, her games had usually involved books, dolls, paper and pencil. But it seemed unkind to spoil their game, and to lose the chance of a bath!

'Listen,' she said. 'We can do some of that, though we'd better not get too dirty because then they might not let us into the Baths at all!'

They spent the next two hours trying all the muddiest, grubbiest, messiest games they could think of. At first Mattie was restrained, but a liberal coating of dirt quickly covered all her embarrassment and soon she was whooping through the bracken, rolling about in the mud and scrambling up and down trees with abandon. It was quite simply the best game she'd ever played and she was sorry when it was over. Jasper was sorry, too. He had not understood the games but had clearly felt the excitement of them. He hopped and fluttered from branch to stone to muddy bank, squawking exuberantly, skipping frantically from side to side and trying to join in at inconvenient moments.

They ran down to the stream and washed off most of the mud, splashing each other, tripping over and falling in, pushing one another in and finally just throwing themselves in. Then with their teeth chattering (for the water was wickedly cold) they ran to the cottage and put on their second best change of clothes, hanging their dripping rags to dry in the decrepit room at the back of the cottage, which had once been a kitchen but now was the living quarters of several dozen mice.

Mattie checked her little purse to make sure she had enough money for the baths and hung it about her neck on a little cord. Jasper fluttered to her shoulder, cawing at the sight of silver coins, which always excited him.

'You'll have to stay here,' she explained calmly. 'We're off to town and it's not a safe place for birds!' She put him on the mantelpiece and gently stroked him until he closed his eyes and made little chirruping sounds, which meant that he was going to sleep. Lizzie came in to watch, and then Tom.

'We'll buy him a penn'orth of seed, shall we?' Tom asked.

'We've a few coins put by,' Lizzie added. Tom gave her a cautioning look.

As they walked up the hill, their clean clothes wrapped into bundles and folded under their arms, Tom asked lazily, as if it were of no real import:

'D'you think, Lizzie, we ort to show her the hidey-hole?'

Lizzie clapped her hands. 'Can we, Tom?' she cried. And they each seized an arm and dragged Mattie off the path into the depths of the woods until they stood at the great oak. Mattie watched in amused confusion as Lizzie climbed up and pulled out yesterday's bread and their few coins.

'Now you knows where it be,' Tom said. 'And if there be trouble, you can run here and find a bite to eat and money for flight. Fine?'

'Right fine!' Mattie replied. She was overwhelmed by their generosity. It was like the widow's mite in the Bible - they had nothing, but what they had they were going to share with her. She didn't know how to thank them, but gave Lizzie a hug.

They replaced the money except for a penny but kept the bread, which they munched on the way to Andover.

'We used to have baths, we did,' Lizzie announced through a mouthful of bread as they tramped the familiar road into Andover. 'Afore the fire, in a big tin contraption wot leaked a bit down one side.'

'Once a week, was it? I can't justly call it to mind,' added Tom.

'Nah! Once a fortnight, if that! Depended whether Dad

was about, didn't it? Mam had a bad back, see,' she explained to Mattie. 'She couldn't drag the bath in and fill it with buckets of hot and cold, not without takin' to her bed afterward.'

'We used to do it for her, once Dad left. We was just gettin' old enough to be a help when Mam died.'

'What did she die of?' asked Mattie.

'Old age, the doctor said.'

'What? How could she be old? I mean, you're young, so she'd be young, too - unless I suppose she married late and...'

'How old was our Mam, Tom? I disremembers now.'

'Nigh on thirty, she were.'

'But that's not old!' exclaimed Mattie.

'Tis when you've worked since you was eight year old! She laboured on the farms 'ceptin' in winter, when she did piecework sewin'. Used to sit up late an' rise early, did our Mam! Doctor Westlake, he said it wore her out. Now, *he* was good to us - used to see to it we got our poor relief when Mam couldn't work and our Dad was away (which he usually was).'

'But then the Union turned Doctor Westlake out.'

'Who are the Union?' asked Mattie.

'The Work'us Union. The snobby gents what runs the Work'us and the poor relief! Don't you know nothing? Well, they got themselves another doctor instead, one what wasn't so easy on folk like us. So this new doctor, he comes to see us once. Not that we ast him to - we'd no money to pay for doctorin'. But he came 'cos we was meant to be on relief. When you asks for poor relief, the doctor he visits for to see if you be proper sick, or just shammin'. So - arter the new doctor comed, the Relief Officer sent word that there wasn't to be no more help, and no more doctorin' neither. Said we wasn't bad enough off and could bide well easy as we was!'

'How badly off were you?'

Tom shrugged. 'Mam couldn't work no more. Tried to, but couldn't stand proper. Had to crawl about to do the chores, some days. Lizzie and me, we went and did some days on a farm, but that ended, too, and the money was soon gone. Weren't hardly more'n a few coppers, anyways! When you be only eight, an' starvin' and desp'rate, they doesn't have to pay you much, does they?'

'And it were worse than the Bones!' complained Lizzie. 'All day in a half-froze field diggin' turmits and pasmets, then puttin' they all in sacks, then draggin' they sacks acrost the field - you couldn't feel your feet for hours arter! Would of helped if we'd had shoes!'

'What?'

'We'd no shoes that year, so we wrapped instead.'

'Wrapped, Lizzie? What do you mean?'

'You takes bits of cloth and winds 'em round and round your feet and up your legs. Better'n nothing!'

Tom was impatient to continue the story. 'So Mam sold the big bed, the one she an' Dad slept in when he was there. Then she sold her bits of jewellery. Then the table and the chairs and such-like - all 'cept her rocker and our one bed what was left. But when it was coldest, we'd no money again. We'd nothin' for the fire neither.'

'We had coal some days,' corrected Lizzie. 'We'd go out arter dark an' climb the wall into the ironworks. Plenty of coal there, though you needed to be careful not to get cotched! An' we couldn't carry much at a time.'

'Mam said it weren't properly right and gived us a good tongue-bangin' the first time we done it. But it weren't wrong neither, she said, 'cos every soul has a right to a fire in winter. And to a little food, too.'

'Didn't have no bath that winter! Didn't hardly take our clothes off! The weather were so outdaceous bad we sometimes stayed in bed all day.'

'Then Mam died. An' there was only the one bed in

the house, so that's where she lay. We went and told the new doctor, who ballyragged us for botherin' him and shouted that 'twas none of his duty. But Doctor Westlake, he got to hear of it and comed out instead. We'd no money for a coffin, we hadn't, but Doctor Westlake he arranged all that. We'd nothing to give him for his trouble, neither.'

'But we had, Tom - we gived him the rocker! He was that touched, too. Said he wished he could of done more. But I reckon there was poor folk dyin' every day that winter.'

Tom continued. 'We had to go register Mam's death. Nigh on two year ago that was. Had to walk five miles to where the Registrar lives. And when we gets there, he'd not had his breakfast yet, so we had to wait outside in the cold till he'd done that. We'd had no breakfast neither, nor nothing to eat the day afore; but we had to wait for him to fill hisself. It's him now what's the Poor Relief Officer - God help the poor! Last of all, there wasn't no proper buryin' service at the Church. The parson, he gets sixty pound a year from the Work'us -'.

'Sixty pounds! That's a considerable sum!' exclaimed Mattie.

'But he never come to see our Mam, nor t'other poor that I knows of! Beggin' your pardon, Mattie, you bein' religious and your pa a parson an' all - but there ben't a church for poor folk. Reckon church is for them as has plenty and don't plan to share it. An' I reckon when the devil dances down in hell, he's galumphing on the heads of vicars and bishops what never cared for nothing but their own bellies!'

'Tom!' exclaimed his sister, scandalised.

'That's all right, Lizzie,' Mattie reassured her. 'I know what he means and I'm - I'm as upset as he is about it. But my father was different - *is* different. I'm not offended, Tom. Do go on with your history.'

Tom paused a moment and smiled at Mattie - the first true smile he had ever given her. Then he continued. 'An' the vicar, he said unless we could pay for a proper service, our Mam must be buried as a pauper - with nothin' but a few mumbled prayers by the grave you know, an' no marker, just a mound of earth.'

'But we got round him, didn't we, Tom? We made her a marker! Stole an old tombstone what had writin' so worn out it couldn't be read and weren't doin' no one no good. We put it at the head of her grave one night. Made our hands raw diggin' a hole for it in the frosty ground with sticks, but we did it!'

'And we didn't know what to write on it - and didn't know how to write it if we'd known. So we just puts "Mam" on it. "Mam Smith" an' the year. It's still there, too.'

'Wrote it with real black paint, we did, an' all! Stole the paint from the ironworks when we went next for coal!'

'Then they put us in the Work'us.'

'Well, it were somewhere to live, I 'spect, though it weren't home. Not that there was much of home left by then.'

We'd sold the bed, see, for to buy food after Mam was gone. After that there was nothin' left to sell.'

'Did your father ever come back?'

Tom made a face. 'When she was took ill, Mam told us he'd gone for good. Found a woman in London a year afore, she said. Good riddance, she said, and God have mercy on the poor trollop. Our dad was a hard drinker, you know? And he liked a fight, even at home, even with a woman. He'd better not turn up again: I'd kill him.'

'Oh, Tom!' cried Lizzie. 'He be our dad!'

'I'd still kill him, I reckon. But he's in no danger, for he'd never find us now, would he?'

Chapter 11 The Workhouse

They had scarcely reached the outskirts of town when a small carriage overtook them. Its driver seemed half asleep, and the horse was making its own rules of the road, trotting almost on the verge. Lizzie pulled Mattie out of the path of the swaying contraption, and Tom shook his fist at the driver.

'Stupid old fool!' he cried.

The man sat up suddenly and pulled the horse to a dead stop. He vaulted from his seat clumsily and turned upon them. They started to run off, but the sight of a pistol being waved in their direction made them pause. Behind the pistol a tall, red-faced gentleman with large red sideburns and a fiery moustache berated them in an uneven, tipsy, military voice. He spoke with a mild Scots accent.

'Damned, dirty good-for-nothing gutter-bred bastards! Talk to *me* that way, will you? Lucky I don't blow your louse-ridden heads off. No bloody respect!'

Uncharacteristically, Tom and Lizzie hung their heads. Tom even covered his with his hands. But it was too late: the man had recognised them. He gave a great laugh.

'Well, I'll be damned! It's young Elizabeth and - and Thomas - come back to us!' He waved the gun wildly at them. 'Didn't hear you greet me, though! Have you lost what few manners you had?' he accused them.

'Evening, Sergeant-Major,' muttered Lizzie, and Tom

repeated the greeting, his face still turned to the ground.

The man looked at Mattie with evident interest. 'And now you will introduce me to your - your friend. Sharp now, Thomas!'

Tom spoke in a dull voice. 'Mr McDougal, this is Matt - this is Matilda Harris. Matilda, this is Mr McDougal, warden of the Andover Workhouse.'

Mattie made a little curtsey. McDougal stood before them, muttering and wiping his face with a large red handkerchief. He seemed to be holding an argument with himself, and the progress of his slow ponderings could be seen in the changes of expression which passed across his flushed, craggy features. Meanwhile, he continued to wave the gun at them. Finally he heaved a sigh and motioned towards the carriage.

'Can't leave you two wandering the streets,' he said to Tom and Lizzie. 'You'd better come back to the House with me.'

'Thank you kindly, sir,' replied Lizzie with careful politeness. 'But we've a place to stay now, see.'

His face fell. Then he said craftily, 'I'll take you there, of course. Not safe for you to be out on your own!'

'There's no need,' Mattie put in hastily. 'Tom and Lizzie are with me. I'll see them home.'

'You?' he queried. 'And who are *you*? You're a stranger to me, young Miss. Whereas I am *in loco parentis*, you might say. God knows what trouble these two have fallen into since they left the House! I'm still responsible for them, and I'll have you know I take my responsibility seriously!'

'I'm sure you do.'

'Damn right I do! Now hop up, you two, and I'll see you to your lodgings.' But Tom and Lizzie were motionless. McDougal smiled triumphantly. 'So, my little vagabonds,' he continued softly, 'where is this place you say you have? ...You won't tell? Can't tell? Well, well.

Might it just be that there's something you don't want me to know? It seems I must either take you to a constable, or go against my law-abiding principles and offer you lodging for - for the weekend, let's say.'

'Why?' asked Tom bluntly.

McDougal put on a hurt look. 'Thomas!' he exclaimed. 'I make the offer from the goodness of my heart! As a good citizen, I cannot turn my back on your - your *situation*. Heavens, boy, my conscience won't let me consider such a thing! And yet - and yet I've no desire to imprison you both. So, let us make a treaty: you will return to the Workhouse. I will have discharged my duty by that. Should you run away yet again - well, that would not be *my* doing, would it?'

'What about Mattie?'

McDougal looked at Mattie again, and Mattie did not like the smile that came to his lips. She reddened and looked away. He said thoughtfully, half to himself, 'Nice girl. *Fine* girl! And where do *you* live, Miss Harris?'

Mattie did not reply. McDougal gave another low laugh. 'It seems you'll *all* have to come back with me,' he concluded, pointing the gun at each in turn. 'Step up, Thomas, if you please. Now you, Elizabeth. And yourself, Miss Harris!'

They climbed into the carriage and he seated himself between the two girls. A strong smell of beer and tobacco smoke rose from his person. He passed the horse's reins to Tom and placed his arms around the girls. 'Not much room in this carriage!' he explained. 'Have to squeeze in close. In - *in loco parentis* you might say!' He gave a short laugh and motioned to Tom. 'Drive, then, Thomas. Mustn't miss curfew at the House, you know!'

The two-storey brick Workhouse was set on a small hill. It looked attractive and new, with large windows looking in all directions. Seen from above, the main building formed the shape of a square cross. The arms left and right housed the dormitories while the top of the cross held the kitchen and dining room. At the base was the front entrance, with a porter's lodge built on. The warden's family lived on part of the second floor. The cross was enclosed by a square of outbuildings, walls and fences, forming yards shared by the chickens, the pigs and the workhouse families.

The large front door was lit by a lantern and there were cheerful lights at some of the windows. The horse made its way to the side entrance without any prompting from Tom. When it halted the twins leapt down, followed by the Sergeant-Major who insisted on handing Mattie out onto the paved drive, his other hand still holding the gun. They left the horse and carriage to a stableman and walked back to the main entrance, where McDougal pulled irritably at the bell rope several times until the door was opened by a serving girl. She hurried to take the his coat.

'Where's your mistress?' he asked her gruffly.

'Please, sir, she's in the sewing room.'

'Tell her I want to see her! I'll be in the admissions room.' And snatching a lamp from a window ledge near the door, he led the three children forward to the end of the wide entrance hall, which was panelled with wood and well-furnished. He pushed through a large door covered with green baize cloth into a second hallway. They turned almost immediately and entered a small, windowless room that smelled of disinfectant. In one corner was a table with an enamel jug and washbasin. There was also a plain wooden chair and a small, lumpy bed. He set the lamp on the table. Without a word to the children he left them, closing the door behind him.

'So what'll we do now?' Lizzie asked Tom.

'He'll have us watched tonight,' Tom judged. 'I reckon

he'd do it hisself if he weren't quotted with drink!'

'But why is he bothering with us at all?' asked Mattie.

Tom pulled a face. 'He don't care about *us* - it's for hisself he wants us here! Must have some shirky reason. Mostly, the gen'lmen what runs the Work'us don't want folks in it. "Make it hard for 'em," they says! "Make it hard, and they won't take advantage of our generousness! Make 'em work hard here and they'll go get jobs rather than relyin' on charity!" Give me a shillin' for each time I've heard such talk, and I'd be rich enough to run my own work'us!'

Lizzie shivered. 'But how're we to get away?'

'He seemed to be saying that he didn't mind us going after the weekend,' Mattie reminded them.

Tom laughed at this. 'You reckon he meant that?' he asked. 'Well, maybe he does – now! But like as not, he'll say different on Monday. Unless -' But he was obliged to break off because the Warden and his wife came to the door.

Mrs McDougal was a thin, sour, greying woman with rimless spectacles and wrinkles about her small, dark eyes. She stood submissively while her husband spoke, her head bowed.

'You see!' he exclaimed triumphantly, as if he were making some important point in a long argument. 'There - three of them! As the parson would say, the Lord provides, ay?'

'Well, I suppose - ' his wife began nervously.

'Suppose? Heavens above, woman! What has supposing to do with it? Enrol them! You won't find three likelier, will you?' McDougal frowned at her fiercely - an exhibition of spleen that was totally wasted since she was not looking at him. She was peering uncertainly at the children and muttering to herself.

'I suppose... the two, they're in the book anyway. Just need to - to *regularise* things. But the girl - I don't

118

suppose your name would happen to be Sissy, would it?
No... silly
question.'

'Of course her bloody name is Sissy!' her husband
growled. 'She'll be whatever you want to call her!' He
turned his scowl upon Mattie. 'While you're here, you'll
be called Sissy!' he shouted. 'D'you understand?'

The man looked so suddenly, frighteningly violent that
Mattie thought he was about to strike her. Her hands
went to her face and she could make no reply.

'She's called Sissy,' he said fiercely to his wife. 'Enrol
her! And you'll need to examine her and the others.
Probably carrying lice and God knows what else.'

'Will you -?' his wife gestured towards the door.

'I'd better stay here with you. She's likely to be violent, that one.'

Mrs McDougal nodded. She turned to Mattie. 'Remove
your clothing then, child!' she instructed.

Mattie blushed.

After the medical inspections, McDougal rang a little bell
to summon the night matron.

'Blimey,' Tom muttered to the others when a large,
stern woman appeared. 'It's Mad Mollie. Just our luck!
No escaping tonight then!'

'What's that?' Mrs McDougal turned upon him
sharply. 'You were speaking before you were spoken to,
Thomas?'

Tom nodded meekly. 'Sorry, Mrs McDougal,' he whispered.

The new woman peered at him. 'It's Thomas,' she
announced. 'Don't ferget faces. 'E's been 'ere afore, so
'e knows the Rules. What's Rule Twenty-six say 'bout
noise, Thomas?'

Tom shrugged.

'Elizabeth?'

Lizzie gave the tiniest of sighs before repeating: "Any pauper who shall make any noise when silence is ordered shall be deemed disorderly and shall be placed in apartments provided for such offenders".

Mad Mollie nodded. 'And it's not just silence at mealtimes that means, young Thomas! It's silence afore your betters and elders till you're spoken to! Bain't it so?'

'Yes, Miss.'

Mad Mollie looked to Mr McDougal with a gleam in her eye. 'Oh, Major McDougal, sir, what can be done wiv a boy like this?' she whined. 'I tries to make 'em behave, sir, but it don't do no good, sometimes. Do you think he needs punishment? Do you, sir? I knows you're a kind man, Major, and punishment don't come nat'ral to you, but we must all of us 'bide by the rules, mustn't we?'

McDougal's voice betrayed none of the kindness she credited him with. 'Lock him in the punishment room for the night, Nurse! And put him on half diet for tomorrow. Perhaps he's been eating too well of late! A little abstinence never harms the body and it's good for the soul!' He unconsciously patted his own well-rounded stomach as he spoke.

Mrs McDougal murmured her agreement. The children stood still, and quiet as stones. Mad Mollie eyed them like a cat waiting for the mouse between its paws to make a doomed run for freedom. Finally McDougal gave a little wave of the hand, passing over responsibility for the children to the women, and strode from the room, whistling to himself. Tom was led off by the nurse and the girls were taken to their dormitory by Mrs McDougal.

There were three dormitories for the females: one for the old, one for women over sixteen, and one for children over seven. The youngest children of both sexes had a dormitory of their own.

Mattie's dormitory was hot and stuffy. It smelled of

sweat and urine. It buzzed with the wheezing of a sickly girl and echoed to coughs and snores, little groans, whimpers of dismal imaginings and the occasional sigh of a child who, having seen little of goodness in this world, was dreaming of it in another. Mattie lay awake between scratchy sheets, wondering when they had last been washed. She was thinking of the events of the day, and burning with anger. She had mattered nothing to the McDougals, nothing! - except that the husband had enjoyed watching her undress, of course! At least Tom had had the decency to turn his back.

She was hardly better than an animal to them. While the three children stood there naked, waiting to be permitted to dress again, the McDougals had carried on a conversation over their heads: as if they were just three stray cats picked up from the streets.

Mattie turned again and again on the hard mattress. Well, at least it was more comfortable than sleeping on a pile of rags stuffed with spiky vegetation. Mind you, there were probably bedbugs in it! She listened to the slow, regular breathing of Lizzie in the next bed and wondered whether Tom was asleep. She tried to piece together a plan for escape and hoped that Dicker's gang had not concluded that the children had simply run off. Was Dicker striding about the camp, shouting at the others and brandishing his pistol? She shivered suddenly. Would he take a shot at Jasper? Or had Jasper wisely removed himself? While she pondered, she grew drowsy. Finally she slept.

Chapter 12 Nobbut Hard Work

At six o'clock in the morning, a handbell was pulled from its shelf and rung severely. The night nurse entered each dormitory in turn, clanging the bell and grimacing at the occupants. Last of all she entered the punishment room and swung the bell vigorously in Tom's face. When he sat up, throwing off the thin sheet, she boxed both his ears and gave him a crooked smile.

'Make haste, young Tom! There's hard work to be done afore you earns yer breakfast! Cook's been told you'll scrub her gruel pots and she's like to hammer you if yer not down in the kitchen afore t'others!'

Tom groaned and stood up. 'Hike off, you raff old hoosbird!' he snapped.

Mad Mollie sneered at him. 'You wouldn't be so brave if there was others to hear you, my fine boy! An' you'll not ferget I'm about tonight agen an' all! I'll 'ev you back in 'ere an' I'll be up ever' hour to thrash you. I've a good mind to give you a taste of it now...' She waved the heavy bronze handbell at him.

Tom took a step towards her and such was the look in his eye that she retreated, despite being twice his size and many times his match for violence. She swore at him, adding before she fled the room, 'Wait till t'night, you'll not be so forward then!' The door slammed and Tom put his head in his hands. She was not exaggerating about what she would do if she got a chance.

Breakfast was at 6.30, after roll call. Around sixty inmates sat at the plain wooden tables, Mattie and Lizzie among them, listening to the rain drumming on the roof.

'Can you smell the gruel?', Lizzie had whispered to Mattie as they were about to enter the high-ceilinged hall. 'It's allus gruel for breakfast!' she groaned. 'But hush now - no talkin' at meals!'

Mattie watched as a thin porridge was measured into bowls: exactly a pint and a half each. Bread was doled out too, roughly a third of a small loaf for women and children, an ounce more for men. Mattie would have refused the gruel but a warning look from Lizzie stopped her from pushing her bowl away. She made herself swallow its tasteless bulk, wishing there was a little honey to go with it. At least the wheaten bread was good, even if not quite fresh. She realised that she was hungry after all and began to eat more quickly. But she halted when she noticed Lizzie tucking most of her portion of bread under her uniform.

'Why -' she began. A kick to the ankle from Lizzie halted her question. One of the supervisors craned her head in Mattie's direction, trying to decide who had been talking. Everyone's eyes suddenly looked down at the table and everyone's eating became studied and noiseless. The supervisor looked away again.

Lizzie traced the letter 'T' on the table with a finger. Mattie nodded. That meant 'Tom' - though what Tom had to do with it, she did not understand. Lizzie paused and tried to write something else - something which went 'Bkn.. dnr.. no dreb'. Lizzie bit her lip and tried the last word again, making it 'bred'. Mattie gave a little smile. She nodded to Lizzie to show that she understood the last two words at least. Lizzie smiled back, glowing with pride at her success at writing.

At another table Tom was chewing moodily through the half rations he had been put on. The Warden was allowed to reduce the diet of anyone who broke one of the numerous Rules. He was supposed to ask the Board of Guardians for permission, but since this was always given, he didn't bother them with such small matters. Besides, whatever the inmates did not eat was added to the Warden's food. McDougal and his wife between them were already receiving six times a pauper's allowance, and more besides for their two children; but another portion of bread and some slices of bacon or an extra wedge of cheese was always welcome!

After breakfast they returned to their dormitories to prepare for work. Mattie copied Lizzie by hiding part of her bread amongst her nightclothes and followed her to the washroom.

'What was that about, Lizzie?' asked Mattie as they queued to wash their hands. 'Why don't we eat all our bread?'

'For a start, Tom's on 'alf rations. He'll be mortal 'ungry.'

'You mean, leer as a gallybagger?'

Lizzie giggled. 'And Sattidays we keeps part of our bread back anyways, to eat with dinner. We gets a bit of bacon and veggytables for dinner on Tuesdays and Sattidays, but no bread. Other days we gets no meat nor veg neither - only bread and cheese. And once a week we gets nobbut soup!'

Mattie was puzzled. 'Nobbut? What's a "nobbut"? And what kind of soup do you make out of it?'

Lizzie burst into peals of laughter.

'You been skisin' in your talkin' lessons, Miss! Nobbut means "nothing but". Once a week, we gets *nothing but* soup for dinner!'

'But when you have soup, surely you've bread with it?'

Lizzie shook her head at the other girl's innocence. 'We don't get a speck, and drot it! It's a pint and a half of soup on Thursdays for lunch, be you man, woman or child - and nowt else! So on Thursdays we most of us does like we done today - we saves a bit of bread from breakfast to eat at dinner time. Else you feels mighty empty all afternoon!'

'Do we get anything to eat between breakfast and dinner?'

Lizzie made a face. 'There's no nunch at the Work'us. No tea, neither. Just breakfast, dinner and supper!'

'What's for supper, then?'

'Supper's allus bread and a bite of cheese, same as breakfast is allus bread and gruel, an' a cup of thin milk. There ben't no cream in it, 'cos the Macs has it skimmed off and takes it all. But quick - there's the bell! That means it's seven o'clock and time for work! I hope we gets a bit of schoolin' today, but I fear we might be on the Bones instead. Come on, Mattie, quick, or we'll get a lick of the cane for bein' late!'

Unfortunately, they were late by several seconds - and so the cane was produced by Mrs McDougal and brought down sharply onto the palms of their hands. Mattie and Lizzie hugged their stinging hands to their chests and tried to pretend their faces weren't streaming with tears. A group of a dozen girls aged between seven and sixteen watched the beating without expression. But when Mrs McDougal turned to put away the cane, a few of them made sympathetic faces across the room.

'There will be two hours of sewing,' said Mrs McDougal. 'My daughter being indisposed, I will supervise you today. After sewing, at nine o'clock, there will be an inspection, at which you will be asked to answer to your names. I promise that I will treat with severity any attempts to enter into conversation with the gentleman carrying out the inspection. He will ask whether there are any matters you wish him to consider: I am sure there are none. If you *should* have any complaints, you are to raise them with myself, *not* with the gentleman!'

She glared at them and made her voice threatening. 'If you raise them with the gentleman, you may lose your place here and lose your entitlement to relief. You would then have nowhere to live and no food to eat. Your families would be thrown out onto the streets! Do you understand?' She looked at them severely. Her small eyes were sharp as needles, darting from girl to girl.

'Yes, ma'am,' they replied, looking down at their laps.

Mrs McDougal produced squares of fabric, already criss-crossed by stitching, and passed them out together with needles and cotton. After lengthy instructions they set to, sewing imaginary buttonholes. From time to time Mrs McDougal would leave the room, when the girls would talk quietly.

'You can be fair pleased it's not her daughter overseein' us,' Lizzie commented. 'She be more of a fecky frump than her ma. Nasty, too!'

One of the other girls added, 'If you disremembers how to do something, Miss McDougal gets in a right ballyrag. An' she's like to give you a bannickin' for nowt some days. Oh, *crimany*! I just spiked meself!' She put a pricked finger into her mouth and sucked it ruefully.

And so the two hours passed in squinting at their bits of cloth, poking it with needles and gossiping; poking their sore fingers instead and swearing; being caught whispering and getting the cane. Just before nine, Mrs McDougal collected in the cloths, giving each a cursory glance and complaining.

'A waste of good material, giving it to you girls! To be sure, you'll never make anything of yourselves - you won't settle to work, will you? Always wasting time! Well, you can take your turn on the bones soon; that'll be a fair reward for your laziness!'

'Oh, Ma'am!' several exclaimed. 'It's not fair, Mrs McDougal - the boys ought to do more'n we, cos we be weaker!'

'Hmph! The boys do their share, and so should you! The hard work's good for you, it teaches you to use your time well. Now, go to the dormitories and stand by your beds!'

At nine o'clock exactly the Relieving Officer, Mr Cooke, entered the Workhouse, rain dripping from his overcoat. He went to the study where Mr McDougal had already laid out the large book in which Cooke was to record the payments and receipts for the week. There were neat piles of vouchers ready for Cooke to look at. Cooke did look at them, wearily. He took up his fountain pen and picked up the first voucher. "Received the sum of one pound, three and tuppence halfpenny for providing the following meats to Mr McDougal -" he began to read, and then laid it down again.

'I had nearly forgotten, McDougal. I said last week that I would carry out a check of the register of those living in the home. Can't have you claiming for paupers who aren't here, can we?' he asked, laughing. McDougal laughed too, then pressed a hand to his head. He'd had a little too much to drink the night before, and his head knew it.

They went from dormitory to dormitory, McDougal holding the register open at the correct pages for Cooke to mark off the names of the residents. Entering Mattie's dormitory, they called the roll. All went well until they came to Lizzie's name.

'I thought the Smith children had left.'

'No, no! Still with us, unfortunately! See - we've listed them and claimed money for them for over a year now. You must recall Lizzie there!'

'Must I? I'm afraid they all look very much of a piece to me, McDougal. But the girl is standing there large as life, so you must be right. And the last name on the list - Sissy Morgan. Which of you is that?'

No one answered, and the girls looked blankly from one to another. McDougal erupted.

'Sissy! You, girl! Answer your name when the gentleman speaks to you!' he shouted, pointing at Mattie, who had completely forgotten that this was to be her new name. She panicked.

'I'm - no - you see - I -'

'That will do!' exclaimed McDougal, pressing his hand to his head again. 'The girl is simple-minded, Cooke. Can't even speak properly! Ought to be in a mental institution! Still, I suppose it's cheaper to keep her here.'

'Oh, yes - undoubtedly! Nothing cheaper than the Workhouse, McDougal.' Cooke looked at the little group. 'Have any of you any matters you wish to raise with me? Any problems? Any complaints?' He and McDougal stood shoulder to shoulder.

Not surprisingly, no one had a single matter to raise.

The Bones were even more dreadful than Lizzie had hinted. Imagine, if you will, a stout open-topped wooden box, about as high as a ten-year-old child's knees and a little wider than it is high. Into this box you drop three or four bones. Usually the bones are large, dry beef bones - though there may be pig, or sheep or even horse bones (once, old human bones were sent from the graveyard, by mistake it was said). Sometimes the bones are green and a little musty. Other times, greenish brown and positively stinking. When the bones are first delivered, some of them are wet. They may even still have meat on them, though this has usually been cooked and then stripped off. What is left is well rotted, but it is often eaten by the Workhouse inmates.

'How disgusting!' cried Mattie when Lizzie told her this. She added severely, 'Are you telling me the truth?'

'Course I am, Mattie. An' course it makes your stomach turn inside out. I never touched meat from the bones, not me! But some of 'em do. The men in pertiklar. A body gets powerful hungry in the Work'us, specially in the winter. Then you thinks you could eat anything - and a nice bit of meat on the bone, if it's not smellin' *too* bad, gets fought over by them as can stomach that sort of thing.'

'Ugh!'

'Anyways, the bones today be mortal dry 'cos they been in the shed, not the yard. That's worse in some ways - means they'll be all dusty when you smashes 'em. Look, you drop 'em in the box. Then you picks up the crusher and wallops 'em hard till they break. Like this!' And Lizzie lifted a wooden pole that stood about as high as her shoulder and was weighted at the end with a heavy iron block. The face of the block was shaped into rows of teeth. It took all of Lizzie's strength to lift the pole and then slam its iron teeth hard onto the bones. One of the bones cracked and splintered, sending a nasty-smelling spray of tiny fragments up towards their faces.

'Whew!' Lizzie cried, waving her hand before her nose. 'What a hogo! Like a rotten egg, that one! 'Ere, Mattie, you have a crack at it. It ben't easy, I warn you!'

Mattie's first attempts were a complete failure. Lizzie and the other girls laughed heartily as she chased a bone around with the crusher, just nipping an end of it each time and sending it scuttling to and fro across the box like a nimble little mouse.

'It's easy to see *you've* not done no crushin' afore this! Hold up, Mattie, and I'll put some more bones in so it's easier to hit 'em!' Lizzie laughed shrilly. 'An' we'll do the smashin' together, each aholt of the pole from oppysite sides. That's how the nippers do it.'

'Nippers?' Mattie asked. 'You mean, children younger than us, even?'

One of the other girls laughed. 'McDougal makes the

boys start when they's just nine! 'E says if they work in twos, maybe they won't crush a hundredweight like the men, or fifty pound like us, but they might just make forty. And any weight's good money in the hand, 'cos they sells the crushed bones for farmers to spread on the fields.'

They worked for nearly three hours, taking turns. While others were crushing, they sat on the floor amongst the bone dust and bone chips, wriggling their fingers so as to bring the feeling back to their aching hands. Mattie had long since given up trying to wipe the dust from her face and arms. It was in her hair, in her ears, up her nose. She stank of bones.

'My hands are bleeding!' she exclaimed just before the bell for dinner at noontime. 'Look, Lizzie, they're covered in blisters, and cracked!'

Lizzie inspected the hands and sniffed disparagingly. 'Them ben't much to complain about!' she judged. 'Wait till you've had to smash bones several days in a row - wiv your fingers raw and bruises all over you an' your back achin' - *then* you can grumble a bit!'

'At least you got both legs to stand on,' added another girl. 'Will Newport, he had but one leg but McDougal made him pound bones like the others. He was one of them as chewed any flesh he found on the bones.'

'And he used to eat candle ends! Worse than the Lewis kids!' said another, peering about to check that no Lewises were near.

'What did they do?' wondered Mattie.

'Last winter, they'd eat whatever was thrown to the chickens in the yard - they'd go right down on their knees and eat the scraps off the ground. Mind, they'd been half starved by the time they got here. It were manna from heaven for they.'

'How revolting!' cried Mattie. But one of the older

girls looked at her seriously.

'Easy for the likes of you to say. You've never starved, I allow. When you're shrammed wi' cold and ravenous, a mouthful of warm slops don't seem so foul.'

They were called from their discussions by the dinner bell. They ran to wash in cold water and lined up for dinner. A bit of bacon and a plateful of swede was their reward for the morning's work. Mattie hated swede but she ate it anyway - and pitied Tom on his half rations. At least they'd been able to pass him some of the bread they'd saved. He'd grinned and shown them his own blistered hands: he had been on the bones while they were sewing.

After dinner they were given more sewing, then an hour's religious instruction from young Miss McDougal (who had apparently recovered from her indisposition, though without any improvement to her famous temper).

During this hour Mattie nearly fell asleep several times from tiredness. When it came her turn to recite the passage from the Prayer Book they had all been learning by heart, which for some reason involved the Lion of Judah, she was quite dozy. Lizzie elbowed her awake. Startled, she stood up and began, still in a dream:

"Tyger! Tyger! burning bright
In the forests of the night -"

She paused. The other girls were laughing. Why was that? She continued while Miss McDougal's worried eyes stared at her in wonder and something near to terror.

"What immortal hand or eye
Could frame thy fearful symmetry?"

'I think that is *quite* enough!' cried Miss McDougal. 'What possessed you to chant such nonsense?'

The other girls collapsed in giggles. Lizzie called out, 'That be potery, Miss! An' she can't help it, her's weak-minded. Her allus talks potery. Can't do no else!' She gave Mattie a crafty nudge. Mattie, noting the long cane at Miss McDougal's side, nodded energetically and smiled at the teacher in her most simple-minded fashion. The girls laughed even more.

'Silence!' cried Miss McDougal. 'Or I'll thrash the lot of you!'

Silence fell immediately.

'You, child – Sissy, or whatever you're called! – come here! Here! Stand before me! Now hold out your hand. Not like that! Palm *upwards*!'

She raised the cane high and brought it down with a sickening slap. Mattie gasped with the pain and pulled her hand to her chest, holding it with her other hand. It had been bruised before; now it was burning with agony.

'Perhaps *that* will teach you not to talk nonsense here!' Miss McDougal cried. 'And if you weren't simple-minded, you would have *several* of those! Do it again, and you *will* have! Do you understand?'

Mattie nodded. She could not speak and the tears were flooding down her cheeks. She looked at her hand, which was bleeding. Miss McDougal looked as well.

'Oh, you *stupid* child!' she cried. 'That's what happens when you try and snatch your hand away! Here, wrap it up with a scrap of cloth!'

She threw a dirty piece of cloth at the girl and waved her back to her seat.

They had an hour to themselves in the dormitory, in which they whispered stories and gossip. Then another hour on the bones. Finally it was time for supper - bread and cheese, washed down with water. Tom nodded to them glumly from the other side of the room as they entered, his half rations finished already. Both girls kept back some of their supper for him, and the two who had been doing the bones with them passed Lizzie part of their own food for Tom. Mattie was touched by this. It wasn't as if they had much to eat themselves!

They managed to steal a few words outside the dining room with a scowling Tom before being sent to their dormitories again. Lizzie hugged him and asked why he was so "pucksome".

'I'm that riled!' he whispered. 'The shirky old rammuck has got me put in the punishment room again! She told Matron I'd bit her - Matron said she'd even seen the bite marks. Reckon the fat toad bit herself! An' she'll be at me again tonight. She'll come in ever' hour and wake me an' hit me an' swear at me like what she did last night. I *will* bite her this time, and serve her right!'

'Oh, Tom!' cried Lizzie. 'You can't do that! She'll have you punished proper if you do!'

'Can't you get out somehow?' asked Mattie, more practically.

Tom made a face. 'There ben't no window,' he said. 'I could try runnin' off when she unlocks the door and comes in to pester me - but the Work'us is locked and barred at night, and there's a nightman what'll come smart if there's a ruckus.'

'Could you get away now, before bedtime?'

'Look over there.'

Mattie looked over her shoulder. A burly attendant was standing by the door, his arms folded and his eye on Tom.

'He'll call me over soon and take me to the room. When you're on punishment, they treats you like a prisoner. Don't mind me, Lizzie. I'll not do nothing rumbustical. But if the Devil so much as touch me, I'll twist her tail hard!'

'The Devil?' asked Mattie, confused.

Lizzie explained. 'That's what they calls her. And it suits, too!'

Just then McDougal opened the double-sized green baize door that separated the warden's quarters from the inmates. He strode towards the kitchen but stopped when he caught sight of Mattie. A smile spread over his face and his side-whiskers twitched.

'Why, I'd quite forgotten you were here!' he cried. 'Though I don't know how I could forget such a fine young girl - a fine young *woman*, I should say,' he added in a lower voice, rolling the words around in his soft Scottish accent. 'Now, let's see. Your name was - Marie? No, let me think: Matilda! You are Matilda. Matilda, dear girl, I do think we need to spend a little time together. Need to - ah - ask you some questions. Nothing frightening, I assure you! I just like to get to know my new girls. And the boys too, of course, of course. Perhaps this evening? No - maybe not. I'm out and the wife's in! Tomorrow then. After church! You know, I've taken quite a shine to you. Such a fine young - woman.' He took her unwilling hand and gave it a squeeze. He glanced back over his shoulder at the green door that was just opening. Mrs McDougal was coming to find him. He dropped the hand and, muttering to himself, pursued his original course to the kitchen.

One of the other girls gave Mattie a sympathetic pat on the shoulder. 'It's all right, girl, just keep out the old goat's reach. 'E can't do much if 'e don't get close!'

'Don't worry about that!' Mattie said through clenched teeth. 'The next time he tries to hold my hand, I shall scream the place down!'

Chapter 13 Skisin' Off

They awoke early the next day. Blazing sunshine had roused the birds and warmed them, and now the birds were rousing everyone else. Mattie sat up in bed and stretched.

'Ow!' Her arms and back ached, and her hands were sore. She looked over to Lizzie who had also opened her eyes. 'How long till the bell?'

'Bout an hour, I reckon. They lets us sleep an hour more on Sundays. Tis one of the good things about Sunday. An' there be no work, neither - that's another good thing. An' McDougal's not about. That's a third, and the bettermost, I thinks!'

'Does he go away on Sundays?'

'No! First off, he's like to be in bed, see, 'cos his head hurts. And it hurts 'cos Sattiday nights he's back late an' stiff with drink. Sings his head off as he wanders up the road lookin' for the Work'us 'cos he can't allus recall where he left it! Then he can't find his key so he kicks at the door till the watchman lets him in - or sometimes Mrs McDougal. But then she shouts at him and he goes wild. Don't s'pose she likes the look of him drunk, for she makes him sleep in a separate room Sattiday nights!'

Mattie went back to her question. 'So he's in bed all Sunday?' She was hoping that his proposed meeting would not happen.

'No - course not! He's up by the time we're back from Church (we all goes to Church, 'ceptin' him), an' he's usually down in the kitchen with the Cook.'

Another girl raised her voice. 'An' from what *I* hears, it ben't cookin' what he's learnin' her! Right fond of Cook, he be!'

Lizzie continued. 'After lunch, there's religious instruction and he keeps away from that. Women's work, he calls it.'

'Men allus says that when they be too lazy or else frowted, am I right?' the other girl called.

'Lizzie - how long do people have to stay here?' asked Mattie. 'And how can they bear it?'

'Oh, they's all sorts in the Work'us. There be old folk wiv nothin' of their own and no one to look after 'em - they'll never leave. Not till they does it feet-first: carried out, y'know.'

The other girl added enviously, 'T'ain't so bad for they - too old to crush bones, don't need so much to eat, don't have to do daft lessons with the Macs. They mostly walks up an' down, or else sits an' stares. The Matron gets 'em to do little jobs some times. She ben't so bad, 'cept once a month. As for t'other folk here, they be families most-like where the man's lost his work and they've no home left. Or girls no one wants 'cos they've been ruint.'

'Ruined?'

'Like Mary over there. See - she's got a big yellow stripe on her dress.'

'A yellow stripe?'

'It means she's had a base-born child. You know, a bastard what'll never know who its pa was. Well, she says it's not her fault - she would say that, mind! Says she was took advantage of. They mostly says something like that!'

Mary, who had been listening, sat up in bed. 'An' it's mostly true!' she complained.

Mattie thought for a moment. 'What about the men?'

136

she asked. 'What sort of stripe do *they* wear if they've fathered a baby and aren't married?'

Mary and Lizzie laughed at her suggestion. 'The men gets away with it!' Mary complained. 'But if a girl has a baby an' the father won't marry her, she's marked for life, right? Even 'thout a stripe, she's a baby to care for, hain't she?'

Lizzie scolded Mary. 'You should've thought of that *afore* goin' with men!'

'That's easy to say now,' Mary answered with a sigh. 'If we all knowed aforehand what we learns behindhand, we'd all of us be dressed in gold!'

'Without a dirty great stripe acrost the middle!'

'An' without a baby to bring up. Ah well, Sunday's the day I likes most. I get to see little Emily for most of the day! They doesn't like mothers an' children to mix in the Work'us, but they can't keep me from my little angel on Sundays!'

Breakfast came soon enough (how quickly you grew tired of gruel!). Mattie had hoped they could have a few words with Tom, but they all had to return to the dormitories immediately afterwards and tidy them for the Sunday inspection. She and Lizzie had to be content with smiling at him as they passed. He smiled weakly in return. His face was pale and there were dark blue rings under his eyes.

'Nasty old witch!' Lizzie muttered, talking of the night nurse. 'Ain't no justice in this world, and that's a fact!'

The sunshine did not last. After inspection the inmates were escorted through drizzling rain to the local church for "divine worship". The preacher for that day was the Reverend Christopher Dodson, who was also the Chairman of the Board of Guardians for the Workhouse. It was he who had personally appointed its warden. For the few hours he devoted to the Workhouse each week, he was paid enough to feed several impoverished families. He believed devoutly in the workhouse system.

Mattie spent most of the service trying to think of a method of escape. She dimly heard the Reverend Dodson launch into his sermon and looked up only when he raised his voice and began to preach directly to the inmates of the Workhouse, who were seated at the back:

'The rich - the great men of this parish - pay for you to be housed and given work. It behoves you to be grateful to them! God has shown you His *justice* by allowing you to fall into poverty through your own sloth and wickedness; and the good and generous men of this parish have shown you God's *mercy*.'

Mattie flamed with anger at the words, and she wanted very much to stand up and shout that he was talking nonsense. Then a thought popped into her head. She looked across the aisle to where Tom was sitting and tried to catch his eye. He was looking down at his blistered hands. Mattie gave a little cough and he turned his head a little, just enough to see her face. She made a fist with the thumb sticking up and signalled towards the side door of the church. He nodded and mouthed the word: "How?". She mouthed back, "Wait!"

Then she leaned close to Lizzie and whispered something in her ear. Lizzie's eyes went very wide. 'I couldn't!' she whispered back.

'Then I'll do it. You and Tom must be ready to go.' And she whispered something more.

'You mustn't!' Lizzie protested, her voice rising. 'Not 'ere! Not in Church!'

Mattie patted her hand. Then, gathering her courage, she rose to her feet. 'I doesn't feel well!' she cried with as common an accent as she could muster. 'I feels sick! What 'e sez is stupid an' wrong an' against God's word an' it makes me feel all sick! I needs air!' And she made as if to climb past Lizzie, gave a terrible groan and col-

138

lapsed onto the girl. She gave Lizzie a pinch. Lizzie shrieked.

'Her's dead!' the girl screamed. 'Get 'er off me, some-one! I can't breathe!'

All over the church people sprang to their feet. Mrs McDougal and some supervisors left their places at the end of the pews and ran to calm the commotion. They scolded the inmates into silence and unceremoniously dragged Mattie's limp body from her pew. A shrieking Lizzie was shushed unsuccessfully before being taken away, too. The band of worshippers jostled one another and strayed into the aisles.

...Outside the church there is an odd sight. Flat on the wet grass is a lanky girl dressed in Workhouse clothes with her feet stuck into boots two sizes too big for her. Two female supervisors of the large variety are bending over her and fanning her with great determination, using Mrs McDougal's absurd feathered hat. Another Work-house girl is sitting on a nearby tombstone, rain dripping from her hair, looking anxiously guilty one moment and pleased as Mister Punch the next. Suddenly she turns her head as if she has heard someone call her name. She looks to the back of the churchyard. She jumps down off the tombstone and runs to the two ladies. She seems to be puzzling over what to say to them but doesn't puzzle long. An idea comes to her. She pulls at the dress of the larger of the two women and gives a terrified scream.

'Oh, Miss!' she exclaims at the top of her voice. 'They's risin' from the dead! They's comin' outa the ground! I seen 'em! Look!' And with one hand she points in one direction whilst using the other to signal the exact opposite direction to the girl on the grass. The ladies drop the Hat and turn fearfully to the compass point indi-cated. The horizontal girl makes a sudden, splendid re-covery and in an instant she is loping to the rear of the

churchyard with unusual agility for a child who had
fainted dead away moments before. Her great boots
trample everything in her path. Behind her runs the
smaller girl, shrieking and squealing about Judgement
Day and Open Graves. They come to the end of the
churchyard and scramble over the wall. The smaller girl
pauses on the top and gives the two becalmed ladies a
great wave. She shouts something rather rude, which
they pretend not to hear...

Tom was crouching on the other side of the wall.
'Down!' he hissed. 'Now do as I do and crawl 'long to
the far end.' They did so. The wall turned a corner and
they followed it to a small orchard. Here they left the
wall, running bent double through the trees to its far
side. They found another wall - higher this time - which
they climbed, scratching their hands on the black flints.
They jumped down. They had come to a street with
houses of the well-to-do on both sides. Tom looked
about him.

'Reckon we can keep to-ard here. Takes us north but
at least that's away from the Work'us. We'll turn renward a good step further on, then turn right again once
we're outa town. We can follow our noses down to
Picket Trenthay and then back to camp. Right?'

Lizzie nodded. Mattie just smiled. Tom laughed at
them both. 'I thinks you both be fettled in the brain,' he
said. 'We could of stayed till tomorrow, an' then they'd
of given us back our clothes!'

'Don't talk tosh, Tom!' Lizzie cried. 'You ben't very
grateful, an' you should! Besides, like as not they'd have
kept our clothes anyway. They was too fine for us, them
clothes, they'd have thought.'

Tom agreed cheerfully. He took Lizzie on one arm and
Mattie on the other.

'I still thinks you both be touched,' he repeated. 'But

'tis whackin' wondrous to be out of that place! And look - sun's out now and there's a rainbow! P'raps we could go find where it ends!' And they skipped crazily down the road, while well-bred persons in the rich houses on either side poked their noses through the chintzy curtains and tut-tutted to themselves about the depravity of the lower classes.

It was late afternoon when they returned to camp. They found a pale, fretful Dicker sitting in the little cave, nursing an equally fretful jackdaw. Man and bird leapt up as one.

'And where the devil have *you* been?' Dicker thundered. Jasper hopped up and down on the table, cawing shrilly at Mattie, scolding her.

'We been in prison, master!' exclaimed Tom brightly. His face was pale and pained, and there was a bruise on one cheek - but he smiled impishly at Dicker. Dicker made as if to box his ears but patted him on the shoulder instead.

'We been -'

'I know,' he interrupted. 'The Workhouse. You're still wearing their uniform - where's your own clothes? And you *stink* of the place.' He took out a gaudy red handkerchief, sneezed twice and blew his nose. 'Thank God I've such a cold that I can hardly smell you,' he grumbled.

'That will be the Bones,' Mattie said, holding out her hand to Jasper who was still complaining bitterly from his post on the table. He proudly ignored her advances.

'We met the Warden!' cried Lizzie. 'He made us go wiv him, Dicker. We had to stay 'cos they had Tom locked up -'

' - such miserable food!'

' - but Mattie figured a way to escape, durin' Church it was. I thought I would *die*, I was that embarrassed -'

' - shrieking out she was sick! Pretendin' to be dead -'

The story went on in this fashion for quite some time, with each interrupting the other, Dicker trying to ask questions and failing to end his sentence, and Jasper screeching at each of them in turn.

'But you're back safe now,' Dicker concluded. 'And you look exhausted. And you smell of Bones, and worse! Before Jasper and I faint from the effects of your delicate aroma, I think you need to wash and change. Put your Workhouse togs in a pile. I shall return them. I shall probably make the Warden eat them!'

'He has our proper clothes, Dicker. The good ones that you and I purchased.'

'I shall extract them. I may need to extract a fair number of Wardenish teeth in the process, but if so, it will be a duty I will enact with the greatest pleasure. Go! At least move off from the windward side of me! And take this bird with you, Miss Matilda. He's been in a foul mood while you've been away. Wouldn't leave me alone. Pestered me by the minute, telling me I should be out looking for you! Once I'd sent the crew out on your trail, he relented - just a little - and became almost good company. In a few hours more I might even have begun to feel pleased that I spared his life a fortnight ago!'

While they were washing, Dicker rode off with the Workhouse clothes. An hour later the rest of the crew came back to camp, having been told by Dicker that the children had returned. Lump was moaning about a blister on his foot and nettle stings. The others were just relieved to see Mattie and the Brats back safe and mostly sound.

'You've a good bruise, there, Tom!' cried Scarecrow. 'Been fightin'?'

'Fraid I larrupped a devilish old frump,' Tom admitted. 'But only once she'd podged me with a brass bell. Just wish she'd stayed long enough for a second round. I'd have made her pay!'

Mattie was about to say that it was always wrong to take revenge, but thought better of it. Instead she said, 'Tom was very patient, really. Lizzie and I had a hard enough time as it was, but nothing compared to his problems.'

Lizzie sniffed at this. 'We was worked too hard for girls! Smashed bones, we did, till the blood was runnin' down our arms and drippin' into the bone box!'

They told their stories in detail and then the Crew told theirs. That is, Pirate told it and the others butted in as they saw fit.

'We had a day or so in town. Then we come back just after nightfall on Sattiday -'

'Later'n that! 'Twere halfway to dawn on Sunday morn!'

'Maybe it was. We walked down the hill quiet-like so's not to waken you -'

'We never did, Jack! You was singin' and fallin' over. I was singin' an' not fallin' over. Lump was fallin' but not doin' much singin', 'cept from the ground, and Stump was doin' his best to pick us up each time - which were hard to do with but one hand!'

Pirate continued. 'Let me tell it my way. You was so bosky you didn't even know we was *in* camp. Anyhow, littluns, there we was in the middle of camp, and maybe the lads did have a bit of a sing-song but I don't remember that part.'

'You sang us "Spanish Main" and "Raisin' the Topsail"! You recalls *that*, surely? And doin' the hornpipe on the table in the cave? You was drunk as a fish!'

'I don't allow that to be strictly true, you lubber, and that's enough of that kind of talk afore the childer! But it's surely the case that only Stump here was totally reliable. He it was that looked in on you and found you wasn't there. No one in the cottage but one bad-tempered jackdaw. The bird went for us like he blamed us for eve-rything. He near poked Lump's eye out!'

Stump said quietly. 'We was that afeared for you all, Miss Mattie. Sobered the lads quick-like.'

'So we forms a search party, even though by now it'd come on to rain.'

'We looks through the woods.'

'It were black as the caves of hell when they ain't got the fires lit, so we had to seek more by touch than by sight. Touched more nasty, slimy things in that one night than ever I've felt in me whole life afore it!'

'Started to search along the road at the top when along comes a bad-tempered highwayman on a horse, a-sneezin' and a-shakin' with ague.'

'Ague?' Mattie asked Pirate.

'Fever, Miss Mattie. 'Twas Dicker, shiverin', sweatin', coughin', shoutin', swearin'! Seems he'd ridden hard and long from wherever he'd been. Was wet through and in a foul mood. Cursed us up and down, called us some names you don't hear in polite society and invented some new swear words once he'd run through his stock of old ones.'

Lump added critically. 'Not that he was bothered about *us* catchin' our death of cold! No, not he! Ranted and raved about you all like he was a damned father. Threatened to shoot us if we didn't find you. Not a word of thanks for us havin' sifted the whole hillside lookin' for you!'

Pirate shrugged at this. 'Dicker takes over next. Goes hisself, ill as he was, all the way to Druddery in case you was there; then back to Miss Bell's; then along to where the Brats used to live. Dawn came and passed. The rain kept on and we crept back to the cave. We was dead on our feet. Said we couldn't go on. Dicker waved his pistol at us, but I reckon we fell asleep as we stood. Can't re-call exactly. Damned bird kept wakin' us, really mad with us he was. Dicker mad, too. But he couldn't do no more, neither. Didn't even have the strength to change into dry clothes. Fell asleep cursing, he did. Never afore seen a man what can curse the devil while unconscious!'

'Is he very ill?'

'Was burnin' with fever this morning. Perked up a little once he had some hot food down him. Sent us out as soon as we was able to move without fallin' over reg'lar-like. And - and that's it. Met us on the road just now and sent us back. Said he was goin' to feed some bones to a Mr McDougal. Don't fancy bein' McDougal when Dicker gets to him.'

'Nor I,' said Mattie. She was stroking Jasper, who had forgiven her and was perched on her shoulder, rubbing his head against her left ear. Lizzie was sitting with her, one arm thrown around Mattie's waist.

'Where's Tom?' Lizzie asked. For an answer, snores came from the floor of the cave. Tom had sat down as soon as Dicker's men had returned, and was now fast asleep.

'Reckon it's bed for us all,' commented Jack the Pirate, rubbing his eyes. 'Lump, give us a hand with Tom here. We'll carry him to his bed, Missies, and then you can settle yourselves.'

Scarecrow grumbled that Dicker wouldn't be pleased if he came back and found the whole camp asleep.

'I'll take first watch,' volunteered Stump. 'Bit too excited-like to sleep anyways.'

Chapter 14 Ancient History

As it happened, Dicker did not recover the children's best clothes. Mr McDougal was away for the rest of the day and Mrs McDougal explained sniffily that there had been no "nice" clothes on or with the children when they had arrived.

'Rags, sir - that is all they were dressed in. Rags! We took them in and fed them for two days: and were they grateful? One might as well expect gratitude from a snake, sir!' And more than this the charming woman would not say, except that the local constable would be calling in at the Workhouse later that day - perhaps the gentleman would return then and discuss the matter with him? She gave Dicker a cunning smile.

Dicker rode back to camp, grinding his teeth and swearing revenge.

A few days later, after a shopping trip to replace the missing clothes, Mattie and Dicker called in at Miss Bell's and collected a letter that she read twice on the way back to camp. At her side in the carriage, Dicker tried to read over her shoulder and was rebuffed.

Dear Mattie

The last few days have been the reindeer's antlers, and no mistake. What with being attacked by a crab & frightened by a panther at midnight (well, perhaps it was smaller than the average panther, but it DID look black and it WAS prowling stealthily in the bushes and it DID make a cat sound...) - where was I? Oh yes, what with attacks, alarums, and Mama being ferocious one morning just because I was making too much noise trying to call a blackbird to me - well, I've hardly had time to study, or write to you.

Mama nearly lost her rag last Friday. I was sitting in a plum tree in the orchard by the house, eating plums in the early evening sunlight and trying to read a rather moth-eaten book from the house full of creatures (by which I mean that the book was full of creatures, not the house - and some of the drawings were absolutely splendid) when this man comes trotting up - that is, his horse was doing the trotting, the man was just sitting there. He reins in his beast and gives me an angry look, exactly the same look I'd had from the crab that morning as he crouched there, bubbling at me and snapping his pincers (- the crab did all that, not the man). The man then asks WHO the devil was I, and WHAT the devil was I doing there, and WHY the devil was I reading a valuable old book halfway up a plum tree?

Rather lost for words, I tell him it's a lot better than doing the French that Mama thinks I'm slaving away at, and I didn't know the book was valuable, but that the old chap who wrote it draws a good picture and tells a good story - and when I'm grown I shall do the same! At that, he takes the crabby look off his face and says he wishes he'd spent more time up that plum tree when he was my age. I nearly fall out of the tree because I realise that I am face to face with Mama's dastardly brother, the one she and Papa talk about in whispers (which always has the effect of making me listen even more carefully to what they're going on about! - adults are quite foolish sometimes, aren't they?).

Evil Robert does not spit me upon a hot sword but he

does pass me the horse's reins and orders me to take the sweating steed to the stable, remove his tack, rub him dry, water him sparingly and feed him a little - then water him some more, sing him a few songs, scratch him on the neck and so on until he's stopped puffing (I'm to do all this to the horse, not to Evil Robert, you understand). Then - and not before - I'm to come inside and report to him. E.R. says all this with a stern look in his eye. Remembering the crab's stern look and the nip he'd given me when I sat upon the hummock of seaweed he was hiding in, I was minded to co-operate! Actually, it was great fun - the horse proving to be a wonderful beast, polite, communicative, appreciative even. Far better company than most people. From knowing the beast, I thought more highly of the man.

Finally I wander inside, to find Papa being gentlemanly and Mama hysterical. She keeps going on about how Evil Robert should have stayed away, and how "Father" was too weak to see E.R. and she was sure "Father" was best left to die in peace, and what a disgrace E.R. had been to the family and how dare he bring that disgrace back into this house at such a time? Old E.R. just sits there, cool as a snake, talking calmly, not snapping his pincers - unlike Mama who scuttles from one tirade to another, shooting him dark looks, beating her arms up and down and generally being embarrassing.

I can see this is going to continue for a while, so I retire to the kitchen where I find the servants talking about E.R. in hushed tones. It seems he and his father had argued about who E.R. was to marry, and the son had gone ahead and wed someone of an inferior class - a schoolteacher or such - and the old man had banished him for it. Then E.R.'s young wife died soon after and E.R. took to bad living. He wanted nothing to do with his father, nor the other way around - and certainly nothing whatsoever to do with Agatha! He's been around the world, and done enough desperate deeds to get him in prison in several countries - at least, that's what the servants said. But the man himself seemed harmless enough, except for the look in his eye when he first found me sitting in his plum tree and reading his book.

They talked Mama around somehow (I think I told you that she's been most unlike herself since we arrived here. She's almost bearable sometimes!). She and E.R. went to see the old fellow together, and Papa says it was a touching scene - crusty old father delighted, return of the Prodigal, feasting on the fatted calf together with a certain amount of complaining from the elder sister.

When they returned down the long, curved, dark wooden staircase E.R. ruffled my hair and gave me a gold sovereign for looking after the horse. I nearly fell over with surprise. Mama sniffed disapprovingly and said that E.R. had always been "exuberant" - which E.R. and I both corrected to "extravagant" at the same moment! He laughed, I laughed, and Mama glowered.

Then - oh, paradise! - E.R. took me out on the horse for a look at a little, hidden beach he used to visit as a boy. I told him about the puffins and cormorants, and he told me about the otters in the river nearby. He said he believed my story about the panther (no one else had given it the slightest credence), saying there were catlike beasts on Exmoor and all points west of there. He'd seen one himself when he was my age, and it was dragging a lamb so I expect it must have been of a reasonably pantherish size.

We had a search along the beach and found the cave he used to hide in whenever he ran off from home, which he said was often. His initials were cut into the rock there. We explored the beach and found a few sharks' teeth and some odd fossils. He started to talk about them - and interesting it was, too - but unfortunately night was falling and we had to go back.

After he'd eaten a late supper, he saw his father again, by himself this time. He stayed overnight and left well before dawn on Saturday. Mama was particularly quiet after that. She was even kind to me in her own fashion. Poor Mama, she hasn't much conversation; yet she talked well enough about her girlhood days and even made us laugh at the pranks she and E.R. got up to - while they were still on speaking terms, before her own mother died and E.R. "went bad" (which I expect was mostly her imagination - any man who explains fossils without sounding like one himself must be some sort of saint, don't you think?).

It is late. I must end this letter because I'm rising early tomorrow. I plan to sneak out of my bedroom window just at dawn, to see the sun rise from that little east-facing beach E.R. showed me. He used to do that when he lived here, and he told me which drainpipe to use.

Many felicitations, and hopes to see you soon.

Hubert.

When they had dismounted at camp Mattie passed the letter to Dicker. He looked through it with a careless air.

'Your cousin is clearly a shrewd judge of character,' he observed, handing the letter back to her. 'But then, like yourself he is yet too young to be misled by appearances!'

Mattie bridled a little. 'So you take the side of the disreputable relation?' she queried. 'You assume that because he is well-spoken he must be a likeable rogue whose heart is in the right place? Someone beaten down by the petty injustices of life?'

'Assuredly so!' Dicker responded, amused at her irritation. 'I'd shake the man by the hand, assuming of course that he would stoop so far as to converse with a lowly highwayman! I might look him up if I am ever in Cornwall. You must tell me his name!'

Mattie thought hard. 'I don't know it,' she confessed. 'I suppose it's the same as Aunt Agatha's last name before she married, but I don't think I ever heard anyone mention what that was.'

'Pity. No matter: I'm sure I would recognise him at once, even without his name. He is clearly a man after my own heart, one who would have the respect of any person of noble character.'

'Except for those who knew him best. His father and his own sister, for instance!'

'And what a sister! But you overlook the most important judge of character in your cousin's excellent letter.'

'Who is that?'

'The horse! If a man has the respect of his horse, he needs nothing else. For, of what value are the opinions of mankind? They are the fluttering, feckless, faithless fixations of small-minded persons desperate to demonstrate their own worth by deriding one person and exalting another! Human friendship is partial, self-serving, unreliable; and the effect of it upon the human soul is always destructive. But the friendship of a noble beast - why, it always ennobles a man.'

Dicker laughed and Mattie realised that he had been teasing her all along, at least in part. She struggled with her temper and managed a grudging smile.

She tried again. 'Did you mean nothing, then, by your - your *pathetic* comments? *Is* the only friendship worth having that of a beast?'

Dicker shrugged his shoulders. 'Horses, at least, do not answer back (unlike some young ladies!). And the companionship of a fine horse is often to be preferred to that of a fine lady - besides being less expensive!'

Jack the Pirate had been standing nearby with Stump, grinning at the conversation. He now put in: 'And what about the faithfulness of a good ship, master? The old *Peerless*, she was more to me than any woman. When she went down off Belle Isle, I thought my heart would break. Ain't that right, Stump?' He put his arm on the shoulder of his companion, who nodded at his words.

Pirate continued, 'She was sweetly built. A crew of three could have sailed her. Matter of fact, we once did have to three-man her – d'you call it to mind, Stump? Lost three overboard in a gale off the Cornish coast and only me, Dicker and one-arm here to steer, pump and see to the riggin'. I prayed like a Catholic that night, I did! We ran her into a little cove and coaxed her into the shallows. Even with a hurricane in her face she steered like a little bridesmaid trippin' up the aisle.'

'And how did you lose her?' asked Mattie.

Pirate grimaced. 'Frenchies holed us, Miss. We was doin' a little piratin' - nothing too wicked, mind, no boardin' of passenger ships and carryin' off the women, just a bit of raidin' where the pickings was rich.'

'That's still wicked.'

'I ain't goin' to argufy the point. The Frenchies, now, they was of the opinion 'twas wicked, too! We'd bothered them all along the Bay of Biscay - took a few gold coins too many and, truth be told, drank too much of their brandy -'.

'There!' exclaimed Mattie triumphantly. 'Drinking again! It's quite wrong, you know! Miss Bell says that alcohol is the source of more evil and sadness than all other - other *causative factors* - put together!'

'That's easy enough for a spinsterish schoolmistress to say! But it may have been true in this case. There we was, anchored off Belle Isle, stars blazin' above us, brandy blazin' inside, and then all of a sudden the Frenchies blazin' away *at* us. We ups and tries to set sail - some of us not knowin' which way up *was*, bein' so drunk an' all - but afore we can get her movin' properly, she takes one right on the waterline, amidships. So we snatches up what we can salvage and leaps overboard. There was a ship's boat but no one thinks of that till we's in the water.'

'Did the French come pick you up?'

Dicker laughed at her. 'You have such a touching trust in human nature - expecting mercy after the act of judgement! But I'm interrupting. Carry on, Jack.'

Pirate smiled at Mattie. 'No, Miss, they didn't come to find us. And if they had, there'd have been hand-to-hand fightin' for sure. They'd be wantin' to finish us off, see; and we'd be wantin' to take their boats. They stayed long enough to see the *Peerless* sink, then went back to some French port and most like had a celebration. We splashed about, clinging to whatever wreckage we found. Some drowned. Some didn't. The sea's an unforgivin' mistress. She takes what you give her and, once you're found wantin', even for a moment, she stands aside and watches you go under, with a hard gleam in her eye, like she reckons you had it comin' to you all along.'

Stump spoke briefly. 'W-wind changed,' he said. 'Blew us ashore. Blew the *Peerless* ashore, too.'

'What was left of her,' concluded Pirate sadly. 'Not much gold, but a few kegs of brandy and some silk and tobacco. Enough to see us back to Portsmouth.'

Lump, who had come out of the cave during this exchange, exclaimed, 'And what's the point of going to sea, then? Give me dry land! It don't throw you over when it's tired of you, like a rough sea or a shirky wife!'

'Who needs a wife anyhow?' asked Pirate. 'I've as much call for a wife as a toad has for a side pocket! But if you be a sea-goin' man, a sound ship's as sweet a woman as ever you'll find - and the sea's as stirrin' a mistress as any man might need.'

'And what about you, Dicker?' asked Lump. 'I'd wager you've got some pretty girls lined up waitin' for you in town! You ain't the lonesome type. Maybe you and me, we'll go out and make the acquaintance of a few perky wenches some time? What d'you say, Dicker?'

Dicker's face did not change, except for his eyes. They became cold, like a bleak winter's morning when the frost blasts the life from the iron ground. 'I have no interest in this conversation, Lump,' he remarked. 'Count me, if you wish, as one of the toads.'

'Come off of that, Dicker!' Lump persisted. 'You ain't tellin' me you never looked at a bit of lace trailin' from a pretty leg! You ain't tellin' me there's been no ravishin' of fair maidens (and some not so fair!) in your life. You're for sure a man of the world like myself. You and me - we could go to some places I know in Portsmouth. Plenty of friendly gals there!'

Dicker ignored him. 'Tom!' he cried instead. 'Lizzie! I promised long ago to take you for a drive. Now here's your chance. Up to now, you've walked into town for your bread. This afternoon, you go by carriage. Only this once, mind! I shan't be spoiling you another day! But if I'm to take you, you'll need to be cleaner than the pair of hedgepigs you currently resemble. Go wash, and change your clothes.'

'What about Mattie?' asked Lizzie.

'She's had her outings. She can stay in camp and cook! You'll see to her, ship's cook?'

'Aye, aye,' said Pirate.

'Good. Then, after bread and cheese (for we've nothing else the nonce), the Brats and I will put on the style in Andover. See if we can make the townsfolk gasp and rub their eyes! Though, if this morning's mist doesn't lift, they may not be able to see us in any case!'

Chapter 15 Tricksy Little Game

Much later, after an outing the "Brats" enjoyed immensely, the mist that had troubled the morning returned as they left behind the last little gathering of houses southeast of Andover. When the sun finally fell it would be black indeed; even now it was difficult to see more than twenty paces forward.

After a mile they came trotting up behind a smart carriage that moved slowly, as if its driver were unsure of the road. Dicker passed the carriage with a polite nod and soon it was lost in the mist behind them.

'By Galls!' cried Tom softly. 'It were the Warden in the carriage!'

'The warden of the Workhouse?' asked Dicker. 'The scoundrel himself? Well, we shall see to him, shall we?'

Lizzie put her hands to her face. 'But there was a driver, too! One or t'other'll recognise us. Please don't do nowt, sir!'

Tom disagreed. 'We could have a fine game of hinders-catch-winkers in this here fog, Dicker! Crimany, but we could lead him a dance, couldn't we?'

Dicker glanced at the woods about him, trying to identify where they had reached. 'You say this McDougal has a weak spot for women, Brats? What kind of women do you reckon he likes best?'

Tom answered, 'He was gamesome with 'em all. But his favourite in the Workhouse was the cook, and she be a fine floddy hulk, master.'

Dicker smiled. 'Well, if that's the lie of it, I reckon we can play a tricksy little game on this lusty gentleman!'

Lizzie moaned. 'We'll be cotched, Master. We'll be shot!'

'No we won't!' And with that, Dicker swung the carriage across the road and down a small path a little ways, far enough for the mist to hide it from the main road. He leapt from the carriage and ran to its rear to open the heavy trunk that was always there.

'Mind you, this has been done before,' he puffed as he pulled off his overcoat and slipped over his head what appeared to be a dress. It *was* a dress! Complete with a built-in bustle at the rear! 'Now, where's me bonnet?' he added in a cracked falsetto, with a merry trilling laugh. He took a large, floppy red bonnet from the trunk and placed it on his head. 'And a slap of face paint - that will do! A highwayman named Old Mob once took money from an Earl this way. How do I look?'

He pulled the bonnet forward so that in the gloom all one could see were bright red lips, the flash of white teeth and a couple of sparkling eyes.

'Gorgeous, but you be the wrong shape!' Tom exclaimed.

'We'll be *killed*!' Lizzie complained.

Dicker pulled a loaf of bread from the shopping basket and tore it in two. He stuffed the halves down the front of his dress. 'Now, aren't I the loveliest gel in the forest?' he asked merrily. 'But whist - there's the carriage! Give me that basket!' He took the shopping basket, bent to snatch some cowslips from about his feet and tucked a few into his bonnet for decoration. 'Wish me luck! And, stay where you are!'

They heard him skip up the track to the main road, where he began to hum loudly as he strolled to the right, in the same direction the carriage would be travelling. Tom climbed out of the carriage and started up the path.

'Tom!' Lizzie whispered. 'Tom, he said to stay here! Tom, you'll be in trouble!' But Tom paid her no mind. She grumbled to herself, 'And I'm right galleyed here by meself. There could be anything hidin' in this fog. Oh, cussnation! Jest you wait till I cotches you, Tom, I'll lam you one!' And she leapt from the carriage and followed Tom to the end of the path.

They hid behind a tree as McDougal's carriage passed at a walk. Dicker could just be seen in the fog, not many paces up the road. He had tied something about the mid-dle of the dress to give him the appearance of a fine waist with massive hips below and enormous bust above. He was humming an Irish-sounding air in what could easily pass as the voice of a young, though very large, woman. The carriage drew level with him.

He turned his head just enough to catch McDougal's eye and then made as if to stumble a little, dropping the basket.

'Oh, sir, you did startle me! See, I've dropped me bas-ket and all me bits is bouncin' about! Tee hee hee! Tee hee!' He giggled famously and bent to pick up the shop-ping. Under his dress the half-loaves of bread bulged and swayed impressively.

McDougal signalled the carriage to halt and leaned out to make conversation.

'And where are you off to, young lady?' he asked.

'Well, to tell truth, sir, I can hardly say in this here fog! My old parents, they do live a little further on, and I lives with them, you understand. Just the three of us, you see.'

'Rather - ah - *lonely*, is it not?'

'Oh, it's lonely enough, sir. You're the only bit of ex-citement I've had for many a month! Hee tee, tee hee! Tee hee hee hur hur de hur!' Dicker tried the giggle again and succeeded well enough to start with, but then it be-came rather more a gargle than a giggle and he had to cover it with a cough. 'This fog don't half get into my throat, sir, though it shouldn't. My people is all gypsies, see. Settled now in a bit of land, proper housewallahs as the gypsies would say, but folk of the outdoors all the same.'

'You're a gypsy lass, hey?'

'A little more than a lass, sir, if you take my meaning.... Tell me, sir, would you be wanting your fortune read, now? For sixpence, say, to read your palm?'

'For sixpence I expect to have more than my *palm* read.'

'Oh, *sir*!' exclaimed Dicker in a scandalised voice. He giggled - and gargled - again. 'Oh, you do make me laugh, sir! Tee hee! Tee hurdy! And you a *military* man, too! You see, I can read *that* much just from what I can see of you in this fog. Who *knows* what I could tell about you from a closer viewing?'

'How much for kiss or two?' asked McDougal in a quieter voice.

'Ah, sir, we'd have to discuss that sort of thing *in private*,' Dicker said. 'Perhaps the gentleman would like to - ah - come aside into the woods here for, shall we say, a more *personal* service? Hee! Hee!' And he led McDougal across the road - to the side the children were on - behind a bank of bushes, out of view of McDougal's carriage. Tom and Lizzie crept near enough to watch.

Dicker had to lift his dress to step over some brambles. McDougal, looking down and expecting to see a shapely leg, was most disappointed. He whispered:

'Goodness sakes, woman - why the devil do you have trousers on?'

Dicker turned quickly and put a pistol to the other man's nose. 'So as to put your money in the pockets, McDougal!' he whispered back. 'Tee hee!' He threw back his head and giggled as before. Keeping to his woman's voice, he issued brief, hardly audible instructions to the man, punctuating them with feminine shrieks, gurgles, squeals and more fatuous giggling.

'Hands up! Higher! Let's feel in your jacket. No gun? Just as well. A wallet though! *And* some money in it! Give me the coat, I'll need it. And the hat. Oh, it's a fine hat! Distinctive! I could have fun with a hat like this. Tee hee! Oh, hee tee hee teetle heetle hurdy turty! Let's try the trouser pockets, now. My, what a big boy you are, Sergeant-major! Hee hee! Turn around! That's good. I'll just put this gag on you, so you won't shout. And tie you to the tree. Is that too tight? It is? Good! Lastly, let's have the boots and the trousers - and your breeches. Oh, what fine red pantaloons they are! Tee Hee! Sorry, but I *must* insist! Oh, *thank you*, Sergeant-major! Heedy hurdy teedly tee!'

He gave the rope a final tweak and bent close to whisper something else before turning to go. He left the naked McDougal gagged and roped to a tree and moved quietly back to his carriage. Tom and Lizzie followed, Lizzie grasping the basket he had forgotten to pick up.

'So you came to watch after all! I hope he didn't see either of you! No? No harm done, then! Lizzie, stow that basket on the carriage. Tom, shove McDougal's things into the trunk while Lizzie pulls this blessed dress off me. I feel I'm like to suffocate in it. How can women bear to wear such things? Oh, the weaker sex are for sure the stronger sex in my opinion if they can put up with ·such constricting slavery to fashion day after day! Now hop in, and off we go!'

He turned the carriage and they went back up the little path to the main road. In the woods to the right of the path, the naked McDougal was kicking his legs and making little grunting sounds into his gag, trying to attract the attention of his driver. The driver, further to their right and on the far side of the road, assumed his master was playing about with the gypsy girl and kept his seat. He knew better than to interfere when his master was enjoying himself!

Dicker turned left, away from their victim and back towards Andover.

'Where to now, gaffer?' asked Tom once they were out of earshot of the others.

Dicker turned a twinkling eye to the boy. He gave a fine giggle. 'Tee hee hee! Tell me, Tom lad, what are you like at climbing?'

'As good as Lizzie, master. And she's fair spry at it!'

'Good! I think you will enjoy the final part of today's entertainment, then!'

The mist cleared overnight. The following morning was warm and bright, with the early light sharp as a good knife. People could pass up and down the street by the Workhouse and enjoy the fine view. Those who did not walk through life with their dull noses pointed miserably at the ground were rewarded with an interesting sight, which they brought to the attention of their friends and later gossiped about in the various pubs that evening. There were perhaps twenty public houses within easy walking distance of the Workhouse, and McDougal's hat was known in most of them. But why his hat should be sitting atop the flagpole that morning was a mystery, especially since instead of a flag the Workhouse was flying a pair of McDougal's boots at half-mast. Above the boots flapped his trousers and, just above the trousers, unfurled nicely by the steady breeze, were his beautiful red pantaloons.

Chapter 16 Final Meal

When the three finally returned to camp, singing lustily as their carriage swayed around the bends of the steep path, they found a meal waiting for them. Mattie's face was flecked with ash from the fire but it shone with satisfaction.

'You'll never guess what I've cooked!' she cried. 'It took me absolute hours - and it's all Pirate's - Jack's - doing, really. I just did as he told me.'

Tom breathed in the meaty, herby aroma that rose from two large black pots simmering on the fire. There was something else in it, too – something suety and doughy. 'Dumplings!' he cried.

'And some variety of stew,' Dicker added.

'Rabbit,' Pirate confirmed. 'Shanghaied a few of 'em in the woods, Dicker; brought 'em on board, you might say. Ben skinned 'em and the Missy here chopped, seasoned and cooked 'em.'

'Messy!' exclaimed Mattie. 'I had to keep reminding myself it would turn into something savoury. Jack also showed me how to do the dumplings - it was much easier than I'd thought.'

Dicker gave her a superior look. 'So the ship's cook has to instruct the refined young lady in the mysteries of rabbit stir-about? I'd have reckoned that Miss Bell's Noble Establishment for the Education of the Privileged Classes would already have enlightened you!'

Mattie placed her hands on her hips and gave him a

superior look in return. 'If you're complaining,' she said, 'you can go without, can't you?'

'Then I'm *not* complaining!'

Lizzie returned from unloading the carriage and began excitedly describing their adventures in the mist. Tom joined in and between them they managed to confuse Mattie so completely that the story had to be told twice.

Mattie thought it a shame that neither child had overheard what Dicker had whispered to the Warden and hoped it was a threat so bloodcurdling that the man would immediately repent of his evil ways.

Dicker thought repentance was out of the question.

Pirate thought a dozen lashes of the cat o' nine tails would have been good for the man's soul.

Lump - between mouthfuls of stew - believed Dicker should have robbed the driver as well.

Tom wished he could be outside the Workhouse when people became aware of McDougal's clothing flapping on the flagpole.

Lump asked what his share of the takings came to.

Scarecrow cackled at Lump's greed and poured a mug of ale over the other man's head, saying Lump needed to be baptised with a more fitting name, like Dragon-guts, maybe? And then there were angry oaths and punches thrown, until Pirate knocked both men down and swore to kill the next person who wasted a pint of good ale like that.

Stump said nothing except that the stew was perfect: just as his own mother used to make it.

A few days later they sat down to their final meal together: and again it was stew, but mutton this time, the meat having been bought by Dicker in Andover.

'The most expensive mutton I could find!' he commented. 'For, it being Mattie's last supper with us, extravagance seems appropriate. The Human Fireball has brought us good luck and fine profits for three weeks; and there's nothing like a mutton stew for celebrating both!'

Mattie smiled and nodded, but said nothing. She felt a little anxious about returning home, and was angry with herself for being afraid.

'Does she have to go?' Pirate wanted to know.

'Her uncle and aunt return to Druddery Hall tomorrow morning, and - apart from any other problems that brings (here some of the men laughed) - that means she needs to be restored to the bosom of her family.'

'She ought to stay!' cried Scarecrow, scratching at his black beard. 'She'll be wasted among the toffs! They don't need no luck, do they? Nor no profits, neither! Make her stay, Dicker, and she can have a full share of our takings. I knows - she can have Lump's share, he'll not mind that! Will you, Lump?' He elbowed Lump and cackled.

'I've earned what little I have, and I'll not share it!' grumbled Lump. 'I'd not give up anything rightfully mine, not to childer, not to the poor, not to a troop of angels, nor the devil neither! If any man wants what's mine, he'll have to cut it out of me, like it was my own heart.'

Jack looked across at Lump and made some rude, piratical gestures in his direction. 'You're a selfish son of a lubber, ain't you?' he said.

'A man has to look after hisself,' said Lump comfortably. 'No one else can do it for him. Reckon if we all looked after ourselves proper-like, the world would be a better place!'

'And w-what about them as can't?' asked Stump suddenly. 'Like me sister? She were half a cripple, Lump, what about her?'

'Folk has to stand on their own legs!' insisted Lump stubbornly. 'Waste of time tryin' to look after others. Waste of good money, too. Let them look after themselves, I say!'

'Enough of this!' Dicker suddenly ordered. 'We're having a party, not holding a meeting of the Cambridge debating society! The next person to mention any matter likely to be contentious will be spending the rest of the evening picking ticks off the horses. And eating them! Lump, take this mug of ale and see if you can drown your ego in it. Jack, I've a bottle of rum in the saddlebags - could you fetch it? She's straight from the West Indies and smooth as Chinese silk. Brats, I've nuts and dried fruit - and even an orange for each of you.'

'A what?'

'Never had one before? Well, there's a surprise coming, then! There's that and some slices of crystallised papaya, with a guava or two. I had some business with a trader from the Indies and he was tickled to provide some diverting items for you to try. For those not desiring strong drink, I've even procured a syrup from him, which can be mixed with water to make a refreshing cordial. Little Miss Muffet, fetch us a last bucket of well water with no spiders in it, could you? And do be careful, Miss Muffet. You know why, of course?'

'Why, Sir Dicker?' Mattie laughed.

'Twould be a tragedy if, having escaped being pushed in, you were to finish up by falling in all by yourself!'

'I shall try very hard to avoid that, Sir Dicker!' she answered gravely, smiling at him.

She fetched the water and returned. They ate a sumptuous meal and piled the dishes to one side. Then Scarecrow fetched his fiddle while Pirate Jack hunted out his pipe. Together they played - a little hesitantly at first but as the mood quickened the music flowed with much skill and great enthusiasm, so that Mattie found it almost impossible to sit still. Jack put aside his pipe and danced with Dicker; Dicker danced with Stump, Stump with

164

Lump, Lump with Pirate and then Dicker with Scarecrow, while Jack made the cave ring with his piping. The Brats danced with one another and then with anyone they could persuade. Mattie was dragged to her feet and soon they formed a circle about her as she danced gracefully, if a little solemnly, until Scarecrow Ben struck up such a whirling corkscrew of a tune that she simply had to leap and spin like a tiny, skirted dervish with Dicker and the others revolving giddily about her.

The tune came to a close and everyone collapsed onto a seat (or in Pirate's case the floor, he having drunk more than his share of the rum). They were a merry group now and even Lump was jovial, beaming at everyone and slapping them on the back. Yet - and this seemed to Mattie to be very odd - Mattie found his laughter made her more uncomfortable than his taunts and jeers.

'Sing us a song!' he cried. 'You promised - remember, Miss Matildy? - you promised that one day, if Ben had his fiddle and so on, you'd not do us a dance, but you would sing. That's right, ain't it, Dicker?'

Dicker looked at Mattie, who rose graciously and stood in the middle of the little cave, her hands clasped before her, her little fingers twisted together.

'Do you know the *Rose of Tralee*?' she asked Ben.

'Oh, I knows *that*!' he cried. He fitted the fiddle under his chin. A sweet, sad music filled the cave. The song flowed sweetly, melodically through the cave and out into the calm darkness of night, in and out of the trees, along the whispering river and away through the soft and formless woodland shadows, beautiful under the bright stars. Mattie worked her way through the lovely verses to the end:

> *"Though lovely and fair as the rose of the summer,*
> *Yet 'twas not her beauty alone that won me;*
> *O no! 'Twas the truth in her eye ever dawning*

That made me love Mary, the Rose of Tralee."

Mattie curtseyed low to all four sides and resumed her seat. They clapped and Lump shouted for more, but she said that she was too tired. And indeed it was past midnight.

'Near time to be going, lads!' announced Dicker. 'One more night exercise for us, our last before little Missy leaves us. I'll have to reckon up her share, won't I? And since she'll not take it, we'll find some charitable endeavour for it instead, shall we?' He gave his men a broad wink.

Ben the Scarecrow grinned. 'Aye, Miss,' he said, turning to Mattie and repeating something that had been said at the night of her kidnapping, 'We're all poor orphan lads what never knew their mothers and is in need of a bit of charity!'

'You never knew your *fathers*, that's for sure!' cried Tom. For this comment he was leapt upon and buffeted about in a boisterous, friendly manner before being set free.

'But we releases you on the condition you does some ennertainin'!' cried Pirate. 'Else it's down the well with you!'

Tom sat up and grinned at them all. 'I was plannin' that, anyhows,' he claimed. 'Just couldn't fit in a whole word till now! Reckon I can tell you the story of the Colt-pixey.'

The others resumed their seats and Tom began.

'Once there wwa a clumsy, puckish fairy stumpin' 'long home when he comes to a narrow part of the path and sees an ugly old woman comin' t'other way. "Oh, kind sir!" she cries, flutterin' her horrid, warty old eyelids at him like as if she was a buxom beauty. "Do stand aside for me!" But bein' an idle pixey, he won't back up to let her pass, but pushes past her. An' bein' so clumsy, he steps hard on her toes, not realisin' that he's trod on the horny foot of a wapsy, cranky crosspatch old witch. Then he laughs to see her hoppin' about holdin' her foot.

'She quaggles with rage and gibbles out at him - "Hulkish, rumbustical shammocky pixey!" she cries. "Cuss you! Cuss you to hell! No more shall you traipse about on two clonky corn-crushers, but down you shall go! Down! From now on, four-foot shall you shamble! And a'cos you be too whacking crummy by far, too hulkish for to fit on the path, I'll make you creeny by half!"

'And she raises her knobbly old arms, gnarled and twisted as tree-roots, and the poor floddy, dumble pixey is transmogrified into two flisky pony-pixeys, the one a colt-pixey and t'other a filly. The colt-pixey looks across and sees the filly and falls in love. Then, bein' as thick as a toad-frog cooked in a pie - that is, as thick as any man in love - he just laughs at the old witch and says, 'But see now, you sawney old batty-mouse! What a sossle you's made of your spell! I got me a pixey-mate now, what I've never had afore - and I'd wager that 'tis more'n you never had, with that scrimpy, sour face like what you've got!"

'The frumpish, wizened old hag screeches at him, for it's true. She's a deep forest witch and can't leave her patch; and no man has walked there for many a year! But an evil glint comes to her eye and she waves her arms again and the filly vanishes. The witch cries out, "Who's the sawney now, Puck? Just you shirk off an' see if you can find your pixey-mate! For now you've seen your beloved, you'll have no peace till she's yours! Tis your punishment to wander the forest till your hooves wear through - whickerin' for your lost love till your throat aches - listenin' for her reply till you goes mad! Ha! And see here, Colt-pixey, you won't know your love till she stands in the middle of the wettest bog in the forest, which is the centre of my domain. And she won't know *you* till the moon is full and has a wheel round it!"

'Still the dummle pixey laughs at her. "Old frump!" he calls. "At least I'll have hope, whereas you - with your face like soured cream - you has none!"

'The witch laughs back. "Ornary puck!" she cries. "Each filly you calls brings a man to me! For though I can't leave this part of the forest, you'll bring me man-flesh enough. By the time you recovers your beloved, I'll have had more husbands than the holly tree has thorns!" And she cackles and screeches and folds her wings and flies off into the night, holdin' tight to her crooky broomstick.

'And so now when the nights be dark, and a traveller is ridin' alone in the forest on his trusty mare, the colt-pixey draws near and whickers hoarsely to the mare, hopin' she be his true love. And she turns and follows him to the middle of the forest, takin' her rider towards the deepest, darkest, wettest bog. And the darkness creeps round her rider and there be voices cryin' in his ears and strange, unearthly, black music and he knows not whether he be north nor south, dead nor alive but is in a maze of stars and planets and unknown creatures that fly about him, round and round, until he falls off his horse in a dizzy faint.

'And when the man wakes in the morning, his horse be gone; and there at his side, cuddled in close with her stubbly chin on his shoulder, there be the old witch, naked, with skin slimy and warted as a frog's, grinnin' at him with a mad gleam in her eye. And, if he don't die of fright then and there, he's struck dumb and can't tell no one where he's been, and why he's returned home with no horse and no tongue!

'And so it will be, till the day the colt-pixey finds his beloved and she stands in the witch's domain beneath a full moon with a wheel round it. Then the colt-pixey will know his true love, and the spell will be broken.'

As Tom finished the tale, Mattie looked around. The little group was silent, enthralled. Lizzie was shivering with excitement, with fear and with the chill of midnight.

'Time for the young'uns to be off to bed,' Stump observed.

'And time *we* were off,' added Dicker. 'Lump, dout the fire and put the cave straight. Ben and Stump, you need to hitch both horses to the carriage. Pirate, you and I can fetch the tools to the carriage.' He glanced over at Mattie and the Brats.

'We'll save our good-byes till the morning,' he judged. 'The crew will be back in a few hours and once we've rested, we can deliver you to Druddery - say, lunchtime?'

Mattie nodded, but again said nothing. There was a sadness upon her that made speech very difficult. She and the Brats rose and went to prepare for bed.

Once the men had gone and the Brats had settled to sleep, Mattie rose again and went to her window. It being a new moon, there was no light except the stars. Yet they blazed so brightly that Mattie ceased to be afraid of the darkness as she gazed upon them. Because her window faced south she couldn't see the Dipper, nor the North Star it pointed towards. But if she craned her neck to look upwards, she could see a group of stars shaped like a "W" - that was Cassiopeia, calm queen of the skies. And to the southwest there was Orion the Hunter again - his great starry shoulders shrugging aside all life's little cares as he strode unchecked through the universe, his belt gleaming with jewels and crossed by the scabbard of his bright sword.

She sighed. This was a dirty, tumbledown hovel, but she would be sad to leave it. That was odd, wasn't it? Tomorrow she would abandon her pile of ferns and sleep in a real bed. She would say good-bye to a band of thieves and a couple of dirty, ignorant orphans. And yet she felt like crying when she thought of it. Ah, well. She said her prayers tonight with her eyes open, watching the stars in their slow dance with the planets and asking God to look after the Brats - no, not the Brats only, but all of them.

From somewhere in the room Jasper gave a tired chirrup. Would he be happy to return to the clean rooms and tidy garden of Druddery? Or would he too be sad? Mattie shook the question from her weary head and settled herself to sleep.

Chapter 17 Lump & Emmet Hump

No one heard the puffing of a solitary shadowy figure as it threaded a winding path near the house some hours later. Pale starlight fell through the slowly waving trees in jigsaw patterns across his large face, sometimes illuminating an eye, sometimes catching on a yellowed tooth as he paused to catch his breath. He came now to the cottage and peered into the filmy windows. His flabby hand patted the knife at his belt and he felt his way to the door.

The door creaked as he pushed it open. He waited a moment in the doorway, listening. There was nothing to hear but quiet breathing from the rooms to his left and his right. He began to walk along the short hallway. Old boards groaned beneath his weight and he cursed them under his breath. He paused again, undecided whether to turn left or right. A small stirring to his right decided him; he went that way, drawing his knife.

Jasper was awake. He slept with only one eye open in any case: you never could tell what might happen. Seeing the knife, and the ugly, round face, and the ugly, cold look in the small eyes, he croaked loudly and began flying about the room, whirring and swishing like a whole flock of bats. The man swore again and slashed about wildly with his knife when the bird suddenly swooped past his face, its wings brushing his hair.

'What is it?' cried Mattie, sitting up, confused, her head still full of dreams and starlight. 'Who? Jasper!

What -'. She quickly pulled on her boots.

A shadow moved across the room and suddenly Lump was standing between her and the window. He had a wicked-looking knife in his hand. He spoke quickly, breathlessly, in a low tone.

'Just you keep quiet!'

'What are you doing here?'

He laughed. 'Not good enough for the likes of you, am I? We'll see about that! There's no Dicker to get in the way, not now!'

As he spoke he moved slowly about the room, trying to catch sight of her in the darkness. For her part, she crawled slowly towards the doorway. He suddenly realised this was where she was heading for and made a clumsy dash for it himself, half-falling against it and then slamming the rotten door against its crooked frame.

From the other room came sounds of Tom and Lizzie awakening. Somewhere to Mattie's right Jasper was making angry little sounds, like the hissing and spitting of a kettle near the boil. Lump bent, picked up a mass of rags and threw it in the bird's direction. The sound ceased.

'Jasper!' cried Mattie. She rose and felt towards him, not caring for a moment whether Lump saw the movement. He leapt at her, his left hand finding the frill of a nightdress. Mattie kicked out with her glorious boots and heard him groan. She ran, stumbling, reaching for the door; but he was there before her again. She retreated. He followed. From Tom and Lizzie there was no sound. They must have fallen asleep again.

'Where's Dicker?' she asked.

Lump gave a low laugh. 'I 'spect they've put him in gaol by now.'

'But why?'

Lump did not answer her. He seemed to be talking to himself. 'A man's first duty is to look after hisself! You

172

can only put up with so much. "Lump, see to the fire!" "Lump, take those ponies to the stream for some water!" "Lump, shut your fat face!" "Lump, here's your share and that's all you get!" I growed tired of Dicker takin' advantage of us, like. Lordin' it over us all! Had to look after meself. So Dicker gets took, like, and I gets what he leaves behind!'

Mattie understood. It made her feel sick. 'You informed on him, didn't you? You told someone! And now he's back in prison and he'll be hanged!'

'If he's not dead already! There was some shootin' up at Druddery.' Lump laughed to himself.

'At Druddery?'

Lump suddenly seemed to see her through the blackness. His eyes gleamed and he began to walk in her direction.

'Didn't he tell you, Miss Special? He was usin' your place for smugglin', wasn't he? He needed somewhere he could meet fine folk, somewhere that seemed legal. An' these fine folk thinkin' you was his niece helped plenty. That way he could get twice as much for his smuggled silk and brandy, and have a place to store it, too! But I woulda thought he'd of tole you all that, you bein' the apple of his eye!'

Mattie retreated as quietly as she could, but Lump seemed able to follow her now, though most of the time she could only tell where he was by the sound of his voice.

'An' he thought so much of you that he spent our money on you, didn't he? He spent my money on trash, on a girl what looks at me and sneers and shivers like I'm some sort of filthy, slimy creature from under a log. Oh, you was kind to the others, after a fashion. But you never talked nice to me. I was nothin' but "Lump" to you - just like I been to all the rest!'

Mattie's heart was thumping now and she began to

move in crabbed, frightened circles. Lump was coming closer with every step, every word, every wheeze of his breathing. She filled her lungs to cry out.

Suddenly the door was flung open and a light blazed. Lump paused, turning to look. In the doorway stood Tom and Lizzie, holding aloft a candle and blinking their eyes in its watery light.

Lump smiled at them. 'Now, ain't that kind, Miss Matildy? Your two friends is come to help me see where you is!' He pointed the knife at Tom. 'Put that there candle down and run off, you two! I don't hold no grudge against neither of you but if you don't do as I ask, by Sodom an' Gomorrah I'll skin you both! Hear me?'

The two looked at Mattie. She bit her lip. 'Go, Tom! Go, Lizzie!' she cried out. 'Get away while you can! Don't mind me!' And yet she hoped they would stay and try to defend her from this hulking creature.

But what hope she had died as Lizzie whispered something in Tom's ear, and Tom nodded and knelt, fixing the candle in a gap between floorboards. They crept away along the hallway. The doorstep creaked as they stepped outside.

Lump turned back to Mattie. 'Ain't got many friends left, have you, Missy?' he jeered. 'So now you know what it feels like to be me.'

Mattie said nothing. Her heart ached. There was a great lump in her throat. She hung her head.

Lump stepped towards her. Then the front doorstep creaked again. There were hurried footsteps in the hall. He craned his head around on his fat neck to see what was happening.

Lizzie appeared at the doorway, grasping something in each hand. She leapt over the candle and threw what she was holding into Lump's face.

'Appy Birfday, y' fat dummock!' she cried, and disappeared the way she had came.

Lump shook dirt from his face and swore profusely. Immediately there was Tom, his hands also full.

'This is for you, you slimy crackspittle!' he said, showering Lump with more earth. As Tom retreated, Lizzie rushed back in, with a second double handful. As Lump stepped towards her, roaring with anger, she launched them straight into his eyes with a new taunt before hopping away nimbly.

Then Lump did a strange thing. He yelped and slapped at his neck. He slapped at his chest and rubbed his hair with his hands, shouting and swearing fit to burst. When Tom leapt through the doorway again, Lump was bent double, swatting invisible enemies like a man possessed. Tom launched his second stream of dirt, most of which went down the gaping back of Lump's immense trousers. Lump howled and threw himself at Tom. Tom dodged. Lizzie appeared at the door.

'Greasy old sludgebag!' she cried. 'Have another hunch of emmet-hump!' Mattie understood now: they were flinging handfuls of the anthill, complete with angry ants.

Lump waved his knife recklessly and lunged at Lizzie. She screamed and jumped back. He seemed ready to pounce upon her when the previous delivery of furious ants took effect. He dropped his knife and began beating at the top of his trousers. A crazed look came into his eyes. He rushed for the door, pushing past Tom who hurled another handful of earth at him as he passed. They heard him crash through the bushes, shouting; and then he splashed into the stream. From the sounds that followed, he was removing his clothes and beating his skin with both hands.

Mattie assumed command. 'Quick, Tom! You and Lizzie get your things! We must get away - now!'

They ran from the room. She turned and threw herself towards a small pile of rags. Lifting it gently, she unwrapped it with trembling fingers until a small, grey-black feathered head was revealed. It opened one eye at her.

'Yuk!' it murmured, and closed the eye again. She kissed the bird and tucked him into her bodice, wrapped in a clean cloth. He muttered to himself in a tired, peevish manner for a few seconds before falling asleep.

Scarcely had she gathered together her few belongings when Tom appeared, shouting for them to be off. She ran from the house after him, Lizzie clinging to her arm. Lump was just emerging from the bushes, naked save for some dripping underclothes. He shouted and gave chase.

Lizzie shouted back. 'You'll never cotch us, Lump! You can't run fast enough to cotch a worm! An' if you *should* get close, there's plenty of emmet-humps 'tween 'ere and the main road!'

This last taunt had immediate effect. Lump stopped dead. He rubbed anxiously at the ant-bites that seemed to cover his body. And having no one left to abuse, he swore at the stars instead. Above him, Cassiopeia continued her calm path across the heavens and paid him no mind.

They had climbed nearly halfway up the path before Mattie remembered.

'My horse! She's still down there!'

'We can't go back now!' Lizzie cried. But Tom surprised them both by saying that he would go for the mare. He shrugged off their caution.

'I can keep in the shadows. Lump won't know I'm there till I be gone!' And he was off before they could stop him.

He walked warily to the edge of the camp and crouched among some low trees. Lump, now dressed, was at the cave. Tom watched as Lump ransacked sacks and boxes, piling items at the front of the lantern-lit cave. When Lump next walked to the back of the cave, Tom scuttled across the clearing and hid among bushes by the stream. He walked along this until he came to the smaller clearing where they tethered the horses. Mattie's little mare was there - Lump must have ridden her back from Druddery and clearly intended now to load her with booty from the cave. Tom whispered to her soothingly, untied her and led her away as quietly as he could.

It would have been foolish to go past the cave again, so he took the mare down to the stream and turned left to follow it. He knew there was a narrow path leading back towards the main one - a path that faltered and ended in a maze of scrub and bramble, it was true: but he had confidence in his ability to feel his way forward from there onward. The horse walked along willingly, snorting a little and pushing him along with her muzzle. Above them the stars still peeked through the darkness; about them, branches snatched and mosquitoes hummed. Tom could see very little. What he could see just confused him.

He came to what might be the end of the path. Trusting to the eyes of the horse rather than his own, he mounted and urged her forward, bent close along her back to avoid a slap in the face from the low branches and rearing brambles - not to mention the nettles that had already stung him left and right. The mare hesitated, uncertain. Then she began to pick her way slowly, moving in and out of deep and deepest shadow like an underground fish winding its way about unseen rocks in a sightless pool. It was an eerie journey from nowhere to nowhere, drawn hither and thither by instinct, by some hidden goodness, by unheard nickering of the colt-pixey, by dark fate or evil design. Pulled onward - to who knew where? Tom, who wasn't much for praying, prayed.

After perhaps ten minutes of this delicate needlework on horseback, they came suddenly to the path - at least, it might be the path. The only way to find out was to turn uphill and see where it led. They did so. Moments later Tom heard a sharp whisper from his right.

'Is it you?' asked Lizzie from the bushes.

'Yes.' He dismounted and stood while the two girls came from their hiding place. He manfully bore the hugs and kisses they gave him.

'Oh, Tom!' exclaimed Lizzie. 'You be all goose-pimply!' Tom muttered something about the night air turning cold and urged them up the path, leading the mare by her halter-rope. Lizzie wanted to talk but he shushed her into silence.

They came at last to the main road, where they halted to discuss what to do. Tom suggested they go to Andover and find a place to hole up for a while.

'So long as it ain't the Workhouse!' Lizzie stipulated.

'We could try the blacksmith's at Picket Trenthay. He's got a small barn with straw in it - we could kip there 'thout him knowing, if it was just for the night.'

Mattie sighed so deeply that the others immediately asked her why.

'I want a bed to sleep in!' she said sadly. 'A real bed, with clean sheets and a feather mattress. I want clean water to wash in. I want a cup of tea from a china cup and a boiled egg for breakfast.' And despite herself, her eyes filled with tears.

Tom said unemotionally, 'An' you think we doesn't? I've wanted that all me life! But they don't give it you just for askin', do they?'

A thought struck Mattie and she brightened at once. 'Of course they do!' she cried. 'You just have to ask at the right place!'

'What?' Tom and Lizzie peered anxiously at Mattie through the darkness. The girl must have come un-hinged.

'Lizzie! Tom! Hop on the horse now. No, me first, then

178

Lizzie behind and Tom behind her. Don't worry, little Greylegs can carry us all. She's had to bear Lump a few times and he weighs more than us three together. No, don't argue! I know a place quite nearby where there's featherbeds for all! Not to mention boiled eggs and tea from china cups!'

'What?' Tom repeated.

'Come on! We're off to Miss Bell's Academy!'

'What?'

'Stop saying that word, Tom. Your mouth will freeze in its shape. Here, I'm up. Pass me your bundle, Lizzie. Now take my other hand and pull yourself up behind. Now Tom's bundle. Oh, do come on, Tom! Miss Bell won't bite you! And - you know, I'd quite forgotten - Uncle Lucid wrote to Miss Bell to say that he would pay for whatever expenses she incurred as a result of my staying there. Well, *you* are my expenses. My guests!'

Less than an hour later they were rattling the gates of the Academy and pulling the bellrope at the porter's lodge. A light appeared in a first floor window. A wiry little man pulled aside the curtains and leaned out, shouting down to them grumpily - and rather sleepily.

'Who in the - who *are* you, making such a racket at this time of night? He peered down at them, rubbed his eyes and peered some more.

'Mr Mills, sir!' cried Mattie, dancing about like a mad fairy at a moonlight ball. 'It's me, Matilda Harris! I've come, sir! And brought some friends with me!'

'Oh, you have, have you?' he asked, not at all amused. 'Well, what makes you think I intend to do anything about it?'

'Mr Mills, don't be such a grouch! We want feather beds - the best, softest, dreamiest beds you can find. We want boiled eggs for breakfast – new-laid eggs, mind you and boiled for four minutes exactly! And we want - we need - we *desperately require* cups of tea served in the best china teacups, the ones Miss Bell herself drinks out of, if that is possible! *Do* you think it's possible, *dear* Mr Mills?' And Mattie flashed him a wonderful smile which, though seen dimly through the pitch blackness about her, would have warmed the heart of the crustiest old gate-keeper in Britain.

'Oh - all right!' he grumbled. 'But only because it's you. And Miss Bell's crockery is off limits! You'll have to have Mrs Mills' special Willow Pattern instead. You hold tight and I'll be down once I've found me shoes.'

Chapter 18 A Strange Homecoming

The next morning Mattie woke late. She lay on her back in a deliciously comfortable, clean bed and tried to remember where she was. She had just recalled that this was the gatehouse of Miss Bell's Academy for Young Ladies when there was a gentle knocking on the door. Mrs Mills entered with a large tray.

'Hello, Matilda dear.' Mrs Mills, a plumpish, peaceful lady with a quiet voice, set the tray on a table by the bed and helped Mattie pile some pillows behind her. Jasper gave a little chirrup from his perch on the window ledge and flew over to investigate the tea things.

'Oh, Mrs Mills!' exclaimed Mattie. 'You're so - so *clean*!'

'But of course I am, dear,' replied Mrs Mills, looking at Mattie in some confusion.

Mattie laughed. 'It must seem an odd thing to say,' she reflected. 'But it feels so *different*, being clean - and having clean things about me - and clean people to look at!' She looked at her own hands. They were still grubby about the fingernails, despite a good wash before climbing into the wonderful featherbed and falling into a deep, deep sleep.

'Cleanliness is not the only thing, nor the best!' Mrs Mills replied, a little primly. 'A little dirt on the outside never made the heart unclean. As the good book says, man looks at the outside; God looks at the heart.'

'I couldn't agree more!' Mattie exclaimed.

Mrs Mills lifted the tray onto Mattie's lap.

'Oh, Mrs Mills!' On the tray were two boiled eggs, several rounds of toast, and a cup of tea in a beautiful, delicate blue willow pattern cup.

'Mills said it had to be in my best,' whispered Mrs Mills. 'And the eggs are new-laid and have been boiled for four minutes.' The lady paused, surprised to see a tear running down one of Mattie's cheeks. 'Are you all right, dear?' she enquired.

'I'm fine,' answered Mattie softly. 'Just - just far too happy!' And after saying her prayers she began to eat while Mrs Mills sat by the bed, sewing a sock and talking.

'I took the same to your two friends. Not that they were allowed to eat their breakfasts until they'd washed their hands and faces, mind! But what faces! The girl's a forest faery and the boy's old before his time, but their eyes lit up and they were children again when they saw the food!'

'I hope they thanked you for it.'

'Of course they did. As polite as the Queen's own children, they were. However, they didn't say their grace before eating, not until I reminded them. And what a grace! Four bare aunts, indeed! But I suppose they've never been taught.'

Mattie coughed and spluttered a little, having swallowed her tea down the wrong way. 'Are they still in their room?' she asked.

'Not they. Mills took the boy with him to feed the horses and chickens, and see to some of the fruit trees. The girl is looking through one of my picture-books and when I go downstairs, she'll help me with my mending. She can come over to the school later today and we'll do some tidying there - you'll recall helping me with the start-of-term clear-out last Easter.'

'I certainly do! It was such a happy time. I was so

happy then, Mrs Mills. Then my parents - then my parents died. And it was hard to be happy after that. I felt like I was being unfaithful to them.'

'And what do you want to do today, Matilda?'

'I must go to Druddery.' Her face clouded as she recalled Lump's words the night before. 'I must find out what has happened.'

'Happened to whom?'

'Everyone. To my uncle, and aunt, and cousin. To a highwayman and his gang. To a carriage load of brandy.'

Mrs Mills dropped her sewing. 'I beg your pardon?' she asked.

'I'm not completely certain about the brandy,' mused Mattie. 'Perhaps Lump invented that part. But something must have happened to Dicker and the others. Probably there *was* shooting. But I can't believe Dicker's been captured, or is dead. He's - he's not the sort to be fooled by someone like Lump. He must have known something was up! He'd have made plans, and when they came for him, he'd have faded into the night. And he'd have saved the others, too!'

Mrs Mills was feeling about under her chair for her sewing. 'That's - that's a fine tale, child. (Gracious me, now where's the needle?) Were you dreaming it when I woke you?'

Mattie finished her tea and spoke long and animatedly to the kindly woman. At the end of it, Mrs Mills still didn't know what to think of it all.

'Well, all I can say is that I'm glad you're here safe and sound. After lunch, Mills can get out the carriage and take you over to Druddery and we'll see what we shall see.'

'Thank you, Mrs Mills. I'm so very grateful to you, and I'm sure Sir Lucid will feel the same. But there is no need for Mr Mills to come with me. Once I'm dressed, I'll saddle Greylegs and ride to Druddery myself.'

'All that way alone - and through the forest as well?'

Mattie laughed. 'It doesn't frighten me to travel alone, Mrs Mills. I feel quite - quite strong now, you know? But I would be grateful if you and Mr Mills could look after my friends for a day or so. I'll have a word with them before I go, and I'm sure they'll agree to be on their best behaviour if I ask them to.'

An hour later, Mattie was travelling back up the road she had journeyed along in the opposite direction in the dark, weeks ago now. Jasper flew about her, cawing and chirping ecstatically, now perching on her shoulder, now pecking in the dust at the roadside, now diving into the bushes. Mattie whistled cheerfully as she went, until she turned into the gate at Druddery.

The Hall was in turmoil. Several carriages were drawn up outside the house and there were men walking about in an important manner. Mattie's heart fell as she recognised Dicker's carriage. She rode up to it and examined it carefully, fearing to find it riddled with bullet holes.

Someone moved out of the shadow of the house. 'And what do you think you're doing, young lady?' demanded a tall man in a dark suit. He was trying to light a pipe, and failing because of the wind.

She studied him. He was clearly a policeman of some sort. Probably from London, to judge from his accent. Probably high-ranking, to judge from his quiet, confident manner. But she sat up tall on her horse, squared her shoulders and spoke to him without shyness. She was surprised to find how much like Dicker she sounded.

'I was not aware, Inspector - or is it Chief Inspector? - that there was a law against a person looking at a carriage standing in her own drive.'

'Oh?' The man was dumbfounded. 'And - and who would you be, Miss?'

'Does that matter?' she asked. 'Does the law make

distinctions between persons? Are we not all of us equals before it? Or is there one law for the rich, and another for the common person?'

'Now, young lady, let us not be hasty with our judgements!'

'Of course not,' she said calmly. 'Perhaps, Chief Inspector, you would be so good as to tell me what has happened here; then we will *both* be able to make our judgements without undue haste.' She smiled at him.

The man smiled back at her. He was clearly not offended, though he was surprised by her manner. 'It's this way, Miss - Miss -?'

'Harris. Matilda Harris.'

'Ah. The niece. Pleased to make your acquaintance, Miss Harris. Sorry not to have known it was yourself. I had expected someone much younger. My apologies.'

She nodded. The man continued.

'There was a fracas last night. A smuggling gang had been using one of the barns as a storage post, in your uncle's absence. We had been alerted as to this and arrived in time to make an arrest.'

'Just the one?'

He eyed her keenly. 'No, Miss, there were two apprehended, as it happens. Had you expected more?'

'You said there was a gang.'

'So I had. But the gang leader escaped, and one of his men. We've been searching the grounds and buildings but they seem to have got clean away.'

'Good!' Mattie could not stop herself from exclaiming under her breath.

'Pardon, Miss? What did you say?'

'It was not important, Chief Inspector. Where - where are the two men you "apprehended"?'

'In Andover gaol, temporarily. I expect we'll move them to somewhere a little less rural in a day or two. But why would you be wanting to know that, Miss?'

'I may wish to visit them in gaol, Chief Inspector. Justice should be tempered with Mercy - is that not what the Bible says?'

'No doubt it does, Miss. But I'd not recommend practising the merciful verses of the Bible on villains like these! These are men with no morals and no conscience, and with hearts black as the devil's own. If you'd been here, they'd have killed you for standing in their way - or they'd have done worse.'

Mattie kept her anger in check. 'Is that true, Inspector?' she asked. 'Is there really no spark of goodness in them?'

'Miss,' he said gravely, 'there's a whole class of criminals on whom mercy is wasted. And if you were to meet half the evil wretches I have to deal with, you'd soon see that I'm right. The prisons and workhouses are full of them! You can thank God you never have to deal with folk like that.'

'Thank you for your advice, Chief Inspector.'

'You are welcome, Miss Matilda. Shall I ask one of my men to stable your mare for you?'

'No thank you. I'll see to it myself. Good day, Chief Inspector.'

'Good day, Miss.'

She took Greylegs to the stable and removed her saddle and bridle. She rubbed the mare down with a handful of straw, then gave her water and some hay. Then she went into the house.

It was a strange homecoming. She did not know how to behave. She did not know how to be a child again.

Hubert came forward bashfully and wrung her hand, then threw his arms about her and gave her a squeeze that a bear would have been proud of. 'Oh, Mattie! It's so awfully good to see you again! And there's such a frightful lot to tell you! But here's Mama - you'd best say

186

hello to her first.'

Aunt Agatha bent her head and they touched cheeks for one of those "kisses" where you make a funny, kissy noise but don't actually do any kissing. Mattie submitted to this with a good grace, though it seemed such a waste of effort to *almost* kiss someone!

'Why, child! How you've grown!' was all the woman could say.

'And you've lost weight, Aunt,' Mattie returned truthfully. 'You look better for it, too!'

'I - you... Why, I thank you, Matilda.'

Matilda looked up at the large, slow, insecure woman and felt a sudden pity for her. She took her aunt's hand. 'I was sorry to hear that your father died,' she said. 'It must be a great sadness for you. From what Hubert has written to me, he was an unusual man.'

'Why - yes - a - a painful matter. Thank you for your - your words, Matilda. But there is really no need to be emotional about it.' Agatha frowned and after a few moments retrieved her hand.

Lucid was standing on the fringe of this group. Mattie ran to him and flung her arms about him. Then she let him go and said awkwardly, 'Thank you so much for looking after me, Uncle Lucid!'

'I? But - ah, Mattie, I don't see that I have done anything of the sort, dear child! But it is kind of you to - ah - think so.' He too was awkward. Then they all stood for a moment in silence, not knowing how to speak or behave. Fortunately, Jasper flew in. Being a bird, he was not at all embarrassed and gave a great screech of joy as he spotted Hubert. He landed on the boy's head and began jabbering at him in Jackdaw, nipping Hubert's ear at intervals so as to secure his full attention. Mattie relaxed immediately and began to laugh.

After lunch Mattie spent an hour in Lucid's study trying

to explain what had happened to her during the three weeks he had been away. He listened patiently and with few interruptions. Then he leaned back in his seat and pondered aloud, touching the fingers of one hand gently against their fellows in the other hand as he worked his way down his list of thoughts.

'You - you say, Mattie, that you wish to visit these - ah, these, er, gentlemen - and I do not see that I can have any objection to that. But justice must have its course. Regrettably. We can do little about that. Perhaps a few words to some people I know. A letter. Yes, a letter. But I fear that is all. You must resign yourself to the fact that they will be in prison for some time. Or - or worse.'

'But, Uncle, it's so unfair! They aren't wicked, really they aren't! Stump, for instance: I swear by all that's good and holy that he's never done anything to harm a fly!'

'I do not say that it is fair. The law *aims* for fairness. I do not say that it always *achieves* it. But I will do what I can. Perhaps there will be more to say on this once I have made a few enquiries. Now, as to the two children.'

'The Brats.'

'A most endearing name. A thought occurs to me. Would they by any chance be twins?'

'Did I not say that?'

'I do not think so.'

'They are twins. Does it change matters, Uncle?'

'Only - only in helping me to imagine their faces. I think I may have met them already. Most - yes, *most* - charming children. And the blacksmith's was exactly as they directed us - "renward" up the Roman Road (gracious, I hadn't known it was Roman, that road, but they did!). I am more inclined to - ah - support your endeavours now that I can picture them. I have a little money put by for - for the unexpected. Perhaps we could do something for them.'

'I'd like to enrol them at Miss Bell's.'

'Oh.' He paused. 'I see. That would be rather expensive, I fear. And you will need to enquire of Miss Bell as to whether they - whether - um, let us say that *she* may not be in favour of such an approach.'

'But of course she will!' Mattie said confidently. 'She's such an intelligent woman, Uncle. And so wise! I wouldn't have been able to educate the Brats at all if I hadn't learned to teach by watching how she does it!'

'Doubtless. Doubtless. One can but - but try, Mattie.'

'Can we send someone to ask the School to look after the Brats for one more night? I asked Tom and Lizzie to wait until I returned, and I think they will, if Mr and Mrs Mills tell them they are to stay there another night. Then perhaps you could come with me and speak to Miss Bell. Mr Mills said she would be back at the Academy tomorrow morning.'

Lucid cleared his throat nervously. 'I - I will do whatever I can, child. But I'm afraid I'm not terribly *good* at speaking with schoolteachers. As a species, they rather terrify me. Wild - *extremely* wild - tigers would be preferable! But I will do what I can.'

'Miss Bell *is* rather fierce,' Mattie acknowledged. 'But I'm certain she will be tame in this respect. I can manage the talking, Uncle, if you will be there to support me.'

Lucid looked at Mattie wonderingly. 'Why, child!' he exclaimed. 'How differently you speak now!'

'Do I? Yes, perhaps I do. But *please* say you will come, Uncle!'

'Of course. I will - um - provide - ah - *adequate support*, I think I can say.'

It was a long, good afternoon she spent getting to know Hubert again - and even getting to know a little of Aunt Agatha for the first time. Then she went for a long walk on her own, searching all the hidden places she knew of, in the hopes of finding an escaped highwayman or perhaps two. But in vain.

When at last she went to bed, she realised that she was exhausted. She trimmed her candle and climbed into the bedclothes, aching and suddenly dispirited.

'Serves them right!' she muttered angrily, talking about Dicker's gang. 'They *deserve* to be in prison!' But she did not really feel that. She couldn't have said exactly how she felt, except that her heart ached and her thoughts were in confusion.

Jasper however was not at all dispirited, and just now he was quite excited by the fireplace. Maybe he smelled the soot and remembered the inch-thick layer of it on the hearth in the cottage, for he pecked all around the fire surround, chattering noisily to himself. Mattie shooed him away and he took up a disgruntled station on her window ledge, occasionally sending her a burst of childish, pouting little cheeps.

'But the Raven still beguiling all my sad soul into smiling...' she quoted, then recalled that it was Dicker who had told her the poem. Irritated, she huffed out the candle and said her prayers in a dark mood.

She fell asleep and - immediately it seemed to her - fell into bad dreams. First, the fireplace opened and a ghost crept out. It was a tall ghost, but very pale and sombre. It sat awhile at the end of her bed, talking to her in some fantastic language. She tried it in French to no avail, then in her snippets of German. Lastly, she spoke in her best Hampshire - but the ghost must have been a Cornish ghost, for it couldn't communicate with her.

Then she awoke. And the fireplace *was* opened, like a door, and there *was* a ghost seated at the end of her bed, talking to itself in a feverish, rambling fashion. And the ghost was Dicker.

Chapter 19 Hard Decisions

He was actually speaking to Jasper, who was perched upon his knee and chattering like an old friend. At a movement from Mattie, Dicker fell silent and turned to her. He was pale and his smile was strained.

'I was wondering when you would wake,' he said mildly. 'Your bird keeps better watch than you do!'

She sat up and pondered. She looked towards the fireplace.

'There is an underground passage. It runs from the house to the old barn - with several other outlets, though some of them are blocked by fallen stones. This is the only good access to it from the house... I hope you are not offended that I came through your fireplace without knocking.'

'Offended?' Mattie was suddenly angry. She tried to keep her voice down, but it was very difficult. 'You use my house for your own illegal purposes. You deceive me! You take advantage of me! You put people in danger. You put yourself in danger! And now you think the only thing you need to apologise for, is not knocking before entering my room!'

'Now, then, my little volcano -'

'I am not *your* little anything! How dare you come here, thinking I will help you, thinking I will lift a finger -'

'Did I ask for help?'

'No, but you will!'

Dicker spread his arms in surrender. His voice

toughened. 'Perhaps I will! But as for apologising for my many failings, I would remind you that I am a highwayman. I don't apologise to *anyone*! I take what I want and make the best use of my opportunities, however they arise and whoever is affected by them!'

'But you said -'

'I said nothing except that you should mind your own business! In any case, I can hardly be said to have taken advantage of you. I took pains *not* to involve you. I even avoided asking you for information; I discovered for myself whatever I needed to know.'

He paused, running his hands through his hair. His spoke in a puzzled tone. 'I don't know why I'm sitting here like this: a grown, dangerous highwayman trying to persuade a child that he's not as bad as he seems! I ought to be cutting the throats of the lot of you, plundering the house and making my escape!'

'Why don't you?'

Dicker frowned and did not answer the question. Instead he said, 'And if we are to ponder such things, then let me ask why you do not shout for help? Why not summon the household to your aid? Why not call them in, have me bound hand and foot, and see me sent to gaol?'

Mattie was troubled by this question. 'I - I don't know why. Perhaps I don't think I'm in any danger. And perhaps I don't really want them to put you in prison. I *ought* to want it, but I - I *can't*.'

Dicker's face relaxed. He sat back with a sigh and began stroking the jackdaw with a gentle forefinger. 'A fine mess this is,' he said. 'A cruel, heartless criminal who won't commit crimes and a hapless victim who won't turn him in! And there's Stump and Jack in gaol wondering what will become of them.'

Mattie said urgently, 'Can't you do something for them?'

Dicker considered. 'I have the glimmerings of a plan, child. But it would involve yourself, and I can see that such involvement might be, shall we say, "taking advantage" of your kindness.'

'Never mind all that! Tell me what I can do.'

'Have you a family doctor?'

'Yes. A Doctor Carter.'

'Local?'

'I think he lives east of here - in a tiny village.'

'Excellent! Not too likely to be known in Andover, then. Would your uncle happen to have one of the doctor's calling cards in his possession?'

'I could look and see. I know where the cards are kept. But how will that help Pirate and Stump?'

'With a little assistance from yourself, it could help them considerably. Are you willing, gal? Or p'raps you be a titty bit timersome?'

'I ben't afeard,' she replied in the same tone. 'But I'll not tell untruths, see?'

Dicker smiled again. 'Leave the untruths to me, lass! Find your doctor's card for me and slide it into the gap around the fireplace. Next, deliver a message for me to the lads. Then, if all goes well, you'll not see me again.'

'Oh.' She brooded on this statement. She ought to have been pleased to hear him say that she would never see him again, but instead she was troubled by his words.

He set out his plans. She listened carefully and then repeated them back to him, word for word. But a thought came to her.

'Why don't you just escape now by yourself, and leave the others? Isn't it risky to stay in the area?'

Dicker was angered by this question. 'Am I to be allowed not a shred of humanity, young'un?' he asked bitterly. 'Am I to be entrusted with no finer feelings, no claims of companionship? No care for anything except my own pocket and my own worthless skin?'

'I'm sorry. I didn't mean it that way. I just thought - no, I don't know what I was thinking. I'm very tired. And I had such a fright when Lump came back to camp that night - only a day ago. I've not thought straight since then.'

'Lump?' he cried. 'What did he do?'

Mattie told him. Dicker's face went white with horror.

'He did that? Tried to kill you? And worse?'

'He was bragging that he'd betrayed you to the police, and so you weren't there to stop him from taking what he wanted, and doing what he wanted...' Mattie had to stop. She was shaking all over now at the memory, and breathless.

'God in heaven, what a fool I am!' exclaimed Dicker softly. 'I thought the man was up to something. But not that! I reckoned he would ride off with a delivery of brandy - he'd be a rich man for that and feel he'd scored off me. I was prepared for that - even hoping he'd try it; I'd have let him go and thought it a good bargain to be rid of the beast. I never dreamt -'

'You really should give up crime,' said Mattie suddenly. 'You're too trusting!'

Dicker smiled ruefully. 'A recent weakness,' he explained. 'Once I have removed myself from the bad influences of good company such as your own, I shall be as hard and deceitful as ever I was.... Were you frightened?'

'Terrified. I - I still am.'

'And the Brats saved you? Well, there's a noble result for you. But Miss Matilda, I am truly - truly -'. He paused. 'Truly sorry. Not something I regularly say. Not something I regularly feel. But the thought of that man - horrifies me. What a fool I was not to see you safely to Miss Bell's Academy, or home. A fool!' He rose, agitated. 'I will return to my dungeon. Do you think you could spare

194

something to wrap myself in? It's cold down there.'

She pointed to some cupboards where bedding was kept. He limped over to investigate.

'You're injured!'

'Slightly. No, do not rouse yourself. I'll just take this. I shall return it. Oh, and one more favour. When you go to the stables to see to your mare, cast an eye in the last stall on the left. I managed to put Night there and would be grateful if you could ensure he's well looked after. It's unwise for me to be seen feeding him just now, don't you think? I shall need him again once you've carried out the task we discussed.'

'But how will you get to him without being seen?' she asked suspiciously.

'Oh, there's no problem about *that*.' Dicker laughed. 'No problem at all, my little Chief Inspector, Inquisitor and Interrogator!'

The next morning she sought and found Doctor Carter's calling card and tucked it into a pocket. After duly poking it through the narrow crack into the hidden passage, she next sought out Uncle Lucid, who was sitting in his study, puzzling over some legal documents.

'Uncle? Could I ask you a favour?'

'Why - ah, certainly.' He gave his papers a final thoughtful glance and pushed them to one side. 'Yes?'

'Please could you come with me to the gaol at Andover? I would like to visit Pirate and Stump.'

'Are you sure you ought to?'

'Yes. I think so. No, perhaps that's not right. I - I *feel* I ought to go. But my mind is not quite clear about it!'

'Ah. Yes.' Lucid thought for a moment and then asked hesitantly, 'What if you should decide *not* to go? How would you feel then? And how would your mind - ah - view your *not* going?'

Putting it this way made the matter suddenly very

simple. Of course she had to go. She laughed. 'My mind would be quite upset!'

'Then I shall accompany you once the carriage is ready. Perhaps you could instruct Jackson as to your - our - requirements? On second thoughts, I will come with you to see him. I have been attempting to understand the final will and testament of Agatha's father, and the - ah - *mystery* of legal circumlocution has been growing on my mind in nightmarish fashion. Why do lawyers take simple instructions and stir them about to make such a ponderous - um - soup?'

Mattie laughed again and they walked from the study arm in arm.

'Did Agatha's father leave much behind to make soup from?' she asked.

'Very little in the way of money, I fear. His family had been fairly well-to-do at one stage, but by the time the old gentleman was born there remained to him the wonderful house and not much else. His own father - Agatha's grandfather - had been an excellent gambler when sober but a rather incompetent one when drunk. He was, unfortunately, drunk more often than he was sober. He died from falling into a canal after a night's drinking and - ah - after misbehaviours of various descriptions.'

Lucid gave an embarrassed little cough and continued. 'Not surprisingly, Agatha's father became a strict teetotalist. For years as a child he'd seen the old man reeling in from the bars, pockets empty and brain pulpy. He made an oath that he would never touch alcohol. And he kept it! And he expected everyone else to keep away from the demon drink, too! He was a harsh man to his family. But by clean living and good management he was able to add to the little money that was left to him. And he made the house into something wonderful, though it needs a certain amount of repair. You must come with us to see it.'

'Does the house belong to Aunt Agatha, then?'

'Ah. Well, this is what I am trying to discover. There is a brother, named Robert. I *think* that *he* will have the house. That is the normal course, you know. Sons inherit; daughters do not. The old man was a stubborn fellow and a man who bore grudges hard, including a long grudge against his wayward son; yet he forgave him in the end. I *think* that Robert - whom I have met only the once - is allowed the house but provided next to no money for its upkeep. Agatha however seems to have a little money, but no house. Because of the - ah - *rift* between the old man and her brother, she had expected to inherit both house *and* money. She is not at all pleased!'

'What was her brother like?'

Lucid stopped and puzzled over this. 'A charming villain,' he said.

Mattie and her uncle went to the stables and found Jackson cleaning out the horses' stalls. The carriage was duly ordered for an hour's time and they were turning away when Jackson called out.

'Sir Lucid - that new horse - begging your pardon, sir, but I was wondering what to do about him.'

'The new horse?' Lucid was baffled.

'The black stallion, Sir Lucid, in the stall at the end.'

Lucid walked slowly to the stall indicated. He looked up at the great, muscled black beast with interest.

'Such a beautiful creature!' he breathed. 'But I have not - *I think* - seen him before.' A thought came to him and he turned to look at Mattie questioningly. 'Have *you* seen him before now, Mattie?'

'He's called Night and belongs to the highwayman,' she said. 'Please may we look after him for now?'

'Of - of course, my child.' Lucid extended a hand slowly and the horse breathed the smell of this new man and snorted comfortably, then gave Lucid a little nudge in the chest. Lucid reached over and scratched Night on the neck. He gave a little laugh. 'I would not wish to ride him, though. He's rather more horse than I am accustomed to!'

'I doubt that anyone other than Dicker *could* ride him.'

Lucid started a little at Mattie's words and paused, thinking about something. He was about to make a comment, but then shook his head at whatever he had been prepared to say. Instead he looked up at the horse again.

'I think, Mattie, from my own knowledge of horses - one of the few subjects I would claim to know much about - that he would permit himself to be ridden by a child such - such as yourself. He has the look: gentle with the weak, stubborn with the strong. Other than that, yes, I expect he is a horse for one man alone.'

The Andover gaol house was a dismal place. Lucid went in with her to ask if they could see the two highwaymen. The gaolers looked doubtful; but one of them called their superior, who recognised Sir Lucid and gave permission immediately.

Mattie was allowed a brief, whispered discussion with the two men while a puzzled gaoler looked on. Then she introduced her uncle to them and it was difficult to say who was the most embarrassed - Stump, Pirate or Lucid. A few minutes more, and she was outside again in the bright sunshine of early September.

They mounted the carriage and Lucid signalled to the driver to start. He turned to Mattie.

'Your acquaintances are - ah - interesting, Mattie,' he said diplomatically. 'I do not know whether they are typical of their class, but I can see why you found their company to be - to be diverting. Were they - I do not know how to put this - were they *gentlemanly* in their treatment of you? Not harsh, not taking any liberties?'

'Their actions were gentlemanly enough,' she answered. 'Their words were sometimes rather - rather *strong*, if you know what I mean!'

'I do. It is not only the lower classes that swear! Or drink! People say "Drunk as a Lord", you know. That presupposes some - er - tendency towards excess in the upper echelons of society.'

They rode in silence for a while, towards Miss Bell's. As they turned into the gates of the Academy, Mattie suddenly burst out:

'Uncle, is it wrong - would it be wrong - for me to help them to escape?'

Lucid was visibly shaken. He opened and closed his mouth several times before finding words. 'I think, Mattie, that it would *almost always* be wrong to help a criminal to escape.'

'*Almost* always?'

'*Almost*. There may be - ah - exceptional cases.'

'How would one know which cases were exceptional?'

'Gracious, child, what difficult questions you ask! Let me see... What would your father have said?'

'Being a clergyman, he would probably have told me to pray about it.'

Lucid smiled at her. 'Then, child, that is almost certainly the right answer. I was not always in agreement with your father's - um - politics, but I could never fault his religion. And what would your mother - my sister - have said? No, I can answer that for you. She would have said that you need to search your conscience, use your mind and then listen to your heart.'

Mattie gazed at him with sudden joy. 'Why, yes!' she exclaimed softly. 'That's just what she would have said! Did - did you know her well, Uncle?'

'I - I loved my sister. She was my dearest friend. We are - were - not alike, Mattie. I could never have been brave as she was. Her faith is - was - quite robust and mine is rather fearful. But we were close as children and remained close up to her - her death. You remind me of her. That is a comfort to me.'

She put her hand in his and smiled at him.

They left the carriage on the front drive and went in search of the Brats. Lizzie was easy to find. She was playing in the garden with an old doll, singing to it in a soft voice. When she saw Mattie, she ran over and squeezed her tight.

'I were hopin' you'd be back afore nuncheon. And oh, Mattie, there *be* nunch here! *And* breakfast, dinner, tea and supper! Miz Mills says she'll let me cook summat myself if I remembers to wash me hands afore meals. - Oh, crimany! It's you!' Lizzie had recognised Lucid. 'It's the kind gennleman! Mattie, he gived us two pennies once! Say, Mattie! They pennies an' all be in the hidey-hole still, ben't they?'

'Good - good morning,' Lucid said shyly. 'You must be Lizzie. Mattie tells me you are a kind and brave child, and I am pleased to make your acquaintance.' He held out his hand and she shook it vigorously.

Mattie explained who Lucid was.

'Crumbs!' exclaimed Lizzie. 'A proper toff! Don't tell Tom though, Mattie, 'cos it might make he a titty bit fierce, y'know?' She looked up to Lucid and confided, 'My brother be pucksome toward rich folk, but don't let that maze you. It's his way, see?'

'Ah.' Lucid was lost for words. However, he was saved by the arrival of Mrs Mills who took them all into the house and went to seek Tom.

Tom came into the house a few minutes later but was sent out again to remove his boots. Then he was sent out a second time to wash his hands. Finally he stood in the drawing room, nodding to Mattie and staring at Lucid.

'Tom, this is my Uncle Lucid,' began Mattie. 'He -'

'I recalls he,' Tom said with satisfaction. 'He ast us where the Smithy was. An' there were this old cow -'

'Tom!' warned his sister.

'I'm tellin' it my way, Lizzie. You gets your turn arter me. This old cow -'

'I really don't think you should talk like this, Tom,' Mattie said hurriedly. 'It's not at all kind!'

'Well, *she* weren't kind. *She* says -'

'I know what the lady said,' Lucid put in mildly. 'And I am sorry for it. My - ah - wife sometimes says things she regrets or - or *should* regret. As do I. As do all of us. I am - sorry.'

'Well, that's all right, then,' Tom said, but he didn't sound convinced about this. 'She ben't here, be she? She could say sorry herself if she was!'

'She's at home,' Mattie said quietly. 'My aunt is at home. But I hope you will meet her, Tom. Perhaps you'll be able to persuade her that all folk deserve respect!'

Lizzie added, 'Even them as doesn't wash proper unner their nails, Tom Smith! And can't speak a dozen words 'thout ten of 'em bein' rude!'

Tom glowered at her. 'Spect a man needs to stand up for hisself, don't he?' he grumbled.

'Quite - ah - quite right, Tom!' said Lucid. 'And to stand up for others, too! But there is no need to be - um - *unkind* with it, I think your sister is saying. But - but no offence taken. Mattie has told me of your - your bravery and faithfulness. I - ah - um - that is, I am most *grateful* to you and wish to accord you the respect you are due.'

Tom nodded in what he hoped was a gracious manner. He hadn't the slightest idea what Lucid was trying to say, but the man's voice was kind and respectful, and he liked the hesitant friendliness of the man. He was seeking in his mind for an appropriate reply when they were interrupted by the return of Mr Mills.

Mills held the door open for someone behind him and Mattie gave a little gasp as Miss Bell entered. Miss Bell advanced to the middle of the room and stopped there, looking somewhat puzzled at this strange gathering.

Mattie stared at Miss Bell, trying to fit her to the picture she had been carrying in her mind of the Great and Terrible Headmistress. She had thought Miss Bell to be tall, immensely tall, her head formidably high and her bearing imperious. But the real Miss Bell was tiny - hardly taller than Mattie herself. Her shoulders stooped a little and her head bobbed up and down when she spoke, like a little bird's.

'Sir Lucid - it is good to see you once again. I was distressed to hear of Lady Agatha's bereavement. I hope that she is bearing her sadness with fortitude. Pray convey to her my condolences.' The voice was assured, firm, clear and level - but it did not ring with tempered steel as Mattie had imagined it. It did not make the walls tremble, and Uncle Lucid was not vaporised in the furnace of the fearful lady's polished phrases.

'And Matilda! Welcome back, dear girl. I understand from Mills that you have had some unusual experiences. But I am sure you have done your duty! Noble blood will always prove itself, my child.'

Mattie did not know how to reply to this. But Lizzie intervened.

'Our Mam had nobles in her blood, too, I reckon. Plenty of 'em!'

Miss Bell turned slowly to look at Lizzie. 'I beg your pardon, child? Matilda's family traces its roots back to Charlemagne. To which noble family are *you* referring?'

Lizzie insisted, 'Our Mam must of had dozens of them roots, Miss, cos she allus done *her* duty, too! An' more'n that mos' days!'

Tom laughed. 'P'raps our Mam had kings in her blood, d'you think, Lizzie? If Mattie has nobles in hers, even though she do have that mangey fellow in it, too, Mam must have had a king or an emperor, for sure!'

Lucid smiled and remembered what he had come for. 'Miss Bell, I wish to introduce two - ah - friends. These are Thomas - I mean *Tom* - and Lizzie, er, Smith. Good and true children, and of great assistance to Mattie in these past weeks.'

'Enchanted,' Miss Bell said a little weakly, extending a hand to the children, which they seized in turn and gave a great shake, as if it were the limb of some tree they were trying to dislodge nuts from.

Mattie thought she should take matters in hand. 'Miss Bell,' she began politely, 'I have told Tom and Lizzie about the Academy and I have discussed my - my ideas with Sir Lucid, who supports me. I - we would be grateful if you could consider enrolling them here.'

Miss Bell appeared dazed. 'Here?'

'At the Academy.'

'Why - yes, I understood that. But in what capacity, Matilda?'

'As students, of course.'

'Of course.' Miss Bell's face became like that of a hunted animal and she appeared for a moment to be considering running out the door. But she took a deep breath and spoke calmly.

'There would of course be the matter of fees. This is an expensive boarding school.'

Lucid said quickly, 'I would pay.'

'Oh. Oh... And the accommodation could be difficult. We do not normally take on boys.'

Tom spoke up. 'You won't be needin' to. I'll not take charity an' I don't need schoolin' anyways.'

'Oh, Tom!' exclaimed Lizzie. 'Don't be so ornery! 'Course we ort to take charity. Only a dummock would

203

thumb his nose at the gennleman's offer!'

Miss Bell bit her lip. 'And the educational differential is enormous. I expect these children cannot even read.'

Lizzie was scandalised. 'I reads *The Little Green Primer* all right, doesn't I, Mattie? Mattie taught us, Miss, and we can do *all* sorts of learnin'! 'Cept I ben't over sharp at the sums, but I reckon that be boy's work and p'raps you don't teach it much here anyways.'

Miss Bell swallowed. 'And there is the little matter of social class. These children would, I expect, feel somewhat ill at ease in a group of children from backgrounds so distinctly removed from their own. Not to mention that - that - Sir Lucid, may I speak plainly?' She suddenly stood upright and for a moment a fire blazed in her eyes. She turned to address Tom and Lizzie.

'I hope you will not be offended if I say what I feel.'

Lizzie shrugged her shoulders and Tom, surprisingly, smiled.

'I been waitin' for you to talk plain,' he said. 'Mattie, she promised us the wondrous Miss Bell what told folks what she thought straight out, like a bolt from heaven.'

Miss Bell looked at him as if not certain whether she should be angry at this rather personal comment. She said, a little haughtily, 'Sir Lucid, the simple truth is that I cannot afford to take these children into the Academy. I might - in time - be able to overcome my own prejudices. I am, I admit, shocked at the suggestion of schooling these two. But that could change. Slowly. However, I could not change the attitude of the wealthy parents who send their daughters to this place. Let them hear that I have accepted two uneducated, unmannered children of the lowest class, and within a week half my pupils will have left. I cannot do it. And - I say this honestly - I do not know that I *should* do it even if I could. I do not know whether it is a good thing for the lower classes to be educated. I do not even know if they *can* be educated. Do you understand?'

Lucid nodded. Tom gave a look to them all, which plainly said that he'd known it would turn out like this. Mattie lowered her head and tried to think of a way around the problem. Only Lizzie spoke.

'Oh, drot it! Cussnation to hell an' back! Now I won't get to see the Book!' She stamped her foot in exasperation.

Miss Bell turned her eyes upon the child. 'Which book, child?' she asked.

'*The* book! The one about the Tyger!'

'Tiger?'

'*You* know! - Tyger! Tyger! burning bright, in the forests of the night - '

And Lizzie recited the whole poem through, without flaw, without stumbling, giving life to its every phrase until the Tyger itself seemed about to burst upon them. She finished and took a deep breath.

'*That* Tyger!' she exclaimed fiercely. 'You has a book by the man what wrote it, what has pitchers in it, too, and he did 'em.'

'Blake's *The Tyger*. I understand now. Child, I have several of his books. All of them complete with pictures he drew.'

Lizzie froze. Her eyes opened wide. She struggled to speak. 'You - you has *two* books he did? *Three*? *More'n three*? Oh, crimany!!'

Miss Bell's voice was soft now, and even apologetic: 'Yes, child, more than three. And although you may not enrol at the Academy, I shall be happy to show them to you.'

Mr Mills, who had stood silent and unmoving through the whole of this long exchange, now gave a small cough.

'Yes, Mills?'

Mr Mills rubbed one worn, wrinkled fist into the palm

of the opposite hand. 'Begging your pardon, Miss Bell, but I have a suggestion you may wish to consider.'

'Pray continue.'

'It's like this. Now, the Missus has taken a liking to the girl, and I've a fair respect for young Tom here. You know we aren't as young as perhaps we might be, and sometimes the work of a caretaker and his wife takes a little longer than is pleasurable. Besides which, some nights it's a little lonely in the gatehouse. Now, what if these two were to decide they could bear to live with us? No charity, mind you, Tom - you'd have to work for your keep, I promise you!'

'Wouldn't stay otherwise!'

'That's right. Now, Miss Bell, perhaps these young things will find our way of life suits them. Perhaps they won't. But for as long as they are willing to live here, perhaps something could be done in the way of schooling, see? Not with the other students, perhaps, at least not to start with; but something provided by The Academy in way of payment for their work about the place, you understand?'

'I understand entirely, Mr Mills. It is a worthy suggestion. Perhaps we all need to have some time to consider it, however. I suggest we take a few days to think it through.'

Tom lifted his voice again. 'One more thing. This eddycatin', you needs to know we already has a teacher. Won't have no other, neither. Mattie learned us well enough and we'll stick wiv her, see?'

Mattie looked at Tom and a roguish glint came to her eye. 'If I be the teacher, Tom Smith, I'll stand no mitchin', see?'

He grinned. 'That depends on the teachin', Miss!'

Lizzie joined in, remembering their first conversation about it. 'Us'll not stand bein' treated as dummles, mind!'

'An we'll not 'bide rafty lessons neither!'

'Ah, well!' Mattie said with pretended weariness. 'Spect if you ben't caddled yet by all me jags and tags of teachin', I can carry on. But I'll find me a flexy cane like Miss McDougal's and larrup you proper if you don't learn!'

And while the others stared, the three children laughed uproariously.

It was a thoughtful Mattie who settled to sleep that night. She hardly dared hope that the arrangements for Lizzie and Tom would work for long, but she couldn't think of anything better. She still didn't know whether she'd done the right thing by helping Dicker. She didn't feel any more hopeful about living peaceably with Aunt Agatha, who had begun fussing again already - about rings and houses and the wastefulness of education for girls, and her wicked, wicked brother who had taken advantage of her father's illness to steal - yes, *steal* - the house from under her very nose!

And she didn't know what had become of Dicker. When they had returned to Druddery, the horse was gone and therefore he must be gone, too: without a word to her. She had searched her room for a letter. She looked around the horse's stall. She even went and asked Mrs Murphy if a letter had been left. Nothing. Not a single word. That bothered her more than she wanted to admit.

Chapter 20 Revelations

Breakfast was proceeding in a stately fashion and they had just completed the muffins stage when the housekeeper entered and said there was a gentleman asking to see Sir Lucid immediately. And he wished to see the young lady, too - meaning Mattie.

'What kind of gentleman is he, Mrs Murphy?' asked Lucid, his butter knife arrested in midair.

'One of those policemen, Sir.'

'Oh. Perhaps - rather than waiting – perhaps he would be willing to share a cup of tea with us. Could you please ask him if he wishes to - ah - do that? And if so, please ask Cook to send up another plate of muffins.'

Mrs Murphy returned with the Inspector whom Mattie had spoken to on the previous day. He introduced himself graciously as Chief Inspector Marriot.

'You may remember meeting me when you returned from Cornwall. I was one of the Inspectors dealing with the robbery.'

'I do recall you, Chief Inspector,' said Agatha. 'You were so kind as to compliment me on the flagrance of my rose garden. My roses are certainly the most flagrant in the area. I recall thinking that it was most unusually observational of you. My estimation of the police was immensely aggravated by that fact!'

After a moment's puzzling, Marriott thanked her for this commendation, accepted tea and then greeted the muffins with great satisfaction, taking one onto his plate with the clear intent of further interrogation of it at a later stage. He looked over towards Mattie.

'I understand that yesterday this young lady visited in prison the two brigands who had been arrested here.'

Mattie nodded. Lucid said apologetically, 'Yes. I - I took her, you see. Was that - did we - that is, did you prefer that we should not have visited?'

'Ah!' The Chief Inspector dissected his muffin neatly. 'That is what I ask myself, Sir Lucid. I do not yet know whether to be pleased or disappointed that you visited. Perhaps you can assist me there.'

'Oh - yes, certainly. Certainly.'

Marriot spread butter on the bottom half of his muffin - thickly and evenly, with certain evidence of great delight. He paused with the muffin halfway to his mouth to ask, 'I would like you to tell me about your visit, in detail. Did you notice anything or anyone unusual? Did you hear anything out of the ordinary? Were the arrangements at the gaol in any way exceptional?'

Then he took an enormous bite of the muffin and sat back to chew it thoughtfully while Mattie and Lucid struggled to recall their visit precisely. They had been at the gaol for scarcely a few minutes... it had appeared quite an ordinary prison, though rather dirty... no, there had been nothing odd, nothing surprising, nothing worthy of particular comment.

'Shocking!' commented Agatha.

The policeman looked at her with friendly interest. She was swathed in an indecent amount of pink fabric; it boiled about her shoulders and swelled in great ruffs and puffs all down her arms. 'Shocking, Ma'am?' he asked.

'Visiting criminals! It only encourages them to take advancement of decent folk!' Agatha rose to her feet in her excitement, a bright pink volcano of rustling crinoline. 'I know, Chief Inspector, I *know*!' (wagging her finger at him) 'Prisons are there for punishment, not as pleasure parks! Criminals should be made to do hard labour! They should be required to do something unpleasant - all day, every day - such as - well, such as -'

Hubert couldn't resist the opportunity. 'Such as doing jigsaw puzzles! Don't you agree, Chief Inspector? Surely that would reform them!'

'Undoubtedly.' Marriot contemplated sending another bite of muffin into that long, dark imprisonment which muffins must sadly suffer. 'However, these criminals will not, unfortunately, have the opportunity of remedial puzzling - at least until they are recaptured.'

'What?' cried Agatha. 'They have escaped? They might return here! We shall be murdered in our beds!'

'Ah. Now, that is unlikely. Unless of course they left some of their valuables hidden here. But we will post a man in the house for a few days, to cover that possibility.' The rest of the muffin disappeared efficiently and Marriot sat in silence while Agatha spoke wildly to Lucid about the need for him to purchase weapons with which to protect them all.

When silence fell again, Mattie asked what had happened. Marriot turned his eyes upon her again - bright, intelligent eyes with a shiny eagerness that reminded her of a pet mouse she had once owned.

'Ah. I *had* hoped, Miss, that you and your uncle might be able to tell *me* what happened. But -' he paused for her to respond. She looked back at him calmly, blankly. 'But I see that you have nothing to add to my knowledge, such as it is.'

He continued. 'The escape was really rather clever. Shortly after you left, the two prisoners began complaining of pains in their neck, under their arms and at the – ah, the tops of their legs. The two guards on duty took little notice until the men began rolling about in - apparently - some pain. Now, it so happened that a gentleman calling himself Doctor Carter - you may know of him? I thought as much. This man had a calling card to match his name and had come to the gaol for some reason - wanting to report a petty theft or some such. He had his medical bag at his side: so the gaolers quite naturally asked him to take a look at the prisoners. He spent a few minutes with them and came out with a face white as a winding sheet. He said the men had the Plague. The Black Death! This is not as unlikely as the uneducated might think, for the men were both ex-sailors, and the Plague does occur amongst them.'

Hubert interrupted. 'Did you know, Chief Inspector, why that is? It's because the Black Death is spread by the species of rat known as the Black Rat, *Rattus Rattus* I think, common on board ship and in ports. Jolly fascinating, don't you think? Thrilling!'

'Undoubtedly.' The Inspector looked anything but thrilled. 'May I continue?' he asked.

'Yes, do!' Hubert replied.

'The gaolers were scared witless. What should they do? The doctor thought for a time and then said that the two men could be taken to his clinic, which had an isolation room he used for contagious illnesses. He proposed that the gaolers allow him to tie the men securely and take them in his carriage. One gaoler, fully armed, could follow him at a short distance in case either prisoner found enough strength to try to break free. Not that this was likely, he said. They were in an advanced stage of the illness and death was no more than a day or two away.'

'Well - the gaolers thanked him, in tears I expect. They let him secure the men and lead them outside. Off he went with his great black horse pulling a carriage-load of Plague, whilst a trembling gaoler trotted behind on his own horse. A little ways outside the town, the carriage stopped and the Doctor jumped down, gesturing for the gaoler to come to him. When he did so, the Doctor brought out a pistol he was hiding in his coat and asked the man if he would kindly hand over his gun, horse and shoes: or alternatively, die like a dog!'

'Golly!' Hubert exclaimed. 'But why do they always say that? About dying like dogs, I mean? Do dogs die in a particularly spectacular manner, Chief Inspector?'

Marriot ignored this new interruption. 'That was the last we saw of them. The highwayman and his rescued assistants vanished into the sunset: going West. I don't expect to come across them again. Not unless there happens to be someone who knows more about them than I do, and is willing to tell...'

He sat in silence for a while, looking more than once at Mattie. She smiled sweetly in return.

Marriot inspected the empty muffin plate wistfully before giving a gentle sigh. 'Ah, well! If you should recall anything, Sir Lucid, I would be grateful to be told of it. I shall leave my card. And I shall ask one of my men to stay here in the house, if you wish it.'

'I am sure there is no need for that -' began Lucid. But Agatha interrupted, almost angrily:

'There is *every* need!' she cried. 'My lovely valuables! The glass case with wax fruit in it - my expensive flower arrangement made of shells - what will become of them? We could be robbed - plundered - *murdered!* '

The Chief Inspector looked to Lucid, who reluctantly nodded his acceptance. Marriot rose. 'I will send a man this afternoon. He will bring a letter of introduction from me, and unless I am very wrong, that will be the last you will hear of this matter for a long time. Men of this sort, given an hour's start, disappear like foxes at the sound of the hunter's horn.'

Once Marriot had left the house, Aunt Agatha went to lie down, but not before ordering the servants to make a search of her rooms, in case a highwayman should be already hidden there - and not before commanding Lucid to purchase some check trousers and a brown frock-coat like the Chief Inspector's! Mattie and Hubert tiptoed away to the stables, accompanied by Jasper.

'Why all this mystery, Mattie, old girl?' Hubert asked cheerfully as they entered the stables through a small side door, ducking beneath its low, crooked beams.

'It's something Dicker said.'

'Who?!'

'The highwayman.'

'Oh, him! I thought you said someone else. What *did* the dread defrauder say?'

'He implied that there was no problem to his getting from the house to the stable without being seen. More precisely, there was no difficulty going from the house to the stall his horse was in.'

'Ah! A tunnel! But, Mattie, that's no mystery. There are tunnels galore beneath us - cellars and underground vaults, chambers, caverns!'

'Oh,' Mattie was disappointed. 'So you know about it already.'

'But I didn't know there was a tunnel to the stables. Matter of fact, I doubt it's so. Someone would have noticed, wouldn't they?'

They entered the stall where Night had been kept. It looked unexceptional - just a square, straw-bedded room with thick planks to all sides and an airy roof overhead. The wood was dented and worn from numerous kicks, bites and rubbings; the floor was just uneven, packed earth beneath the straw. Mattie and Hubert kicked and prodded for some time without success. Then Hubert clambered on top of the close-boarded wall and looked around.

'Say, Mattie! Come have a look at this!'

She pulled herself up beside him. The timber lining of the stall was solid all right, and eight feet high; but between it and the side of the stable was a gap a foot wide. This gap was bridged by a heavy board - except at the far end. Here, a shorter length of board was hinged so that it could be pulled open. It was open now. Mattie peered down the hole, which was slightly broader than a man's shoulders.

'It's black as night.'

'Black as the inside of the earth! Though that's not true, you know, Mattie. They say the earth has a lake of fire within - a great, molten, glowing core. Like the fires of hell, only not quite so hot!'

The jackdaw peered into the hole as well and made dark, gloomy noises.

'Jasper! Come away from there!' Jasper paid no attention and began strutting back and forth along the side of the hole, muttering grimly to himself.

'We'll need a candle, or a lantern,' Mattie said.

'There's a lamp at the stable entrance. I'll fetch that and light it.'

Hubert returned soon, the lantern sputtering weakly in the daylight. But once he lowered it into the dark gap, it seemed to strengthen, sending out fiery rays, casting great, gloomy shadows.

'Oh, I say....'

There were steps below them, leading down behind the wall and then turning under the stall itself. Mattie and Hubert slid along the top of the wall until they came to the start of the steps; then they descended, Hubert first. Jasper stayed on the wall until they had nearly disappeared from sight. He then gave a peevish squawk and fluttered down to sit on Mattie's shoulder.

The air was cold, still, musty and a little damp. Their footsteps made a dull, deathly sound, like the muffled scrabblings of a mole burrowing somewhere deep in the ground. Down they went, and round and down again, until they were well below the surface of the ground and facing a tunnel. The roof of the tunnel was hardly wide enough for one man, and so low that they had to stoop to enter it. Mattie squeezed up as close behind Hubert as she could get, peering over his stooped shoulder to see ahead as far as the flickering pool of lantern light permitted.

They soon came to a junction. Tunnels ran off in three directions.

'And this is where we turn back,' said Hubert wisely, his voice echoing in the gloom. 'I know what happens if we continue: we'll get lost. And we'll *never* get out. Never!'

'But *he* found his way.'

'So he did!'

'What about footprints?'

They studied the dusty earth. Footprints went in all directions.

'Please, Hubert!' pleaded Mattie. 'Just let's have a quick look down each tunnel.'

'No more than ten paces down each!'

'All right. To your right, first.'

They entered the right hand tunnel. Hubert stopped immediately. 'Not this one, old sport!' he cried. 'Look ahead!'

Mattie peered before her. Someone had scratched a skull and crossbones on the ground and on the sides of the tunnel. Beneath each picture was written the simplest of messages: "No!".

She laughed. The sound echoed dismally about them, but she laughed again, anyway. 'Dicker did that! I know he did!'

The left hand tunnel was marked with a picture of a barn, complete with a drawing of what might be a family of rats. 'Not this way, either!' said Hubert. He turned to the straight on route. 'But here's a drawing of the house. And if we look behind us, down the tunnel we came from - yes, there's what might just be described as a horse scrawled on the wall!'

And so it was at each crossroad and fork: a picture or message. Finally they came to a turning to the right, marked with an arrow and the message: "Little Miss Fireball".

'That's me!' Mattie cried.

'Shh! We're under the house now!'

On they went, and then up a steep gradient, ending in twenty rough-hewn steps between old stone walls. Then the tunnel stopped abruptly, its end blocked by a sheet of heavy black metal. Tucked into the edge of this sheet was an envelope, with Mattie's name upon it.

Hubert made approving noises. 'This outlaw chap has some style, you know! What does the letter say, Mattie?'

She opened the envelope and withdrew a sheet of paper. Hubert held the lantern so that she could read:

Dear Explorer

I expect you won't be long in finding this, perhaps from the direction of the stables (yes, I caught the bright, suspicious gleam in your eye when we were speaking of the latter!); or from your room. If not, I shall draw it to your attention when next I have time and safety on my side, permitting me to write again.

Thank you for your kindness on behalf of the lads. And on my own behalf, I thank you for - well, for many things. For your brave heart; for that sudden blaze of light in your eye; for words kindly meant, though they sometimes scorched where they touched; and for a smile that recalled another smile, very long ago.

This is not the place for a man to justify himself. But in case this is the final opportunity I have to write, let me at least claim to belong to the more gentlemanly of the two traditions of highwaymen. For there are two tradi-

tions. I stand, I hope, with Robin Hood, and Old Mob, and Captain James Hind. With Hind I say: "I have not wronged any poor man of the worth of a penny, but I must confess that I have made bold with many a rich bumpkin or a lying lawyer, whose full-fed fees from the rich farmer doth too much impoverish the poor cottage keeper".

And now some information. First, the tunnels. You should not investigate these. They are dangerous! However, I expect you will ignore this good advice, and therefore I have marked each junction. Do not enter any sections where I have drawn a skull and crossbones.

Second, entrances and exits. You will have to work out most of these for yourself. But I can tell you that the fireback to your room opens by pulling down a small latch you will find at the top, back, right hand side (as you stand in your room). It looks like a small ridge in the metal. To open from the other side - well, I trust you can use your own intelligence for that.

Lastly, I offer you proof that I am not totally without regard for another's property. I believe your aunt has lost a small ring. I saw it atop the cupboards in the scullery, together with a quirky collection of glittering items gathered by your jackdaw. I expect it to be worth a small fortune: enough to feed an impoverished family for a few years at least! But you may return it to your aunt with the compliments of:

Your prior employer and - I hope - in some respects your friend

Robert Dicker

Mattie read this aloud, though in places her voice went a bit shaky. As she read the final few words, Hubert gave a long whistle.

'Well, who'd have thought it!' he exclaimed softly. 'Poor Mama! What a shock *this* will be! Mattie, promise me you'll let me be there when you tell her about it. I'd not miss this little drama, not for all the spice of the Indies - nor the gold of the Andes - nor the tea in China!'

'Why should she be shocked?' Mattie asked, puzzled.

Hubert looked at her blankly. 'Oh,' he said. 'Oh!' Then he grinned. 'If you don't mind, dear cousin, I shan't explain, not just yet. Best to wait until after you've told my stepmother.'

Mattie nodded. 'Let's see about opening the fireback, then,' she suggested. They felt around its grimy top and soon found a small latch to their left. After wriggling it in various manners, they tried pulling it down. There was a small click and the fireback was free to swing towards them. They pulled it fully open and proceeded to climb out of the tunnel into the large fireplace, Mattie first.

There was a scream. Mattie straightened up suddenly and banged her head against the underside of the fireplace. While she was shaking the stars from before her eyes, Hubert climbed out beside her. Another scream, and this time Hubert bumped his head.

Aunt Agatha was in the doorway of the room, staring in at them but clearly not seeing them for what they were.

'Jackson!' she cried. 'Jackson! Come now! Bring the shotgun! The highwaymen - in this room!'

Jackson appeared at her side, a shotgun in his hand. But he immediately pointed it to the ground, unhinged it and calmly removed the cartridges.

'We'll be killed!' Agatha moaned.

'Beggin' your ladyship's pardon,' Jackson said apologetically, 'I expect that's unlikely. These two may be dirty, but I wouldn't reckon them to be dangerous. With your permission, Ma'am, I'll put this gun away. I'm not over fond of firearms in the house.' He withdrew and his slow, even pacing could be heard as he walked away.

Mattie stepped out onto the hearthrug. 'It's us, Aunt Agatha! Hubert and Mattie.' There was a noisy, screeching grumble from her shoulder and she added: 'And Jasper!'

Agatha stared. Her vision seemed to clear. 'Oh. It's you! I thought - I heard noises in the wall. I looked into your room and I thought -'

'Hello, Mama!' said Hubert cheerfully, joining Mattie on the hearthrug and rubbing his head ruefully. 'We've found your ring! That is, the ring is found. No - that's not it either. What I means is, we know where the ring *is to be* found! Where someone else found it, in fact. Where someone - some*thing* - else hid it. But you mustn't blame Jasper. Jackdaws aren't thieves, not really, not in the conventional sense. Not like highwaymen. Though some might argue that not all highwaymen are thieves, either! It's just in their nature to take bright objects and hoard them. Jackdaws, that is, not highwaymen. Especially when the male birds are trying to attract females. Or perhaps it's the other way round... well, whichever it is, it's really the same sort of thing that humans do, you know, using glitzy bits of metal and stones to attract the opposite - uh, the opposite gender.'

'I see,' said Agatha, a little testily. 'I see! You have both gone mad! Here am I, worried sick about brigands and villains and there are you, hiding in fireplaces so as to leap out when I pass. Then you talk crazily about jackdaws. I see! The young have no respect for their elders!'

Lucid, who had just then wandered up, was puzzled. 'Respect, my dear? What - ah - what manner of disrespect *is* implied by discussions concerning jackdaws?' he asked.

Agatha glared at him. He apologised immediately.

'Sorry, dear one... I - um - was just wondering.' He looked in at the two children. He looked past them. His face lit up.

'You've found the entrance!' he exclaimed. He came bustling into the room, almost skipping with excitement. 'You know, we'd always been told - as children - that there was an entrance to the tunnels from the house. But we couldn't find it. There's an entrance in the cellar, but you can only get to the barn and the orchard from there: the one side passage is blocked by a landfall. Why, this *is* an achievement!'

They began telling him about it - hurriedly, excitedly. He beamed and nodded as Mattie explained how they had found the tunnel, guided by hints from the fleeing highwayman.

Agatha caught at a few words and repeated them wildly: 'Highwaymen? Tunnels? Smuggling? Good heavens! And Jackson said there was no danger! Lucid, I am a moral terrier!'

Lucid gazed at her helplessly for a moment. 'Oh. Mortal terror,' he said at last. 'Is that what you mean, dearest? That you are in mortal terror?'

'That is precisely what I said! Your hearing, Lucid, is not what it was!'

She turned on Mattie. 'So!' she cried. 'This is what befalls, is it? Not content with simple disobedience, you conjoin with thieves and aspersions, whom you shelter from the proper jerkings of the law! And you shelter them here, in the house no less!'

'He is not an - an *assassin*. And as for being a thief - well, yes, I suppose he is -'

'Ah ha! You permit that, do you?'

'Yes. But is he therefore to be totally condemned? Is he to receive no respect at all? Is he to be declared inhuman, unworthy of mercy, unworthy of understanding?' Mattie was once again surprised to find how like Dicker she sounded.

Agatha's face reddened. 'We are not talking of gentlemen!' she objected. 'We are talking of common footpads! Of the low, mean, *dirty* class of people with whom persons of good breeding do not associate! You have too much kindness, Matilda. You are like your mother: more kindness than sense! You imagine something can be made of folk of low breeding. But no! A thousand times no! They have their place, those people your father used to associate with: and they need to remain there, in the positions society wisely gives them. They can be taught to respect their betters, to work quietly, to say their prayers even. But the best of them is only a step above the gutter. Show them a chance of easy money and they'll slit your throat for it. Or worse!'

Lucid put his hand gently on Agatha's arm. 'I - I do not think that is entirely fair, my dear,' he said quietly. 'Money does not make a gentleman, nor do fine clothes provide a man with a good - um - conscience.'

'Ha!' Agatha retorted. 'And what of the conscience of this highwayman? He has broken into our home! I daresay he has removed several items of value. Lucid, call the servants! We must search the house to see what he has stolen!'

Hubert laughed. 'But he has stolen nothing, Mama!' he cried. 'In fact, quite the opposite! He has provided something! Your ring! He found your ring for you! He's told Mattie where it is in a letter, and we'll go fetch it for you - once you've stopped slandering the poor man before you know anything about him!'

Agatha sniffed. 'So who is this polygon of virtue?' she asked. 'Who is this gentleman I'm supposed to be grateful to for not killing me and taking all my valuables? And for what reason did this robber decide to excuse us from theft and bloodshed?'

Hubert looked to Mattie, his eyes dancing. 'Mattie will

tell you, Mama. Go on, Mattie!'

Mattie looked down at the letter she still held in her hand. At her shoulder Jasper was muttering in her ear. She pushed him aside with a gentle hand.

'He - he *is* a bit of a brigand,' she answered her aunt. 'I can't deny that, and in fact he'd be angry if I tried to say he wasn't one. His gang - I don't think you'd like them. *I* didn't, to start with. But they were - *are* - people. Even Lump - Lump, evil as he is: he is a person, too. I hate him, I can't help that, though I know I shouldn't... shouldn't hate. But the others, they are almost like family. More than family, some of them. I'm not saying this well, Aunt -

'I don't know what you're going on about!' Agatha snapped.

'I hardly know myself. Except that Dicker, though he was bad, was in some ways so good, too. Better than he would admit himself.'

'Who? Who?' Agatha's voice rose.

'Dicker. He called himself Sir Dicker, but that was a private joke. He said he was Sir Dicker, highwayman by appointment to the Queen. But he was plain Robert Dicker, of Cornwall.'

Agatha's eyes became very large. Her mouth opened once or twice but no words came out. At her side Lucid was nodding his head vigorously, and the look on his face showed that he had suddenly made sense of something.

'Oh, no!' Agatha said weakly, and then she fainted.

Chapter 21 A Long-awaited Bonfire

November 1st, 1845
Somewhere in Cornwall

My dearest non-relation

I expect that by now you know my guilty secret. Had you guessed? I wonder how my sister has taken it! Do pass to her my best wishes and a promise that she is unlikely to see me again: the latter will no doubt be of more value to her than the former!

It was a surprise to me to discover, on my first visit to Druddery, that your step-aunt (is there such a term?) was my very own sister, whose company I had successfully - and happily! - avoided for ten years. My clumsy attempts to pretend to be an Irish-born relation of yours became an amusing mirror for the "real" relationship. Between the two angles of the mirror and its reality, images of the past came back to me - those haunting voices of childhood - an ageing, rigidly moral and straight-spoken father; games and fancies; a young man's courtings and fond hopes; the sweet waving of a slender hand: ah, bittersweet are the remembrances of gentler times.

Enough of that! You will wish me to provide hard news.

Firstly, the lads. They have recovered miraculously from their bout of the Plague and are in rude, rumbustical health. They send you fond greetings. I despair of their being any use to me in the near future, for they are no longer quite bad enough and - until their money runs out - no longer <u>poor</u> enough for piratical deeds! However, once I have regained my own enthusiasm for my chosen employment, I expect I will be able to encourage them sufficiently. If not, I will have to seek out a new band of black-hearted men!

As for myself, I am considering leaving this country. If a man is to live on the lonely outskirts of polite society, he may as well do so in a place where it is warm enough for him to enjoy his own disgraceful behaviour for more than two months in the year! There are passages on a ship travelling from here to the southern states of America, and I may persuade the lads to take them up with me.

And now a little business. I have written separately to your good Uncle Lucid, enclosing various legal documents. You may know that my father left to me an unusually interesting house, complete with odd parcels of furniture, poor plumbing and crumbling roofs. Perhaps he had some hope that this would encourage me to settle myself there as a gentleman, spending my remaining years playing penny whist and attending tedious church fetes. Perhaps he had some absurd idea that my sister and I might be reconciled and maintain the house together. Neither is possible! Yet I would be unhappy to sell the house, which is - though I scarcely know how - part of myself. What to do, then?

What I have done is to transfer the property to someone who is not quite a legal relation: a sort of half-step-cousin: yourself. Your uncle will, if he agrees, hold the property on trust for you, maintain it and so on. When you come of age, you may use it as you wish - perhaps to set up a "Ragged School" for the poor, such as they have in the larger cities? Or a nursing home for retired gentlemen of a piratical persuasion? I do not mind what

you do, so long as you do not bother me with unneces-
sary expressions of gratitude!

Lastly, two little matters bearing a monetary value.
Firstly, I hope that by now you have found the way into
the fireplace in your room. If not, there is a small ridge of
metal at the top right hand side of the fire backplate: pull
that until it clicks, when you can push the fireback open.
There is a letter for you on the far side of the plate - it
will probably fall off as you open the door. Secondly, I
had promised to take you moonraking. I'm afraid you'll
need to ask the Brats to stand in for me. But I can tell
you where best to try your hand. You will find your share
of the takings - and the Brats' - in a barrel at the bottom
of one of the pools on the River Test. I have left full di-
rections in that convenient storage place for Dicker
memorabilia - the raised tomb: you recall?

With kindest regards

Sir Dicker

Mattie folded the letter and replaced it in the envelope. It was rather tattered already, for she had read it
several times in the past two days. She smiled once
more at the thought of running a home for retired gentlemen of "piratical persuasion". Calling to Jasper (who
was investigating fireplaces again), she went to stand at
the open double doors of the study.

It was a mild night for the 5th of November. The
frosts of the week before were forgotten and the only
reminder of them was the largesse of leaves snapped
from the trees, now raked into huge piles and fuelling the
Guy Fawkes Night bonfires.

From beyond the dark lawn came great shouts of
laughter as the gardener lit their own bonfire. Hubert was
at his side; he had been in charge of the building of the

pyramid that was slowly conflagrating before the gathered group of family, servants and a few friends. Mattie tucked the envelope into her cloak and went to join them. Her great, shambling boots stomped and clomped comfortably on the pebbled path that led from the house to the croquet lawn, by way of a tangle of "flagrant" rose bushes.

On the lawn itself, Agatha was fretting aloud amongst her little circle of well-to-do ladies. She paused in her flow of words as Mattie approached and waited until the girl had passed before resuming her commentary. Mattie went to stand with Hubert, and Jasper swooped down to land upon her shoulder.

Hubert's face was glowing with exertion and the heat of the fire. 'What a night!' he exclaimed. 'Stars blazing, fire blazing, Mama blazing!'

Mattie giggled. 'Do you think she'll calm down soon about me inheriting the house in Cornwall?' she asked.

'The trouble is, old girl, that she can't bear the idea of the poor becoming rich - it's even worse than the thought of the rich becoming poor! She wouldn't enjoy that passage in the Good Book where Jesus says the First on earth will be Last in heaven, and the Last will be First. Poor Mama, she'd rather lose a fortune down a hole than see someone else enjoy it!'

'At least she has her ring back!'

'And at least she's mad at *you* again for a while. That lets *me* off! She's taken no interest in my education for weeks! I've been able to spend most days up to my ears in Nature! Ha ha!'

'You seem very happy.'

'I am, Mattie, old girl, I am! And there's one more thing!'

'Oh? What's that?'

Hubert danced a few steps, most clumsily and amusingly, before coming close and whispering in Mattie's ear.

'You didn't!' she cried.

'I jolly well did! And I shall dance, dance, dance!' He tried his ungainly little jig once more and nearly fell over.

Just then Agatha hove into view, like a great floating hulk looming up suddenly on a dark sea. 'Hubert!' she ordered, in a sugar-sweet voice. 'Hubert, my dear boy! Come here!'

'I *am* here,' Hubert replied, a little nervously.

'I was congratulating the gardener on the bonfire. He says it was *all* your doing. Is that true, Hubert dear?'

'Oh - mostly. Mostly.'

'I see. It is an *excellent* bonfire! Quite the most striking fire I have ever seen! And what, pray, are those little boxes on top? The ones the guy is sitting upon?'

'Those, Mama? Ah. Yes. I had some - er - items I no longer needed.'

'They appear to burn rather well.' Lady Arbuthnot stepped a little closer to the fire. One of the boxes spilled open and its contents dribbled down the side of the piled wood and leaves. She peered into the flames and stiffened.

'Hubert! Hubert! Come here! *Hubert*! Where are you?' she cried. But Hubert and Mattie had tiptoed away and had lost themselves in the party of guests.

'Hubert! How dare he! All his precious, precious jigsaws!'

~ ~ ~ *end* ~ ~ ~

Historical comment

Until 1834 the poor could call upon the parish they lived in to help them through their worst times, for instance by providing food when they were starving. Then the "Poor Laws" created the Workhouses, including the one at Andover.

The purpose of the Workhouses was to save money. The wealthier citizens resented having to support the poor in their area through local taxes, and Workhouses were seen as a way to reduce this "burden".

Extreme poverty was common. England was one of the richest nations in the world but the wages of its poorest workers were barely enough to survive on. When the work failed in the winter, as it often did in rural Hampshire and elsewhere, the poor faced freezing and starvation. Unless they turned to crime they had only two choices: either keep their few miserable possessions and die; or else give up everything they had and enter the Workhouse.

Once there, they were fed a carefully calculated meagre diet, just above starvation level. This was intentional – the theory was that the pauper in the Workhouse should be no better off than the poorest person outside it.

Inmates there were often treated like prisoners or even slaves. The scenes recorded by Dickens in "Oliver Twist" were terrible enough, but not as terrible as the truth.

The Andover Workhouse came to the public's attention in 1846, with reports in the Times newspaper of cruelty, abuse, deprivation and starvation. All the dreadful things mentioned in this book actually happened there, and worse.

Although some reforms were made after the scandals in Andover and elsewhere, the Workhouse system continued until it was abolished in 1929.

Hampshire dialect

Tom and Lizzie use words that were common amongst the poor of their time in Hampshire but were not well known to the wealthier classes and are certainly unfamiliar now! Most of them can be guessed. Some of the harder words are:

Ballyrag	- to swear	Ruffatory	- rude, boisterous
Bibble	- to drink	Rumbustical	- as Ruffatory
Bosky	- drunk	Sawney	- simpleton
Caddled	- annoyed, confused	Scrimpy	- mean, small
Cranky	- peevish, cross	Shammocky	- shambling, idle
Crummy	- fat	Shirky	- deceitful
Dubby	- short, stubby	Shrammed	- chilled to the bone
Dubersome	- doubtful	Sidy	- surly, moody
Dumble	- stupid, slow	Skise	- frolic about
Dunch	- deaf	Skise off	- skive off work
Eenamost	- almost	Sossle	- a slop, a mess
Feck	- worthless	Taffety	- dainty
Fessy	- proud	Tickler	- puzzle
Floddy	- stout	Timersome	- timid
Frowted	- scared	Titty	- small
Frump	- cross old woman	Tongue-bang	- scold
Galleybagger	- scarecrow	Wapsy	- spiteful
Goggle	- shake, tremble	Wheel	- halo of moon
Hoosbird	- disreputable woman		

Ballyrag - to swear
Bibble - to drink
Bosky - drunk
Caddled - annoyed, confused
Cranky - peevish, cross
Crummy - fat
Dubby - short, stubby
Dubersome - doubtful
Dumble - stupid, slow
Dunch - deaf
Eenamost - almost
Feck - worthless
Fessy - proud
Floddy - stout
Frowted - scared
Frump - cross old woman
Galleybagger - scarecrow
Goggle - shake, tremble
Hoosbird - disreputable woman
Hudgy - thick, clumsy
Huffled - angry, offended
Hunch - solid lump of something
Janty - showy
Jawled-out - tired
Jobation - lecture, reprimand
Larrup - thrash, beat
Leer - empty
Maze - astonishment
Miff - offence
Mitch - to idle, shirk
Mizmaze - confusion
Muggle - muddle
Mullock - confused heap
Nobbut - nothing but
Ornary - common, mean-looking
Peel - Upset state ("in a peel")
Rammucky - dissolute, depraved
Rampagious - riotous, noisy
Rattletraps - things lying about in disorder (like Alice W's room!)
Renward - to the right (& To-ard = to the left)

Ruffatory - rude, boisterous
Rumbustical - as Ruffatory
Sawney - simpleton
Scrimpy - mean, small
Shammocky - shambling, idle
Shirky - deceitful
Shrammed - chilled to the bone
Sidy - surly, moody
Skise - frolic about
Skise off - skive off work
Sossle - a slop, a mess
Taffety - dainty
Tickler - puzzle
Timersome - timid
Titty - small
Tongue-bang - scold
Wapsy - spiteful
Wheel - halo of moon

Plus some useful swear words:

Cussnation!
Crimany!
By Galls!
Drot it!
I'll be drattled! (hanged)
Hike off!
Shirk off!

Some other books by Ed Wicke

BULLIES

Alex is an expert at outsmarting bullies. But when he starts at a new school, he finds that he's out of his league. Will he get through the year in one piece? And can he keep his crazy little sister from starting a pirate mutiny and kidnapping the head teacher's crocodile?!! The only book in the world with a fairy who conducts anti-bully warfare using beetles, a snowman that talks in riddles, a school assembly taken by a talking bear, and a boy who turns into a bird after Christmas lunch! A book that's serious about bullying. But crazy about everything else! (new edition December 2003)

NICKLUS

A talking cat, the "coolest cat in England". A nine-year-old boy who hardly talks at all. A lost mother he's determined to find, even if it means walking every street in London. A mad scientist and her crazed henchman. A grandfather done in by his young wife, the Lady Emmeline Jasmine de Rocheman Tiroli Deptford-Jones - who is also the scientist planning world domination and the extinction of all the cats in England!

Nicklus and Marlowe the cat make an unusual team as they join forces to upset the clever plans of the Lady Emmeline, and to find Nicklus' mother. But how? (to be published January 2004)

See also the next page...

Some other books by Ed Wicke

AKAYZIA ADAMS AND THE MASTERDRAGON'S SECRET

A school visit to London Zoo causes Kazy Adams to swap the rough streets of East London for a world of magic and danger. With a creature she frees from its cage, she and her grandmother flee a band of hooded Watchers and enter the Inner Lands. They find themselves in a world where caravans fly quietly across the skies; lightstones glow with the wave of a hand; and dragons make good but enormous pets. Humans rub shoulders with the bear-like Hrakkú, while friendly goblins have taken over the northern parts of Old London and winged horses roam the ancient woodlands.

She is enrolled in Old Winsome's Academy, where half the pupils are Hrakkú. Together they study Magic - the Magic that powers the swooping airboards on the sports field and protects them from the power of the Shadowmaker and his cruel allies, the Werewitches.

And in amongst the Ordeals of skill and magic, there is a mystery to solve: the disappearance of nine pupils during the Headship of the Masterdragon Tharg, at the time of the Goblin Wars...

A book for all fans of magic and mystery.
(to be published December 2003)

See also previous page....

Printed in the United Kingdom
by Lightning Source UK Ltd.
9826900001B/1-24